# A SPY IN VIENNA

## A PAUL MULLER NOVEL OF POLITICAL INTRIGUE

WILLIAM N. WALKER

ISBN-13:978-1983986888

ISBN-10:1983986887

*A Spy in Vienna* is a work of fiction and a product of the author's imagination. While the story endeavors to recapture historical events accurately and to portray real places and institutions, it does so in an entirely fictitious manner reflecting the author's opinions and conjectures.

The novel refers to many historical figures but they are characterized as the author imagines them. Dialogues and descriptions are fictional and are not intended to depict actual events or to alter the entirely fictional nature of the story.

Any resemblance to actual persons or events is entirely coincidental.

# DEDICATION

*A Spy in Vienna* is dedicated to my wife, Janet Smith Walker without whose love, unflagging support, and encouragement, this book–and much else as well–would never have come about.

My thanks as well to my children, Gilbert, Helen and Joanna whom I know I can always count on.

# ACKNOWLEDGEMENTS

I extend thanks to my editors, Rhonda Dossett and Marian Borden, who were both efficient and very helpful.

I am especially indebted to Colonel Ernst M Felberbauer, Austrian National Defence Academy, Vienna, for fact-checking and correcting German language errors in the book.

After reading my earlier book *Danzig*, Col. Felberbauer sent me a congratulatory message saying that he had "rarely read a historical novel that finds the right tone for the period and its historical setting." When I responded that I was working on a new novel concerning the Austrian Anschluss, he volunteered his services to review and comment on an early draft, which I found very helpful.

Col. Felberbauer has enjoyed a distinguished career as an Austrian military officer, with extensive deployments in international service in the Balkans, New York and Geneva. I am greatly complimented by the favorable reaction of such a knowledgeable commentator to *A Spy in Vienna*.

Cover photo used with kind permission of the Austrian National Library. ANL/Vienna, Lothar Rübelt, http://data.onb.ac.at/rec/baa3066138

# FOREWORD

A spy in Vienna is a novel; Paul Muller, the protagonist, is a product of my imagination.

But as in my earlier novel Danzig, I have used Muller's fictitious character as the vehicle for trying to create and capture for the reader, an authentic account of the actual historical events that are the centerpiece of the book.

Here, the focus of the story is Hitler's bellicose campaign in 1938 to take over Austria and incorporate it into the German Reich. From the safe remove of nearly 80 years, we have the luxury today of looking back, knowing that the Austrian Anschluss, as it is called, was one of the decisive events leading directly to the outbreak of World War II less than eighteen months later and the calamitous consequences that would follow.

But participants in the events of those parlous times knew none of that. They knew only that they were caught up in a whirlwind of confusing events in which the very existence of Austria seemed at stake. Hitler unleashed furious Nazi pressure to seize control of the country and the Austrian leadership, in particular its Chancellor, Kurt von Schuschnigg, mounted a fierce campaign to resist the German onslaught. A series of seemingly daily crises–each appearing more serious than the one that had preceded it–erupted in Vienna in early 1938 as this struggle reached its dramatic climax.

This is the fraught period of time which the novel seeks to capture. I have endeavored to offer the reader an authentic account of the history itself while, at the same time, inviting the rich cast of largely fictional characters in the surrounding story to experience the events and react to them. So, we watch Muller and his colleagues trying to sort out events that unfolded in a fog of uncertainty, wondering what might happen next, and speculating about how the tumultuous events that enveloped them might influence their lives.

What to us is history was, to them, a chaotic present leading toward an obscure and highly uncertain future. Offering readers the opportunity to watch historical events play out in the lives of unknowing contemporaries is the opportunity and challenge for the novelist.

# TABLE OF CONTENTS

# CHAPTER 1

In the end, he decided to take the train instead of trying to fly.

It was all very well that engineers had lately made big improvements in the radio signals that could direct the new generation of twin engine commercial airliners. But they still hadn't figured out how to take off from Geneva's tiny airport in the thick fog that regularly formed a leaden ceiling over the runways. Most winter days, moisture from the lake rose to create cloud cover which was trapped between the Jura Mountains to the west and the higher Alps rearing up to the south, completely blocking out the clear air above. Every skier was familiar with the experience of driving up the mountains in grey fog, then suddenly breaking into bright sunshine and blue skies as the car climbed to a higher altitude, leaving the cloudy soup below.

But at the airport, the foggy overcast was impenetrable. If a plane were to take off, it would fly blind until it broke through into the sunlight like a skier–or until the pilot became disoriented and flew the plane into the side of a mountain or crashed into the lake; everyone knew it could happen.

So, there was a certain resignation among passengers waiting in the small terminal that foggy afternoon in early January 1938. They smoked, sat, paced, occasionally stepping to the window to see if there were any sign of improvement, then, seeing none, sighing and buying another cup of bad coffee or a whiskey from the concession. Every now and then a Swissair official would mount a small platform and say what everyone already knew: weather conditions continued to be unsafe to take off.

And it was not just his flight to Vienna that was delayed. Flights to Paris and Milan and elsewhere were grounded too. Moreover, planes couldn't land in these conditions either, so incoming flights had been diverted to Lyon or Grenoble, or somewhere else. That was always a problem for the airlines; where did you land when Geneva was socked in, as it so often was. This had led to the widespread practice of not taking off from wherever the point of origin was, unless there was assurance from the Geneva tower that the weather was clear enough to land. This made flight schedules both in and out of Geneva into a highly inventive and reliably unreliable gamble.

Paul Muller pulled the Geneva Cornavin Station timetable out of his briefcase for the tenth time and reconfirmed that the Express train through Zurich to Vienna was scheduled to depart at 7 PM. It was already late afternoon. January daylight–what there was left of it beneath the gloomy cloud cover–would soon be gone and the chances for flights taking off in the dark weren't very promising.

He shrugged mentally and told himself that at least he'd be able to get a good meal in the dining car with as much wine as he needed. He was sufficiently accustomed to sleeping in the moderate comfort of a first-class compartment that it would be a routinely survivable overnight train experience. Finally resigned to making the change, he signaled to a porter to recover his luggage and made his way to the small taxi stand to catch a cab to nearby Cornavin.

It seemed to be such an innocent decision.

# CHAPTER 2

Muller awoke the next morning to grey overcast skies above the snow-clad Austrian countryside that was passing by outside the window of his compartment. There had been delays in departing Geneva and again in Zurich, where he'd been awakened by a noisy banging of cars coupling, being removed and added. Still, it had been a passable trip.

After using the lavatory at the far end of the corridor and washing up in the tiny sink, he made his way to the nearly-empty dining car for breakfast. The headwaiter led him to a table and explained that they would not reach Vienna until close to noon.

He glanced idly at the wintry Austrian countryside as he sipped his coffee and awaited the eggs and sausage he'd ordered.

Suddenly, without any warning, the train braked sharply and with great force. Muller grabbed his table, which was firmly affixed to the floor, holding on with as much strength as he could muster and watching as glassware and china flew across the car and loudly splintered into pieces. His waiter fell heavily, grabbing futilely at table legs as he tumbled down the dining car's aisle, his tray with Muller's eggs and sausage crashing to the floor.

It was total bedlam. Muller crouched, redoubling his grip on the table and ducking to avoid flying debris.

Finally, the train came to a grinding, screeching halt as the brakes locked and a huge burst of steam enveloped the train. Muller slowly stood, shaking bits of glass and porcelain from his suit jacket. The waiter who had fallen groaned, holding a leg that had seized up against one of the dining settees and he seemed unable to rise. The headwaiter appeared at Muller's elbow, a napkin pressed against a bloody gash on his forehead, and began apologizing.

"I'm so sorry, sir; I have no idea why this happened."

Muller glanced out one of the dining car windows and saw men running toward the train, some of them waving clubs and making threatening gestures. A hard object, a brick or a rock, Muller guessed, crashed against the dining car wall, narrowly missing a window.

Muller turned and hurried back toward his compartment. He could see conductors scrambling to lock doors against the intruders. He reached his compartment and shut the door, turning the lock and pulling down the curtains. He reached up and yanked his valise down from the luggage rack. Quickly unlocking it, he pulled out the contents, placing them on the seat and worked the secret false bottom, extracting a set of brass knuckles. He shoved his things back into the valise and returned it to the overhead rack.

He slipped the brass knuckles into his suit jacket pocket, then stepped to the compartment window and raised the curtain. It was hard to see much as the attackers were now alongside the train. He could also hear loud voices and shouts. Carefully, he lowered the compartment window and edged his head around the window frame to survey the scene.

The train's attackers were all dressed in Nazi Brown Shirt uniforms and more than a dozen were now trying to board the train. One of them, glancing up, saw Muller's head peering out the window and threw a large rock in his direction that harmlessly bounced off the train's siding. Muller saw a doorway open and the attackers scramble aboard. An insider, thought Muller.

He could also hear the men shouting.

"Jews out!"

"Get rid of foreigners!"

"Out, out. Keep out the fucking Bolsheviks. No more!"

He pulled up the window and locked it tightly, then sat, his anger growing; Storm Troopers. He'd seen them before; trouble makers and very dangerous. Attacking an international train? Who knew what they were planning to do? His blood up by now, he stood and drew a deep breath. Damned if he'd just stand by and be pushed around.

Muller could hear sounds of struggle within the train. With a loud crash, the window of the compartment next to his broke and he heard one of the attackers cursing the occupants.

"Out of here you dirty Jews. Get off the train–this is as far as you go." He heard the sounds of punches being thrown and shrieks of fear and pain from a woman in the compartment.

Muller opened his compartment door and saw the back and booted legs of a Brown Shirt beating someone inside the next compartment. He slipped on his brass knuckles and moved to the compartment door, behind the attacker, who now stepped fully into the compartment, punching two elderly women who cried out and tried to shield themselves from the blows; a grey haired, slender man, bleeding from his nose, had collapsed at the attacker's feet. The attacker turned to try and disentangle himself from the bodies of his victims. He glared menacingly at Muller.

"Stay out of this mister or you're next," he said.

Muller's knuckled right fist caught the attacker flush on his mouth, crushing the bridge of his front teeth, sending a jet of blood into the air; his knuckled left fist struck the attacker's right jaw and Muller could feel the cheekbone fracture. The attacker's eyes rolled up in his head, and as he began to slump to the ground, Muller hit him in the gut, feeling his ribcage crack. Muller stepped back and let the man collapse.

He stepped over the prone body and began disentangling the two women and the old man.

"Can you stand?" he asked.

They responded and slowly gained their feet, looking from Muller to the bloodied attacker, frightened and utterly bewildered.

"Here," said Muller, stretching out an arm, "step over him and get into my compartment."

They held on to Muller and one another and staggered into his compartment, collapsing onto the seats.

"Lock the door," Muller commanded.

Returning to the corridor, Muller saw a train conductor and one of the Brown Shirts in a struggle several compartments away. The Brown Shirt's back was to Muller, so he swung a knuckled fist into the man's kidney. He let out a yelp of pain and turned toward Muller with a look of shock and surprise. Muller struck him hard, on the side of the head, and the man collapsed, apparently unconscious.

The conductor straightened himself wiping blood from his mouth.

"Thank you, sir, Mr. Muller, isn't it?"

Muller nodded. "What the Hell is going on?"

The doors farther down the train were closed and he couldn't see if there were more fights going on.

"We've received threats from Nazi gangs before," replied the conductor. "They've thrown rocks at us and tried to harass passengers they accuse of being Jews and foreigners, but this is the first time they've actually mounted an attack on a train."

The conductor moved toward the end of the corridor and opened the door to the next car, where there were more struggles going on.

Christ, what a mess this is, Muller thought to himself.

Suddenly, he saw a Brown Shirt running in his direction waving a club with a large metal ball on the tip. A conductor stepped out of a compartment and tried to intercept the attacker. They both went down in a heap and Muller ran forward, delivering a kick which caught the Brown Shirt in the neck. Muller reached down to wrestle away the club and swung it at the man, but somehow missed and hit the door of the compartment with a blow that jarred the weapon out of his grasp. He and the attacker both grabbed for it, but the conductor shoved the Brown Shirt away. The man freed himself and stood, but instead of attacking, he wiped a bloody nose and turned, running toward the rear of the train.

Muller and the conductor regained their feet but decided against pursuing the man.

By now Muller could hear whistles and sirens and he saw cars marked Railway Police pulling up beside the train.

Entering a vacant compartment, he pulled down the window and looked out to see several bloodied figures in the snow, which he took to be passengers who had been thrown off the train by the attackers. As police reinforcements began to arrive, he heard the Brown Shirts yelling at one another to get off the train and run for it, which he could see them doing.

The police entered the train and raced forward to search for attackers. They ran past Muller and the conductor, then slowed where the two prone Brown Shirts lay, still unable to rise.

"Well, well, what have we here?" said one of the burly policemen roughly pulling up the heads of one, then the other Brown Shirt and letting them fall again. "I don't think these boys are going to give us any trouble for a while."

"Anyone know who took care of them?"

The conductor gestured toward Muller. "Mr. Muller is a passenger who resisted the attack. And pretty successfully, too," he said.

"I should say so." The policeman stood to appraise Muller. "Looks like you're handy with the knuckledusters," he said, smiling.

Muller took off the devices and slipped them back into his suit pocket, shrugging.

"I bought them in Chicago last year," he said vaguely. "I've never used them before, but they seemed to be useful."

Muller strode toward his compartment. "The passengers in the next compartment were being attacked, so I intervened. When I subdued that one," he pointed to the first attacker who was beginning to move, moaning hoarsely, "I put them in my compartment to wait. They may be injured and need help."

Muller rapped on his compartment and when the occupants raised the curtain and saw him they unlocked the door. Muller entered, accompanied by the conductor, the policeman observing from the hallway.

Muller knelt in front of them as they cowered against the compartment wall, still terrified and uncomprehending.

"It's okay now," he said gently, reaching out to touch them reassuringly. "They're gone. You're safe; it's over."

They looked at him, still too shocked to speak. Then the man began to sit up and recover his wits.

"You saved us," he said. "You saved us." And he fell back on the compartment settee.

"Are any of you injured?" Muller quietly asked.

"We were beaten," replied the man, "but I don't think any of us is seriously hurt. Magda, Harriet?" he said looking inquiringly at the two women. They shook their heads.

Muller stood and turned to the conductor.

"Let them stay here, since their compartment got pretty broken up."

The conductor nodded. He reached for Muller's luggage. "I'll move you to another compartment and put their things in here."

"I'll return to speak to you later," said the policeman, striding toward the rear of the train.

In his new compartment, Muller lowered the exterior window. He could see train personnel and railway policemen tending to the victims in the snow and moving them back on board. Looking forward, he saw a Railway Police truck winching and dragging an obstacle of some kind that the Brown Shirts had placed on the track to force the train to brake. Then he saw two policemen open a compartment doorway, tossing the two Brown Shirts he had fought with out onto the snow. They then disembarked and each picked up one of the prone bodies, threw it over their shoulder like a sack of grain and began trudging back toward the rear of the train, where some kind of operations center had been set up.

Muller decided matters were under control, so he walked to the lavatory and stood above the small sink, his hands on either side and took a long look at himself in the mirror. He saw the reflection of a trim 30-year-old, with brown hair and brown eyes and a determined look on his face. He filled the sink, dashed cold water on his face and washed his hands, which shook a little, but he was surprised to discover they didn't hurt at all. He saw he had bloodstains on his shirt and suit jacket, but no other evidence of his fights. He took several deep breaths, trying to calm himself.

He'd never thought he'd actually ever use the brass knuckles when he'd bought them in Chicago, during a visit to his sister over a year ago. He was walking in one of Chicago's gritty neighborhoods when he happened to glance in a storefront pawn shop window and saw several sets of brass knuckles offered for sale. He'd walked on a block or so, then stopped and retraced his steps. He'd remembered a dark night in Danzig a year earlier when he was summoned to a meeting that could have been an ambush. He was locked in a struggle with the local Nazi party as a diplomat in that Free City, which was supposedly under protection of the League of Nations. So, he'd had plenty of enemies who might want to send him a message. He'd wished then that he had brass knuckles, which might offer him some kind of protection–or at least reassurance. In the end, the meeting turned out to be a clandestine warning from friends about a Nazi assassination squad that had him as a target. So, he'd not been attacked and he had been able to defuse the assassination threat. But afterward, there had been a lingering thought that having access to brass knuckles might prove useful sometime in the future.

So, standing in front of that Chicago pawn shop, he'd decided to humor himself. He'd walked inside and talked with the shop owner, a seedy looking individual with heavy jowls, unkempt hair and an edgy demeanor. The man had let him try on several pairs and recommended one particularly nasty looking set that was broad enough to cover his whole fist and had small studs on the heavy metal cover above his grip.

"This one'll cost you $1.25," he'd said, "an extra quarter for the high quality."

And so Muller had acquired a set of knuckledusters as they were called in the trade.

They'd come in handy today.

He toweled off, went to the dining car, still a shamble of broken china and glassware. He was able to get a mug of hot coffee and several croissants which he took back to his new compartment, and sat down, his mind spinning.

# CHAPTER 3

It was only two months earlier that Muller had returned home to Zurich after a year of overseas travel and had accepted his father's invitation to join him for what he had called a small discussion. It had turned out to be much more than Muller expected.

They were sitting in his father's book-lined study, a small fire warming the November chill, Muller on an overstuffed sofa next to his father's handsome leather chair which faced the fireplace.

Muller leaned forward, elbows on his knees, and responded carefully to what his father had just told him.

"Let me try to understand this. You're proposing that I go to Vienna as an undercover Swiss intelligence officer–a spy, if you will–but on an informal basis, as the Swiss Government doesn't have an Intelligence Service. I'd be reporting to someone who's not a government official but an influential government advisor and my cover for this unofficial espionage work would be a League of Nations diplomatic appointment.

He shook his head, trying to absorb what his father was suggesting. "This is very bizarre, Father. I think you better go back to the beginning–and also explain to me what your role is in all this."

Karl Muller fixed a steady gaze at this son. "It is very bizarre, Paul," he said. "But we live in strange times. And I'm dead serious about this." Karl did not smile.

"My role is easily explained," he began. "It's an outgrowth of our compulsory military service program, which I've now been a part of for over 40 years. You and your brother have your backpacks and rifles to do your military training exercises–well, you've been away, Paul, so you've been exempt for the past several years, but you know what I'm talking about."

Muller nodded. "I confess that I haven't missed marching around in rain and snow and heat with my pack and rifle, training to defend Switzerland."

He grinned. "But I'm all for it, Father. It's really important; I'm just glad others have been doing it in my absence."

"It's something every Swiss male does." His father nodded. "But I've traded in my backpack for a different role."

"I haven't spoken about this to you or your brother–or frankly even very much of it to your mother," Karl continued, "but over the years, I've come to assume positions of increasing authority in our civilian-military hierarchy and I now count myself among the handful of leaders. There are actually six of us. One is a banker like me, another owns a watch factory, the others, well, let's just say they're prominent Swiss citizens. We all have our occupations, but we meet to consult one another on a regular basis about our nation's business.

"It should come as no surprise to you that we view the current state of affairs in Europe with great concern and that we are taking steps to prepare for whatever may come. I hope we don't find ourselves facing a new war, but it would be irresponsible not to look to our interests."

"But Father," Muller interrupted, "surely you're not gearing Switzerland up to take sides in these European quarrels."

"No, not at all," Karl replied. "The preparations we're making are designed to permit us to maintain our neutrality. That's not such an easy thing to do."

He paused. "One of the subjects I try to keep tabs on is intelligence. We'd like to know as much as we can about what our neighbors are planning to do so we can figure out how *we* ought to respond. But unlike our British, French and German friends, each of which has quite sophisticated networks that we know about, and sometimes encounter, there is no Swiss intelligence service. Our Defense Ministry has exactly three people that are assigned to tasks remotely resembling collection of foreign intelligence.

"So, you've set up a secret network, outside the government," said Muller.

"That's right," said Karl. "I'm not going to tell you much more about it at this stage. But yes, we have a network that I want you to join. Right now, we need someone to operate in Vienna."

"And you want me to be that agent," Muller said.

His father nodded. "That's right."

They both grew quiet and gazed into the fire, reflecting on what Karl had proposed.

"You will understand that what happens in Austria is important to us," Karl said, breaking the silence. "Among other things, we share a long border. You're also aware that Hitler has been running an increasingly aggressive campaign to absorb Austria into Germany."

Muller nodded. "He's made no secret of that. Even the American press reported that much. But what's his rationale?"

"Hitler's embarked on a massive rearmament program," said Karl. "Austria has valuable assets–coal, iron and steel industries, for example, industrial chemicals and machine tools; there's a long list. We think he wants to seize them and put them to work building still more arms for the German military.

"And there's one more thing; he's running short of money," Karl said. "Rearmament is very expensive and he needs more money to finance his program."

"So, what's his solution to that problem?" asked Muller.

"Steal Austria's gold and cash reserves," Karl replied. "We believe that's Hitler's principal goal in wanting to take over the country." He sighed and ran his hand through his thinning hair. "The reality is that if Hitler sets his mind to taking Austria there's not much we can do to prevent it. But maybe we can find a way to limit the damage by diverting the funds he wants to seize."

Muller stubbed out his cigarette. "And the role of this agent you're talking about–that is, me–would be somehow to get hold of Austria's money before Hitler does?"

Karl nodded. "That's about right." Again, he didn't crack a smile.

And so that's how it had begun.

But as Muller was to discover, there was more to it.

There always is.

# CHAPTER 4

Hans Hausamann was 40 years old, medium height and trim, with an athletic bearing. His level eyebrows combined with a long aquiline nose to suggest the letter T above a wide mouth. He radiated an image of intelligence and energy.

They were sitting in a comfortable office in Teufen, Switzerland, a village in the Canton of Appenzell situated 90 kilometers east of Zurich, close to the southern shore of Lake Constance and the border with Germany. Hausamann had invited Muller to visit him there following Muller's discussion with his father.

"Hausamann is the man you need to see," Karl had told him. "He's the man who runs the secret intelligence system and he's the man you'll be reporting to. The organization is called ¨ Büro Ha– the letters of his first and last names–and he's really the only one that knows what it does."

"Which is fine with me, incidentally," Karl added. "It limits the opportunity for leaks."

The invitation had been delivered to Muller in an unmarked envelope setting a date three days later at 10:00 AM, clearly timed to give him time to travel from Zurich by the 8:00 AM local train.

Muller took the steps down to the street from the Teufen station platform and a stout man in an ill-fitting suit approached him.

"Mr. Muller?" he inquired. "My name is Rudi Dunkel; I'm to drive you to your meeting."

Dunkel led him to a small Renault and opened the rear door for Muller to enter.

The trip took no more than five minutes. Dunkel braked in front of what appeared to be a small factory; a sign above the entrance read *Optik Werke*. Dunkel guided him to the doorway of an office building set slightly apart from the factory. The door was locked, but Muller found a button, pushed it and heard an entry bell ring inside. A woman in a smock opened the door and motioned him to enter.

"Mr. Muller?" she inquired.

"Yes," Muller replied.

"You are expected. Please follow me." She led him down a short corridor, rapped on a doorway, opened it and announced, "Mr. Muller is here, Mr. Hausamann."

Muller entered the office, was greeted by Hausamann with a brisk handshake, and took a seat which Hausamann proffered, in an upholstered chair, kitty-cornered from the chair Hausamann took. The chair was hard and uncomfortable, not intended for long, relaxed conversations, Muller decided.

"I asked your father to recruit you for Vienna," Hausamann said.

It was an abrupt way to begin, Muller thought. And it soon became clear that Hausamann was a very direct man who got right to the point. Muller thought to himself that the stiff chair he was occupying was very much a part of the business-like atmosphere Hausamann projected. No small talk or let's-get-acquainted preamble; Hausamann was a man with a plan. And without any further introduction, he began to speak.

"I was a Swiss military officer sent to Berlin in 1936 as an official observer of the war games that were being conducted by the German army. One of their exercises was a plan to take over Danzig. So, we had to study the situation there closely. Commissioner Lester played a weak hand very skillfully for the League of Nations in Danzig, staving off both the German government and the local Nazis and keeping the Free City out of their clutches. You were an indispensable part of that effort. So, you became a marked man in the index I maintain."

"We know that Danzig was a stressful assignment," Hausamann continued, "and that after returning to Geneva you resigned from the League to travel for most of the last year–mainly in the United States. When I learned that you were back in Switzerland, I suggested to your father that he have a word with you."

"My becoming a marked man appears to be a compliment," Muller said.

Hausamann smiled. "Oh yes," he said, "marked for bigger things–as now, in Vienna."

All right, Muller thought; two can play the game of being abrupt.

"In that case, Mr. Hausamann, kindly explain Vienna to me. What is to be my assignment?"

Hausamann replied without hesitation. "It's been decided by Swiss leaders that absorption of Austria by Germany would be detrimental to our interests. Consequently, we will attempt to prevent it from happening. Our ability to influence events decisively is limited, however; so, as a fallback plan, in the event Germany succeeds, we'd like to minimize the financial assets which fall into their hands.

"Those are our goals. That's what I'm working on and your assignment will be to help me–us–succeed."

"With all due respect, sir, that covers a lot of ground and doesn't offer much guidance," Muller said.

"I try not to elaborate any more than necessary, Mr. Muller," Hausamann replied. "You will find that my explanation will be a bit terse. I don't expect that you will ever wind up in a cold, dark, cellar room stripped naked and tied to a chair with no bottom, with some Gestapo torturer affixing electrodes to your dangling testicles which he can attach to a small generator and, in an instant, deliver you into a universe of such engulfing and agonizing pain as to force you to divulge any information they ask for."

"Still," said Hausamann, "it's best to be careful."

Muller felt his stomach drop. He'd accepted that there would be dangers associated with his new position and he knew from prior experience that Nazis played for keeps. But Hausamann's graphic description was decidedly unsettling. The image it conjured up caused Muller to wince, his back twitching involuntarily, as if to distance his body from the implicit threat.

In truth, he had not really thought about having to endure torture at the hands of the Gestapo.

Hausamann, however, seemed unaware of the effect of his words, speaking rapidly, but calmly. He conveyed a sense of quiet confidence that Muller found reassuring, even with his offhand, almost business-like, invocation of the lurid prospect of Gestapo brutality.

"I am a soldier, Mr. Muller," Hausamann continued. "I hold a senior rank in the Swiss Army and am trained in military doctrine and military intelligence. As I told you a moment ago, I spent a year in Berlin observing the *Reichswehr*, which, as you probably know, was the tiny German Army that was permitted under the Treaty of Versailles, composed of only seven infantry divisions and three cavalry divisions.

"I also became privy to the illegal German military rearmament program that gave birth to what's now openly called the *Wehrmacht*–the current German army, which is a lot bigger and much more menacing–and I became very well-acquainted with the German military leaders who supervised that buildup.

"I continue assiduously to maintain and deepen those relationships and seek to use them in furtherance of the interests of Switzerland." Hausamann fixed Muller with his eyes, as a way to emphasize his words. "I perform these duties, even in the face of the kinds of risks I just posed.

"I am also a businessman," he went on. "The factory next door manufactures very high end optical products widely used in precision products, including ordinance, aircraft and cameras. These products are of considerable interest in certain German military procurement circles.

"So it is, Mr. Muller, that wearing these two hats, I spend very large portions of my time in Germany. I cultivate the contacts I maintain there to serve our intelligence needs. Let me say, simply, that I am very well-connected and, as a consequence, privy to very sensitive information.

"In this case, unlike the conventional role of espionage agents with which you may be familiar, your role in Vienna will be less about informing me of events occurring in Austria than it will be to inform Austrian officials of information that I will see is passed to you.

"If we cannot prevent Herr Hitler from plotting to take over Austria–and I'm afraid we can't stop him from trying–we can at least try to thwart him, by seeing to it that our Austrian friends learn what the Germans are planning, and hope they will be able to take action to evade or block their plans."

Hausamann paused.

Muller sat back in his chair reflecting on what he'd just been told. He reached for his cigarette case, extracted two Gitanes, offering one to Hausamann who accepted. Lighting them both, Muller exhaled a large billow of smoke through which he gazed at Hausamann.

"So you want me to serve as a link to pass intelligence to the Austrians," he said; "that covers the part about trying to prevent a German takeover. What about the second part–limiting the damage if Hitler succeeds in his takeover plan?"

"That's where we hope your League of Nations cover comes into play, Mr. Muller," Hausamann replied.

"You're to become the League of Nations Commissioner General for Austria. Rather a nice title, don't you think? And it is–well, more accurately, it was–a powerful office, at one time actually running the Austrian economy. Those powers have expired. But the office retains residual authority that I expect will offer you–us," he added, actually smiling for a moment as he said it–"some leverage if it gets to that point.

"Anyway, there's a man at the League offices in Geneva whom you need to see. He knows nothing about me or the fact that you will be working in Vienna as a Swiss agent. But he knows a lot about Austria and its finances.

"We tend to think that he might be persuaded to empower a new Commissioner General to take steps to help achieve our second goal, of diminishing the financial gain that Hitler might realize from taking over Austria."

The meeting concluded and Rudi Dunkel drove Muller back to the tiny station where Muller found a seat on the platform to await the next local train back to Zurich.

He reflected on his conversation with Hausamann. The man was obviously serious, and also very cautious; he hadn't revealed any details about his network or how it worked. As Muller was leaving, Hausamann told him that Dunkel would visit him in Zurich in the next week to brief him on communication procedures and complete the paperwork on his new assignment.

"But don't expect much," he'd added. "It's very un-Swiss, but we minimize organizational structure and avoid conventional bureaucracy. You'll find that's a relief when you're in the field–which is where you'll be."

Interestingly, he'd never asked Muller to confirm that he was taking the job; it had just been assumed–and, Muller acknowledged to himself, he'd certainly played along with that assumption.

Muller sighed. Was he doing the right thing to accept the assignment? He didn't really know much about Austria and nothing at all about its finances. As a tri-lingual Swiss he would face no language issues, since German–the lingua franca of Austria–was the mother tongue of his native Zurich–along with his fluent

English, spoken at home since birth, and French, learned early in school and widely used in the years since then.

He guessed he could learn the issues quickly enough. He'd started out in Danzig with no knowledge of the situation there and had soon mastered it. Once again he'd be opposing Hitler–and in that role, he'd be no better, or worse, than any other diplomat; the reality was that no one could predict what Hitler would do in any given situation.

Muller's mind drifted over the short history. In January 1933, Hitler had been appointed Chancellor of Germany, still then generally referred to as the Weimar Republic, which was governed by a Constitution and had at least the trappings of a democracy. But, within six weeks, he'd abolished the parliament, eliminated any political opposition, overturned the courts and made himself dictator of a new Germany Reich. In June 1934, he had unleashed the Gestapo in an orgy of savage violence, murdering nearly 100 of his perceived enemies and cementing his absolute power over the nation. He had proceeded to employ his authority by unleashing an aggressive assault on existing European institutions. He'd resigned from the League of Nations with no repercussions, he'd re-occupied the Rhineland without a shot being fired, he unilaterally repudiated the hated Treaty of Versailles and he then proceeded to shred disarmament commitments and embark upon a massive program to enlarge the German army and build a powerful new German air force.

He had become, Muller thought to himself, a seemingly unstoppable juggernaut, showing himself to be both willing and able to upend European politics. He had pursued this aggressive agenda while shamelessly proclaiming his commitment to peaceful resolution of political disputes and, at the same time, he'd issued new demands and threatened to unleash violent reprisals if they weren't met.

Muller stood and began to pace on the platform, putting up the collar of his overcoat against the winter chill.

He realized that this was the maelstrom he would be confronting again if he accepted Hausamann's assignment. He had been in that position once before. As Secretary to Sean Lester, the High Commissioner of the League of Nations in Danzig, he'd spent two years working to stave off a Nazi takeover of what had been designated in the Treaty of Versailles as a Free City under the protective mandate of the League. It had been a trying and–at times–intimidating role.

But he had come to relish it and had thrown himself into the task, honing political and diplomatic skills to resist the Nazis, their hateful ideology and their thuggish behavior. And repeatedly, he and Lester had been undermined by a timid and ineffective League, which proved powerless to confront aggression–not just in Danzig, but in Spain and Abyssinia too. Ultimately, he and Lester had managed to preserve a stalemate in Danzig–a kind of fig-leaf that camouflaged the reality of Nazi rule. But it had been a dispiriting and disillusioning outcome and he had returned to

Geneva, resigned from the League and set off for a year of travel to clear his mind.

Now he was back; what was he going to do with himself? He'd asked himself that question countless times. His family bank, Muller & Company, was very successful, managing money, safeguarding valuables and keeping secrets for wealthy families in Europe and elsewhere. His father ran the bank, his brother was the next in line and Muller had never had the slightest interest in being involved in the business.

Meanwhile Hitler's looming presence in Europe had continued to grow. There was open talk of the risk of a new war–a prospect viewed with utter horror by the democracies, but which they seemed unwilling to confront. France was politically riven and convulsed by repeated changes in government and Britain continued to pursue a policy of appeasement, offering one concession after another to Germany in hopes of satisfying Hitler's ambitions in order to keep the peace.

Muller had grown to detest Hitler and what he stood for. He'd seen first-hand in Danzig the casual violence of Nazi Party members and their contempt for democratic values. Traveling in the United States, he'd been able to avoid watching the spectacle of Hitler's aggressive behavior. Americans weren't interested in the subject; it wasn't covered in the news and people rarely spoke about it. Like his American hosts, Muller found that he could simply ignore what was happening in Europe.

Except, he couldn't. Europe kept beckoning him to return. And once he was back, the growing Nazi menace had recaptured his attention. He realized that it was a subject he knew better than most people. Then suddenly, his father had proposed that he talk to Hausamann about becoming a Swiss agent and try to help deter Hitler's plan to annex Austria. He'd gone along with the idea, really without giving it much thought.

But now, as the locomotive pulling the local train rounded a bend and approached the station, puffs of black, sooty smoke billowing out of its stack, he felt a sense of comfort descend. Hausamann's assignment was a good opportunity, he decided. He smiled as he mounted the steps to board the train.

This was something he ought to be doing. It was time to get on with it.

He buried any thoughts about Gestapo torture chambers.

## CHAPTER 5

Several days later, Muller found himself in the offices of Jose Maria Oquendo, a Paraguayan national, who was Chief of the Financial Section of the League of Nations.

"So, you're to become the League's new Commissioner General for Austria."

"Yes. I'm told that I'm to be appointed by the League Council later this month," Muller replied.

Oquendo was an acknowledged, almost legendary, expert in the League's vast array of financial interventions around the globe. What Muller had been instructed to do was to tease out of Oquendo an understanding of the position that had been selected as his cover in Vienna and begin to plan how to accomplish the goals of Büro Ha.

So, he'd come to Geneva and this meeting at the offices of the League.

The Palais des Nations, site of the League's headquarters since 1920, was a large and imposing structure with a five-story brick and stone façade dominated by tall marble columns. It was situated alongside Lac Léman in Geneva, facing east toward the Salève, the steep mountain abruptly rising above the lake, and on the occasional clear day it offered views of the Swiss Alps and a gleaming Mont Blanc summit in the far distance.

But no scenic panorama was on offer outside Oquendo's office window that early December afternoon; leaden clouds turned the lake a gunmetal grey, flecked with windblown whitecaps. Combined with the shadows of oncoming twilight, the view conveyed a melancholy appearance that Muller decided seemed to fit the circumstances.

Sitting in the anteroom awaiting the summons to Oquendo's office, he had reflected on how different things felt that morning, going through the tedious process of getting signed up again as an employee of the League.

Back in the summer of 1933, when he'd been hired the first time, he had been an enthusiastic new recruit, excited at being admitted to a vibrant institution that was brimming with energy and self-confidence. But this morning, he'd found it to be a diminished place. There was no longer the bustling impatience and boisterous enthusiasm or the sense of urgency that reflected the importance of the work the League was performing and the significance of its mission. Now, three-and-a-half long years later, having been repeatedly shown wanting and having failed to meet its own and the world's expectations, the League had become a shambling bureaucracy and the staff seemed to be going through the motions. Back then, the shabby offices and overcrowded corridors had seemed to be a badge of honor, reflecting higher priorities; now, they weren't as crowded, certainly not as important–and they had deteriorated from shabby to downright seedy.

"Mr. Muller."

He snapped out his reverie and stood to shake hands with Director Oquendo.

Following him into his office, Muller saw a short, wide man–not fat, but stocky, like a hydrant–with a bald pate and longish white hair. Muller took him to be in his early 60's. When he sat and faced Muller, piercing black eyes dominated his appearance. Rimless glasses couldn't camouflage the intensity of Oquendo's gaze.

"There was a time, Mr. Muller–and not so long ago–that appointment as Commissioner General in Vienna would have made you a very important figure indeed," he began. Then he paused; "but it's a little late in the game, don't you think?"

Oquendo's gaze was unwavering. It was an unspoken accusation that there was something decidedly odd about appointing a non-career, non-diplomat–and not even a financial industry expert–to the Commissioner General post now, at the end of 1937, when Austria was under intense pressure from Germany and the League wasn't in a position to help it resist.

"I'm told, the appointment was made specifically *because* of current circumstances," Muller responded, returning Oquendo's gaze. He hoped that would be a sufficiently ambiguous response.

"I'd like to engage your expertise in exploring how the office might be adapted to the situation."

Oquendo continued his intense gaze for several long moments more, then, evidently having made a decision, he sat up in his chair, reached into a desk drawer and produced a bottle of red wine and an opener.

"Fair enough, Mr. Muller," he said. "We've got the rest of the afternoon to talk about Austria, then. But since it's a dreary day in December, and the story we're to discuss is itself a little sad, we should fortify ourselves a bit. This is a ten-year old Gevrey-Chambertin. Will you join me?"

"Gladly," replied Muller.

Oquendo reached behind him, removing two glasses from a shelf, and placed them on the desk. He deftly uncorked the bottle and poured a splash into one of the glasses. He swirled it, and took a long sniff to test the bouquet, then slowly tasted it, moving his tongue to savor the texture. Nodding, with a smile indicating satisfaction, he proceeded to fill both glasses to the halfway point.

Together they lifted their glasses and clinked them. "Santė," they murmured to one another, then took a sip.

"Superb," said Muller. "Thank you."

"So, Mr. Muller, let's begin by speaking about the Austro-Hungarian Empire," said Oquendo. "Probably not an area of your expertise," he smiled as he continued without awaiting Muller's response, "but history can inform us in useful ways.

"In 1914," he began, "at the start of the War, Austria-Hungary was a great power, its 52 million inhabitants spread out over 415,000 square miles making it the second largest and third most populous nation in Europe. It had been ruled by the Habsburg dynasty since the thirteenth century, yet it was hopelessly divided.

"Indeed, you can make the case that Austria-Hungary had ceased to exist in all but name long before the War began. The Emperor resided in one capital, Vienna, but there was a second capital in Budapest, the seat of the Kingdom of Hungary. There were two competing parliaments each with separate and conflicting agendas. Then there were all the other ethnic enclaves: the Croats; the Slovenians–not to be confused with the Slovaks; the Czechs, of course, made up of Bohemians and Moravians; there were the Poles, the Romanians, and the Ruthenians."

"Ruthenians?" inquired Muller.

"That's what the Ukrainians living up in Galicia were called," Oquendo replied.

"Anyway, no one got along with anyone else; something like 21 languages were spoken–they actually issued bank notes in eight different languages–and there was no real sense of nationhood, except for the tax authorities, the army and the secret police that they deployed to keep order."

Oquendo paused, sipped his wine and accepted Muller's proffer of a Gitane, which he lit for them both.

"So, they marched off to war, and by the end, found they'd marched off a cliff. I don't have to tell you that the costs of the conflict were horrendous, not only in the number of soldiers and civilians killed and wounded, but in the political upheavals that were unleashed."

"In the end, as you know, Austria-Hungary was broken up. Czechoslovakia and Hungary declared independence; the Balkan territories of Slovenia, Croatia, and Bosnia were absorbed into the new Serb-dominated Yugoslavia; the Romanians annexed Transylvania; the region of Galicia became part of a newly independent Poland; and the Italians laid claim to the Southern Tyrol.

"So, Austria emerged from the debacle as a shrunken nation of only 13 million square miles, with a population of just 7 million, smaller even than Czechoslovakia."

Muller stubbed out his Gitane. "I read about the exploits of the Czech Legion and how that led to establishment of the Czech nation when I was at Cambridge," he said taking a sip of wine and holding out his glass for the refill being proffered by Oquendo.

"Ah," exclaimed Oquendo approvingly. "What a story that is: 50,000 Czech POWs–mainly deserters from the Austro-Hungarian army–forming an army in Russia that controlled nearly all of Siberia in 1918. Not many people are familiar with it.

"But since you're aware of it, let me show you something,"

Oquendo stood and crossed the room, picking up a framed photo from a shelf which he handed to Muller. The grainy photo showed a group of smiling men with ammunition bandoliers over their shoulders holding rifles and sitting astride the front cowcatcher of a locomotive with a large star affixed to it.

"That's my father-in-law on the far left," he said. "They had captured a Red Army train somewhere east of Irkutsk, near Lake Baikal, and for weeks they blocked any Bolshevik movements in Siberia."

"He must have some fascinating stories to tell," said Muller examining the old photo before handing it back.

"Unfortunately, he didn't survive," said Oquendo. "In fact, my wife never even knew that he'd been part of the Czech Legion–only that he didn't return after the war. Then, one evening fifteen years or so ago, we were at a diplomatic dinner here in Geneva and my wife happened to be seated next to a Czech diplomat–who turned out to be the guy next to her father in this photo."

Oquendo pointed to the grinning face.

"The two of them began conversing and sharing memories of growing up in what was then Moravia. My wife told him her maiden name, Evinka Hradecky and somehow it came up that her father had been killed in the war. The diplomat looked at her in astonishment. 'Was your father Konstantin Hradecky by any chance?' She said 'yes'. The diplomat proceeded to stand up, push his chair back to kneel before my wife, kissing her hand and bursting into tears.

"Well, no one at the dinner party quite knew how to react," Oquendo continued, "including me; I was seated several places away. All the guests stopped conversing, looking on in bewilderment, and the room fell silent. The diplomat finally regained his composure and stood, still gazing at my wife. 'Konstantin Hradecky was my dearest friend and one of the bravest fighters in the Czech Legion,' he said. 'I owe him my life. And now I have the great honor to find myself seated to the daughter I never knew he had.

"'I am overcome with joy' and he kneeled to kiss my wife's hand again.

"As you can well imagine, Mr. Muller," Oquendo continued, "this ranks as the most remarkable diplomatic dinners I have ever attended. The diplomat–Radoslav Kubilek is his name–became a good friend and was able to tell my wife something of her father's life with the Legion, and his death in a firefight with the Red Army. Kubilek had somehow gotten his hands on this photo and he made a copy for us.

"And here it is," he said, returning it to the shelf where he displayed it.

Muller smiled broadly at Oquendo.

"That's a wonderful story," he said "and what an extraordinary memento that photo must be for you and your wife."

Oquendo nodded.

"She passed away two years ago," he said, "and I decided to keep it here in my office instead of at home.

Oquendo waved away Muller's offer of condolences.

"I wanted it here not just for its sentimental value," he said, "but as a reminder of the opportunities events sometimes offer statesmen to affect the arc of history–and the consequences that can ensue if they fail at their task.

"Think of it," he continued, "this ragged army of Czech deserters from the Austrian Army became a fighting force that controlled the whole of Siberia and the Port of Vladivostok. They blocked any supplies from flowing west to the Red Army, which was desperately short of arms and equipment. At the same time, the British landed troops at the northern Russian port in Murmansk, halting any supplies coming from there too. And of course, the German army blocked any access to Europe. So here was this new Bolshevik Russian state, completely surrounded and cut off from every outside source of supplies. There was a chance to destroy it, and the Communist menace it posed, right then and there."

Oquendo paused, smiling. "Wouldn't that have made life a lot better?" he asked rhetorically. "No Soviet Union, no Comintern, no Lenin or Stalin." He shook his head.

"But it didn't happen. Leaders failed to grasp the opportunity and it slipped away."

Oquendo smiled wanly.

"Which brings us back to Austria, doesn't it?

"Will some leader assert himself in this crisis and make a difference?" He again fixed Muller with his penetrating gaze.

"We'll soon see, won't we?" he said. "In the meantime, we should continue preparing you for *you*r leadership role."

Muller smiled, acknowledging the challenge implicit in Oquendo's remark.

Muller lit another Gitane and Oquendo poured more wine before continuing.

"So, there was Austria after the war; stripped of its empire and reduced to a small shadow of its former greatness. It still had the Habsburg palaces with their fabled architecture, and, of course, a strong and unbending Catholic tradition. What it didn't have, though, was enough food to feed its citizens.

"Austria, and particularly Vienna, experienced the worst famine in post-war Europe; people literally starved to death. The Allied blockade had created shortages throughout Germany and Central Europe, but it was worst in Austria. There were tales of aristocratic families sitting down to dinner around polished Louis XV tables in ornate dining salons, with plush Persian rugs on the floor and old master paintings on the wall, serving Delft porcelain dishes holding only half a cold sausage to eat.

"And it persisted. The Empire had been organized so food, fuel and other necessities produced in the far-flung regions found their way to Vienna through well-established commercial networks. But, those networks had ceased to exist. And the Viennese starved.

"The economy cratered too. By 1922, the currency had devalued so that, like in Germany, people carried their worthless Austrian Crowns around in wheel barrows. Austria was truly in a state of collapse. And that is when the League first got involved."

Oquendo glanced at Muller. "No, I was not here then," the older man said with a thin smile. "But I've been here a while so I can tell you what happened."

"Please proceed," Muller replied. "I'm particularly anxious to hear about the role played by the Commissioner General."

"Well, it was a central role," Oquendo replied. "The League organized a loan guaranteed by Britain, France, Italy and Czechoslovakia. The central bank was reorganized and a new currency, the Schilling, replaced the Austrian Crown. Austrian assets were pledged as security for the loan and Austrian customs revenues and revenues from the tobacco monopoly were pledged to service the loan. Control over the Austrian economy was handed over to an official of the League, who was awarded the grand title of League of Nations Commissioner General for Austria–the very position you are about to assume," he added, tipping his wine glass to Muller.

"This was one of those historic turning points symbolized by your photo?" Muller asked.

"I hadn't thought about it quite that way before," Oquendo replied, "A Dutchman named Zimmermann assumed the office," he continued, "and he literally ran the Austrian economy. He reorganized the government, raised taxes, cut pensions, eliminated the deficit and oversaw all public investment. It was a very powerful position. His title was Commissioner General, but for practical purposes he was Czar of Austria, answerable only to the Council of the League of Nations.

"And the plan worked. By 1926, the economy was stable, Austria was prospering and the League and the creditors agreed to remove direct controls over the economy and return responsibility back to the Austrian government.

"So, yes; this was a case where decisive League intervention worked, Mr. Muller."

Muller acknowledged the point, but he was troubled by what he'd heard. Oquendo's description conjured images of the Commissioner General's authority that were at odds with Muller's idea of the low-profile diplomatic cover he was supposed to use for his upcoming intelligence mission. He decided to probe further.

"What happened next,' he inquired, "after the Austrians resumed control?"

"At that point, Zimmermann resigned as Commissioner General," Oquendo replied, "and he was replaced by another Dutchman–actually your direct predecessor–a man named Rost van Tonningen.

"Van Tonningen didn't have the same dictatorial authority as Commissioner General that Zimmermann had enjoyed. But he still had control of the revenues generated by Austrian customs and the tobacco monopoly that had been pledged to service the loan, and this made him a very influential player in Austrian financial circles–and, it has to be added–in political circles too."

Oquendo poured out the last of the wine. Muller's apprehensions were growing.

"So this van Tonningen became a political leader as well as a key economic leader?' he asked. The last thing Muller wanted was to be thrust into a prominent post where he would have trouble operating behind the scenes as he envisioned the role described for him by Hausamann.

"Actually, no," replied Oquendo. "Van Tonningen proceeded to marginalize himself and significantly eroded the influence of his office."

Muller's spirits rose. "How did that come about?" he asked.

"Van Tonningen became a very early supporter of Hitler and the Nazis," Oquendo replied, "and his vocal embrace of them did not sit well in Vienna. Austria's government then–and it's still the case today–is modeled along the lines of Mussolini's Fascists but it's also closely tied to the Catholic Church. The ruling party is called the Fatherland Front, but it's widely–and in my view accurately–portrayed as a Clerical-Fascist alliance and it has stoutly resisted Hitler ever since he seized power.

"You'll remember that Hitler was born in Austria, so right from the start, he began meddling in Austrian affairs and our Mr. van Tonningen was right there, urging him on. The Austrian Chancellor, Engelbert Dollfuss retaliated by banning the Nazi Party, but Hitler's supporters continued to agitate against the government and in July 1934 they attempted to overthrow it. A gang of Austrian Nazis invaded the Chancellery and murdered Dollfuss–shot him in the head–then took over the radio station calling for a popular uprising. Government loyalists quickly put down the revolt–Mussolini even threatened to invade Germany if it moved against the Austrians–and the plot fizzled."

Muller leaned back in his chair, running his hands through his hair.

"I confess I'd forgotten about that incident," he said. And it was true; he'd been at Cambridge when news of the Dollfuss assassination broke, and he'd paid little attention to it. It was shocking to be reminded of it now, when he was on the verge of assuming a role in Austrian affairs. Shamefacedly, he asked Oquendo to elaborate.

"Is there a legacy I should know about?" he asked. "A violent act like that must have provoked a huge backlash."

Oquendo nodded. "Absolutely; it still resonates–and not just in Austria, but in both countries. Austria cracked down hard on the Nazi Party; it executed a dozen or so of the ringleaders and expelled many Party members to Germany. Hitler, for his part, imposed a rule banning Germans from visiting Austria; no more ski trips to Kitzbühel," he added with a smile.

"The impact of the ban on the Austrian tourist business was devastating," he said. "Hotels, resorts, and restaurants all over Austria cater to European tourists and they were badly hurt when Germans were forbidden to visit– and this came at a time when the Depression was already cutting into their business.

"The attempted coup also left a legacy of violence–on both sides," he went on. "The fact that the attackers stormed the Chancellery and murdered the Chancellor in cold blood led the

Fatherland Front to strengthen its own paramilitary forces, the Heimwehr, to counter the Nazi goon squads. You're going to find these contending forces still battling on the streets of Vienna when you travel there next month, Mr. Muller. You'll do well to stay out of their way."

"What became of van Tonningen with all this going on?" Muller inquired.

"There was never any evidence that van Tonningen had been involved in the attempted putsch," Oquendo replied, "but as a Nazi sympathizer, his influence was severely impaired. In fact, he played almost no role at all in the subsequent financial crisis that nearly sank not just Austria, but most of Europe, too."

Muller's ears pricked up; was this crisis an event that could reveal a way to protect Austria's reserves from Hitler?

"I'm afraid, I'm not very well informed about the crisis you're referring to, Mr. Oquendo," he said.

Oquendo nodded, as if expecting Muller's response.

"I'll give you the short version of what is in fact a very long story," he said. Muller thought he detected a patronizing inflection in Oquendo's voice.

"In the spring of 1931, there was a run on Creditanstalt, the biggest Austrian bank, presided over by none other than Baron Louis de Rothschild, the foremost financier in Europe. What became our terrible Depression was then in its early stages and the sudden failure of this supposed pillar of financial stability provoked a panic that spread like wildfire to other European banks and threatened a continent-wide collapse.

"The only possible solution to the panic was some kind of multi-country refinancing program. But the French had their own agenda and they proceeded to fan the flames.

Oquendo allowed himself a wan smile in Muller's direction.

"I think you'll find this a particularly informative vignette, Mr. Muller," he said.

Muller leaned forward, listening intently.

"In 1930, Austria and Germany had agreed to form a customs union in a bid to strengthen both economies. This was long before Hitler, Mr. Muller; it was predicated strictly on trade and economic factors. But it infuriated the French, who feared a resurgent Germany and had long made it a centerpiece of their foreign policy to prevent just this kind of potential merger of the German and Austrian economies. They had even written a prohibition to that effect into the Versailles Treaty and had made it a condition of the 1923 loan to rescue Austria. Now it appeared that the customs union they had so long opposed was suddenly about to happen.

"Seeing an opportunity in the Creditanstalt crisis, the French government pounced. It secretly encouraged French banks to withdraw funds from Austria, worsening the crisis, then as Austria teetered on the edge of collapse, it offered a huge financial rescue package–but with the proviso that Austria must abandon the customs union–and, to rub it in, they demanded a response within three hours."

"This blatant exercise of French monetary muscle outraged Montague Norman, the head of the Bank of England and the most powerful Central Banker in Europe. He proceeded to arrange an immediate Bank of England loan to the Austrian government so they wouldn't have to comply with the French demands."

Oquendo smiled. "I'll bet you didn't know that central bankers engage in these kinds of petty exercises in one-upsmanship, Mr. Muller," he said.

"But they do."

"So how was the issue finally settled?" asked Muller. "Is the Bank of England still on the hook for its emergency loan?"

Oquendo shook his head. "No, that was just a temporary fix. In the end, the bankers worked out a comprehensive refinancing package. But it came with a price; the French–supported by the Italians–insisted that the Austrians must abandon the plan for the German customs union, and the Bank of England reluctantly went along. So that's the package they offered to the Austrian government.

"Well," said Oquendo stubbing out the remainder of his cigarette, "they had the money so they prevailed. But it was very contentious; the Austrian parliament voted to accept the loan by only a single vote–81 to 80. But, again it worked; the crisis was averted, the Austrian economy recovered, and the Austrian National Bank wound up with a new 25-year 570 million Schilling loan that extends to 1959."

"And the Commissioner General?" asked Muller.

"The position remains." Oquendo replied. "His authority over the revenues from Customs and the tobacco monopoly is still in place, and those funds remain the crucial link to pay the debt service on the new loan."

That's an interesting bit of information, Muller thought.

"And what became of Mr. van Tonningen?" he asked.

Oquendo hesitated. "I mentioned earlier that he became an outspoken Nazi supporter and lost much of his influence within Austria as a result. His political stance also made him a bit of an outlier here at the League; not many of us embrace Herr Hitler or his party, and a German takeover–which he was advocating–would be in conflict with the new loan that the League had helped to organize. So, there was a lot of tension with van Tonningen professionally and on a personal level as well. Finally, about a year ago, to everyone's relief, he resigned and as I understand it, he's become head of the Dutch Nazi party.

"His position–the role you're about to assume–has remained vacant until now," Oquendo went on. "And meanwhile, Hitler's campaign to take over Austria has become even more insistent; a lot of us think it is only a matter of time until Hitler succeeds–maybe as little as a year.

"I count myself in that camp," he added.

"And suddenly you appear, rather out of the blue, if you'll excuse me for saying so, to assume this vacant position. Please tell me, Mr. Muller; what is to be the role of the League's

Commissioner General for Austria in the current toxic environment?"

Muller returned Oquendo's gaze.

"We'll have to see, won't we, Mr. Oquendo?" he replied.

Muller rose from his chair and strode to the window, peering out at the grey lake, now barely visible in the gathering twilight. He paused, his mind working, then took the final sip of wine from his glass and turned to face Oquendo.

It was time to see if he would rise to the bait.

"Tell me Mr. Oquendo, with your detailed knowledge and long experience, have you given thought to how, in the event of a threatened German takeover, the Commissioner General of the League of Nations for Austria might exercise the authority remaining in his hands to move financial assets out of Austria that might otherwise fall into the hands of the Nazis?"

Oquendo reacted as though someone had jolted him with an electric shock. He sat up straight and slapped his open hand on the desk in front of him. Then he proceeded to burst into laughter, his face wreathed in smiles.

"By God, Muller," he said, "I was hoping that you might raise that subject." He laughed again. "Yes, I have thought about it."

"I just wish I had another bottle of wine to open."

# CHAPTER 6

Nearly an hour passed after the attack before an Austrian Railways Police Superintendent rapped on Muller's compartment door. Muller slid it open and shook hands with a large, burly man. He had a shock of white hair, with a bushy mustache, and a hard face; the look of a cop, though he was wearing a friendly smile. Muller took him to be in his mid-fifties.

He introduced himself as Superintendent Schönen and showed his credentials. Obviously the senior inspector, Muller thought.

After exchanging pleasantries and delivering the now routine and still unsatisfying apologies for the incident, Schönen asked Muller for his papers, which he examined, and after handing them back, asked him to tell his story of what had happened.

As Muller spoke, Schönen took notes in pencil on a form tucked into a clipboard.

He only interrupted a few times.

"You saw they were in Brown Shirt uniforms when they attacked the train?"

Muller said he was certain. "I lived in Danzig for two years. I know what a Brown Shirt uniform looks like."

Schönen nodded. "It's strictly forbidden to wear those uniforms in Austria. They were making a political statement by doing that. No attempt at all to camouflage themselves as some kind of outlaw gang; they wanted everyone to know they were Nazis."

Muller said he'd heard them shouting threats to Jews and foreigners as they attacked.

"I've heard the same thing from others," Schönen said nodding his head. "The usual Party drivel. But they seem to eat it up. The young men, particularly outside the cities–like the place where they mounted the attack–they're just crazy for Nazism."

Schönen devoted a page of his notes to recounting Muller's description of using the brass knuckles to subdue the two attackers he'd confronted. Schönen asked to see the two pieces and proceeded to try them on, making a few feints, as if to throw a punch. He looked at them admiringly, and handed them back to Muller.

"I should probably classify these as dangerous weapons," he said with a friendly smile. "But I don't think that's warranted in this instance."

As Schönen rose to leave, Muller stood up with him, putting his hand on the Policeman's shoulder in a companionable way.

"Superintendent," he said, "you've seen my papers so you know that I'm a diplomat and traveling under diplomatic protection."

Schönen nodded. "I noted that in my report; a League of Nations representative."

"So, I think you can understand why I would like to avoid being implicated in this incident–certainly not publicly and I'd prefer not officially, either," Muller said quietly; "especially the part about punching out a couple of those characters."

He looked Schönen in the eye. "That would not be a good start to a diplomatic assignment," he said in a firm tone.

"So," he continued, pulling his cigarette case out of his breast pocket and extracting a Gitane which he offered Schönen, "I'd like you to step into the corridor out there and enjoy a Gitane while I remove from your clipboard the page of notes you wrote about my encounters with the attackers."

Muller flipped open his lighter to light the Gitane which he handed to Schönen and reached down to remove the clipboard from Schönen's grasp.

Schönen stiffened, then relaxed, accepted the Gitane and Muller's light and released his grip on the clipboard, stepping into the corridor, but blocking the doorway so no one could see in.

A moment later, he re-entered the compartment, stubbed out the butt of the Gitane and picked up his clipboard.

"Funny how pages of reports sometimes get misplaced," he said.

Then as he turned to leave, he leaned back toward Muller. "We'll see to it that nothing about you gets into the press. Good luck Mr. Muller, but I wouldn't throw away those knuckledusters if I were you."

# CHAPTER 7

The train finally reached Vienna's Westbahnhof in mid-afternoon. Muller disembarked, swinging down from his compartment to the station platform and reaching back to gather his luggage and valise. As he did so, the window of the adjoining compartment, where the party he had rescued was staying, slid down. The elderly man, wearing a white plaster to cover his wound, fumbled with the door handle, then, opening it, stepped spryly down to the platform next to Muller.

"I want to thank you again, more formally, for intervening on our behalf this morning, Mr. Muller," he said. "I learned your name from the police superintendent," he added.

Seeing Muller frown, he said, "Oh don't worry; no one else knows. The conductors are all sworn to secrecy."

He smiled. "I would like to deliver a more tangible token of our appreciation for your action, but a train platform is hardly a suitable venue for that." He reached into his waistcoat and extracted a stiff cream-colored card which he extended to Muller. "I would be grateful if you would call upon me."

Muller took the card without reading it. "It was nothing sir," he said, lifting his valise to go. "And I'm glad to see you're feeling better."

"Shall we say two o'clock tomorrow afternoon?" the man said in a firm tone that made plain he was accustomed to being obeyed.

Muller put down his valise and turned the card so he could read it.

**"Friederich P. Baer**

**Chairman, Baer & Company"**

There was an address that meant nothing to him.

The older man again smiled. "I think it would be useful for the new Commissioner General of the League of Nations to meet with me, especially as you have rendered my family and me such valuable assistance." He reached out and shook Muller's hand. "Go now and get settled," he said. "We will meet tomorrow."

He stepped back up into his compartment without waiting for Muller's response.

Muller shook his head, but pocketed the card, picked up his luggage and headed toward passport control at the end of the platform.

A small suite had been booked for him at a hotel named The Continental, which was located just off the Ringstrasse, on Wipplingerstrasse, not far from the Finance Ministry, where his office was situated. As Muller settled into a taxi, he felt a frisson of excitement. Here he was in storied Vienna, seat of the Habsburg Empire for all those centuries, the site of great architecture and home to Mozart, Mahler, Strauss, and countless other geniuses in his pantheon of musical heroes–and as he rode, he could see that there really did seem to be a coffeehouse on every corner, as everyone said. To be sure, he was entering a political cauldron which he didn't fully understand and danger lurked; but here he was, finally. A sense of anticipation lifted his spirits.

His second-floor hotel suite was bright and airy. Tall windows looked out over a tiny park with benches clustered between two tall, bare trees and a street below led toward the junction with a wider thoroughfare. There he spotted an attractive coffeehouse, a sign identifying it as the Café Louvre.

That looks like a handy place to have nearby, he thought.

He had sent his trunk along earlier, so he proceeded to unpack, hanging his suits and formalwear and finding drawers for shirts, socks, neckties and underwear. He lined up several pairs of shoes on the closet floor and made room next to them for his tennis racket, which he hoped he'd have chances to use. He pushed the trunk into a corner and locked it, placing the key securely in his wallet. He would not disturb the false bottom and the Luger pistol and forged documents it contained.

The suite had its own bath and toilet–a nice luxury–so he took a long, soaking tub, washing away the accumulated travel grime. He shaved, changed into a fresh suit and rang for housekeeping to take away his travel clothing–first checking to be sure that the bloodstains from the fight on the train now resembled gravy stains and wouldn't attract attention.

Before leaving the suite, he took a page of white paper from a pad he'd set down next to the phone and placed it on the window casement so it would be visible to a passerby walking from the thoroughfare toward the hotel, who would be looking for it.

Muller was hungry and wanted a beer, so he strolled up the street to the Café Louvre. He found it to be L-shaped, a bar on the right giving way to a high-ceilinged room with small chandeliers hung above clustered tables and booths along the wall. Tall windows faced the street and an outdoor terrace, awaiting warmer weather.

Looking for a table toward the rear so he could watch the crowd that was beginning to assemble, he suddenly heard a loud argument being carried on in English, emanating from one of the booths.

"Boothby, you are so full of shit," said a thin cadaverous-looking man in a wrinkled brown suit with wispy hair. He had a high-pitched, penetrating voice. "You always make excuses for the lies these press handlers make up to keep us from finding out what's really happening. You're as bad as they are."

The man he was speaking to fired back. "Fuck off Hamilton. As usual, you don't know what you're talking about."

"Goddamn it, Boothby, Hitler's trying to twist his arm and we're supposed to sit here and ignore it all?" Hamilton replied testily.

Several other voices drowned one another out as the argument escalated in intensity and loudness. It was evident these were Western journalists all trying to snoop out the next breaking story in the tug of war between Germany and Austria.

"Schuschusnigg's gone all quiet."

"So what? He's Chancellor; he's got a full plate and just maybe he's got a plan to get Hitler off his back."

"Von Papen's circling like the snake he is. Some Ambassador; he's Hitler's lackey and he's got something up his sleeve."

"Hamilton, will you leave it alone?"

Back and forth they went with other voices chiming in.

Muller sat at a nearby table, ordered a large glass of beer and a sausage with slices of glazed liver and eavesdropped. Journalists were like moths circling a flame–swooping and diving, jostling one another for position, offering and withholding information; it was a game–but deadly serious, often played out in noisy arguments like the one Muller was listening to and nearly always, as here, lubricated by ample quantities of alcohol.

One of the journalists noticed Muller's inquisitive attention and slid his chair over to his table.

"Practicing your English language skills?" he inquired with a grin. He was a short, balding man with thick glasses and a suit in need of being pressed. "Or just listening in?"

Muller reddened. He hadn't realized he'd been noticed. "Well, not actually," he sputtered, responding in English, "um, I, ah…." He cleared his throat.

"You found it interesting–no translation needed, I gather," grinned his interlocutor. "Well if you're going to eavesdrop then you need to buy at least the next round."

He stuck out his hand. "Bill Shirer, *CBS News*."

"I'm Paul Muller," Muller responded. "Shirer? You're the radio guy I heard last fall when I was in the U.S. You and that other guy; what was his name?"

"Murrow," replied Shirer. "Ed Murrow."

"Right," said Muller. "I remember being impressed at hearing you guys reporting live from Europe. I'm pleased to meet you."

Shirer guided Muller's chair over to the booth and interrupted the argument, declaring, "We have a curious neighbor who's not only buying the next round but has already declared himself a fan of *CBS News*."

Shirer introduced Albert Boothby from the *Hearst Press* in Chicago and Nigel Hamilton from the *Daily Telegraph* in London. There were several others whose names Muller didn't catch, including what appeared to be a married couple from the *New York Herald Tribune*.

"Paul Muller," said Muller shaking hands around and signaling the waiter for a new round.

"So what brings you here, Mr. Muller?" asked Hamilton.

"Well, I've just arrived and took a room at the Continental down the street," Muller pointed. "I'm in Vienna as a representative of the League of Nations."

As one, the journalists all turned their full attention to him, their arguments put aside.

"What?" said Hamilton. "A new initiative from the League to save Austria from Hitler's clutches? Well, you have to tell us all about it."

Muller looked at their expectant faces and suddenly realized what had happened.

"No, no," he said with a big smile raising his hands in mock surrender. "No new initiative. I'm no senior emissary sent here to broker a settlement; just a bureaucrat filling a vacancy.

"Sorry to disappoint you," he added, seeing the looks on their faces.

"Well, shit," said one of the journalists whose name Muller hadn't gotten. "I thought we might actually have some news. In that case, you'd better buy two rounds."

Laughter followed and several of the journalists went back to arguing over whether or not Hitler was orchestrating a new squeeze play on the Austrian Chancellor.

Muller observed to Hamilton and Boothby, who were sitting next to him along with Shirer, that he didn't think the League had much energy left for any new initiative, let alone one to block Hitler's aggressive agenda in Austria.

"Germany's not even in the League anymore," he reminded them.

"Right; they walked out in '34 over some French disarmament proposal they didn't like," said Hamilton. "Then the League proceeded to show the world it couldn't do anything about Italy's invasion of Abyssinia or the Civil War in Spain–or much of anything else, really."

"So, congratulations, Mr. Muller," he added, "in coming to visit us from a useless organization. At least you're buying."

"Little Austria really is all alone in this fight with Hitler," Shirer said, drawing on his long thin pipe and returning to the subject they were all consumed by. "The French are paralyzed by musical chairs governments that change every few weeks, Chamberlain in Britain is ready to give Hitler anything he wants in order to forestall war, and Mussolini seems to have decided that Italy should sit this one out.

"The Czechs are sympathetic–they're in Hitler's line of fire too with all that propaganda he's spouting about how they're mistreating the Sudeten Germans. But Czechoslovakia's too small to matter much and, besides, Schuschnigg can't abide even being in the same room with Benes, the Czech leader.

"And, as you point out, Mr. Muller," he added, "the League's not even thinking about riding to the rescue.

"I wonder how much time we have before this thing blows up."

The conversation ranged back and forth over the intricacies of Austria's predicament, with Boothby and Hamilton resuming their argument about whether a new threat was underway.

Muller found the discussion interesting and the journalists were certainly entertaining. But he decided it was time to go and, after buying another round –was it his third? –he excused himself and prepared to leave.

As Muller paid the cashier, Shirer came up to him. "I'll walk with you to the hotel then go on to my apartment. I have a very pregnant wife who deserves more of my attention.

"You certainly got an earful tonight," he said as they buttoned their coats and headed out the door.

"I enjoyed it," Muller replied easily. "I have a lot to learn pretty quickly if I'm to do my job," he added.

"Which you haven't done much to describe," Shirer said with a smile.

"No, no," he said, as Muller began to protest. "There'll be time."

"Look, Muller, Vienna is right on a knife's edge," he continued. "Two dictators are facing off and they're both playing for keeps. One's got 66 million Germans behind him; the other only 7 million Austrians.

"Oh, yes," he said, seeing Muller's startled glance. "Schuschnigg's a dictator too. His Fatherland Front rules Austria with a Fascist iron fist. Parliament was abolished years ago and democracy is a distant memory. Schuschnigg employs untrammeled authority, first to prevent the Left from regaining any power and second to fend off Hitler's power play.

"He's not as overtly menacing as Hitler. He doesn't throw Jews or gypsies into concentration camps. But he's got his own paramilitary gangs that are a match for the local Nazi thugs and you don't want to get on the wrong side of them."

"So, you see this as a stand-off for now?" Muller asked. It was only his first day in Vienna, but one of the first questions he wanted to answer was how much time he was likely to have to do in his job.

"Ha!" Shirer barked a short laugh. "Wouldn't we all like to know," he said. "It probably depends upon what Hitler decides to do. If he suddenly decides to invade and settle the dispute with his new army, it could end in a day or two. I don't think we're quite there yet," he concluded as they drew up to the hotel entrance; "but I don't think this 'standoff', as you called it, will make it to summer. I'd expect some resolution sooner rather than later."

"One last question," Muller said, pulling Baer's cream-colored card out of his pocket and handing it to Shirer. "Does this name mean anything to you?

Shirer turned to the lighted hotel doorway to read the card and nodded, handing it back.

"Baer's one of the wealthiest bankers in Vienna," he said. "Why do you ask?"

"He wants to meet with me," Muller replied.

Shirer smiled and gave Muller's shoulder a comradely pat.

"Then I'd recommend accepting the invitation."

# CHAPTER 8

Muller strode to the Hotel's front desk to ask for his key and the attendant handed him an envelope as well.

"This was delivered while you were out, sir."

The signal, Muller thought. They'd seen the paper he'd been instructed to place in the window. He slit the envelope. Empty as it was supposed to be.

He placed the envelope in the inside pocket of his suit jacket and handed the room key back to the attendant, buttoning up his coat again.

"I'll be back later."

Walking briskly over to the Ringstrasse, Muller had only a short wait for the next tram, which he boarded, then exited after two stops, checking to see if anyone else got off. He stepped into the shadow of a nearby building and waited for several minutes. He saw no suspicious movements. Then as the lights of the tram going in the opposite direction appeared, he crossed the street and boarded the oncoming tram, disembarking at the fourth stop and again stepped into a nearby shadow. Satisfied, he turned left and entered a neighborhood of crumbling apartment houses, most with coffee shops on the street corners that lit the narrow streets.

From the next street corner, he saw, a block away, a sign for the Heinrichshof Café; he walked the block and, seeing no movement behind him, entered what was a small, badly-lit establishment. He took a seat near the wall toward the back, ordered a mokka, the Viennese version of an espresso, and lit a Gitane. Looking around him, he saw a few small clusters of men sitting quietly around tables. Several minutes later, a man, wearing a coat seemingly too large for his spare frame, rose from a nearby table, walked by him and entered the WC. He wore a wool cap with a small visor that obscured his face, but he was carrying a rolled-up newspaper under his right arm, as Muller had been told to expect.

The man exited the WC, walked to the cashier's desk to pay his bill and left the café. Five minutes later, Muller stood and entered the WC. He removed the rolled-up newspaper from the trash can and opened it to page 5, where he saw "Franz" written in pencil. He returned the newspaper to the trash, then walked back to his table and lit another Gitane. Minutes later, stubbing it out, he got up, paid his bill and retraced his steps back to the tramline, crossed to the other side and entered a very similar neighborhood to the one he'd just left.

A sign on his right identified Café Franz. Muller walked in and spied the spare man wearing the visored wool cap. He sat down at the adjoining table.

The man turned to face him. Framed by his cap, the man had what appeared to be a square face, with a prominent jaw and a wide mouth beneath a dark mustache that was tucked under a large nose.

"Welcome to Vienna, Mr. Muller," he said. "It's nice to meet you. In honor of our first meeting place, why don't you call me Franz?" He leaned over to shake Muller's hand. "You've only just arrived, but anything I should know?"

Muller had decided not to share his experiencc on thc train. IIe had been told that this contact person would be his principal communication link to Hausamann and Büro Ha. He assumed that the contact, Franz–he now had a name–had radio links into the Swiss network and that arrangement appealed to Muller. He didn't want to be tied to a wireless set with its transmission and receiving protocols and the added risk of detection. Whoever Franz was, Muller assumed he had been selected for his ability to act as an intermediary; that was fine and Muller was prepared to proceed in that way. But he wasn't ready–at least not yet–to confide fully in the man.

"I overheard a pack of foreign journalists speculating that Hitler' hatching a new plan to destabilize Schuschnigg but that the Chancellor's gone silent and maybe has something up his sleeve."

"Right," said Franz. "There is something afoot, but we're not clear yet what it is. Our mutual friend is working on that."

Franz turned to Muller and spoke in a soft voice. "You'll be invited to a diplomatic reception in two days. Our friend will arrange for certain individuals to introduce themselves to you during the event. They will reference your preference for Gitane cigarettes. These are persons with whom you should develop relationships and who will serve as communications links.

"The paper in the window seems to be a good signal for you to contact me. If I need you, I'll leave an empty envelope with the concierge. That will signal 7 PM the same night at Heinrichshof. Any questions?"

Muller shook his head and Franz stood, buttoned his coat, and departed the café without a backward glance.

# CHAPTER 9

Muller struggled to wake up as his hotel phone rang insistently. He fumbled to switch on the bedside lamp and lifted the black phone receiver.

The voice on the other end didn't wait for his greeting. "Franz. Get to Teinfaltstrasse immediately." The line disconnected.

What the Hell? Muller glanced at the bedside clock. 5:30 AM. Christ!

He splashed cold water on his face and dressed quickly. There was a taxi stand next to the hotel. Muller had to rap on the window to awaken the sleeping driver.

"Teinfaltstrasse? Yes sir," he said crisply in a show of wakefulness, gunning the car after Muller climbed into the back seat.

Moments later they were stopped by military vehicles pulled up as a roadblock two blocks from their destination. Muller paid the driver and walked quickly around the vehicles. As he got closer, soldiers with rifles at the ready stopped him.

"No further. There is Army activity underway."

"I know. I'm a diplomat; that's why I'm here," Muller showed his credentials and, with a confidence he didn't feel, marched past the guards.

Just off to his left, where two roads met and offered a glimpse ahead, he spied a group of men in civilian dress, so he hurried over to join them. They were talking excitedly.

He immediately identified the loud nasal inflection of Nigel Hamilton, his new journalist friend.

"Hamilton," he said, "what's happening?"

Hamilton's voice nearly cracked he was so excited. "Muller, right?" he said recognizing him. "Glad you're here to see what's happening. I never thought he'd have the guts to do it. But look, he's raiding the Nazis. Whoo!"

As if on cue, a spotlight from one of the vehicles was switched on, bathing the scene in cold harsh light. The building directly in front of them bore a large sign reading 'German Tourist Bureau' and the façade featured a large portrait of Adolf Hitler.

"It's the Brown House, Muller; everyone calls it that. It's the unofficial, official headquarters of the local Nazi Party and Schuschnigg's shutting it down. Who would believe it?"

Sure enough Muller could see Austrian soldiers carrying boxes and file cabinets to waiting trucks. Then he began to see men in Nazi uniforms–Brown Shirts and Black-Shirted Gestapo–being roughly led out in chains and tossed unceremoniously in the backs of Black Maria vans.

"Look," cried Hamilton. "They've even got Leopold–the big cheese himself."

Muller saw a stout man in a Brown Shirt uniform being hauled out of the entryway, his handcuffed hands trying to hold up uniformed trousers with no belt that kept slipping down his legs. He seemed to be trying to maintain a dignified posture but kept having to pull up his trousers and his predicament triggered hoots of laughter from onlookers.

Leopold was followed by another Brown-Shirted figure, smaller and even more undignified as one pant leg was loose and forced him to stumble repeatedly.

"Hey Tavs, how's that feel?" Hamilton shouted, followed by a whoop of laughter. He turned to Muller. "That's the Deputy leader. Just yesterday he was bragging to us all about how his Nazi gang was completely in sync with Hitler. They walked around inside that place with their Nazi costumes saluting and 'Heil Hitlering' one another. 'Schuschnigg and his so-called government can't touch us,' he'd said. Ha! I wonder if he likes *this* kind of immunity!" Hamilton broke into peals of laughter again.

"Put your pants on, Tavs!" he shouted.

In moments, the raid was done. The trucks piled with file cabinets and boxes of documents and the vans holding the prisoners all pulled away in formation and the roadblocks and guards moved out too, except for a detachment that was left behind to guard the entrance to the building, which was sealed by barriers and coils of barbed wire.

"Pretty efficient operation," said Muller as the onlookers began to disperse.

"Damn right," said Hamilton. "They came prepared."

Hamilton flashed Muller a wide grin. "This calls for a celebration. Come down the street with me; we'll have a coffee and a double schnapps."

That's what Hamilton ordered as they found seats in a nearby café. Muller settled for coffee and a hard-boiled egg.

"This really throws down the gauntlet," Hamilton said as he took a big gulp from his heavily-laced coffee mug. "The Brown House was an open secret; everyone knew it was the Nazi headquarters here. Schuschnigg let it go, probably because it was easier to keep tabs on than if he drove it underground. But something obviously happened that caused him to change his mind and lower the boom. Maybe he found out about a new threat from Hitler; maybe he just got pissed at the insolent bragging by Tavs. Who knows? But by God, this raid will get Hitler's attention, you can be sure of that.

"I'd keep my ear to the ground, Muller," he said as they got up to leave. "I expect you'll hear another shoe drop before long."

# CHAPTER 10

Muller returned to his hotel to shave and change into business attire. He then paid his first visit to the Office of the League of Nations Commissioner General for Austria, which was situated within the Austrian Finance Ministry at the Prince Eugene City Palace.

Even though he had read a brief description of the Palace in a Vienna guidebook, Muller was unprepared for the extraordinary splendor of the Baroque masterpiece that he encountered as he strolled along the Innere Stadt to the narrow street at Himmelpfortgasse and the Palace suddenly materialized before him. It had a three-story creamy white façade, with portals and a decorated balustrade that conveyed a nearly palpable sense of grandeur. He stopped before the tall wooden entry doors, situated directly below an ornate balcony with vertical piano nobile windows and a massive Austrian Coat of Arms.

Summoning the courage to enter the building, he was directed up a broad marble staircase alongside a massive statue of Hercules; looking up, he could see a brightly painted ceiling fresco. Upon arriving at the second floor, an attendant pointed him to a doorway down a corridor to his right. As he approached it, he saw a large embossed leather frame encasing a sign.

**Office of the League of Nations Commissioner General for Austria**
**The Honorable Paul Mu**ller

Muller squared his shoulders.

Opening the door, he entered a suite of high-ceilinged offices, where he introduced himself to the receptionist, Frau Metzinger, and the secretary, Fraulein Heinz, who were both visibly excited and nervous at his arrival.

"Commissioner Muller, we are both very pleased to welcome you and to restore this office to active service after what has been a long and trying year without a League representative in residence," said Frau Metzinger, a little breathlessly. "The Ministry tried to evict us at one point, and they actually took away the other two rooms that we had occupied behind those doors." Frau Metzinger pointed to two tall dark wooden doors on the wall to the left.

"But we kept this suite intact," she said triumphantly, "and now that you're here, we won't have any more trouble."

Frau Metzinger's territorial priorities were clear, Muller said to himself.

His office was large, with tall windows and a high ornate ceiling inlaid with small frescos. Bookcases lined one wall. There was a conference table to the left with four comfortable-looking chairs and a polished wooden desk with a large padded chair behind it.

"Where is the safe, Frau Metzinger? Muller asked.

"Here, sir," she replied, showing him a wall receptacle to the right of the entrance. "I've placed the combination in the desk drawer."

Muller thanked them, closed the door and sat down at his desk.

Well, he thought, this is certainly an elaborate and extravagant arrangement I've been handed; he shook his head.

He began idly to pick through the mail that had been laid on his desk and found the invitation to the diplomatic reception that Franz had mentioned. It was scheduled from 7 to 9 PM at the Chancellery. Formal attire was expected.

Muller spent the next several hours familiarizing himself with the filing system. He was going to want to spend time on the 1923 Loan Protocols that held his grounds for financial control of the customs and tobacco funds.

Then he went out, lunched at a nearby Café and, at 2 PM, presented himself at the offices of Baer & Company, which were only a short walk through the Innere Stadt. They bespoke wealth; an austere, understated exterior that gave way to high-ceilinged interior rooms, walls clad in creamy silk and hung with elegant oil paintings mounted in gilded frames.

He was promptly ushered into the offices of Friederich Baer, who rose from his desk to greet him with a broad smile and outstretched hand.

"Welcome Mr. Muller. I'm very pleased to see you again," said Baer, steering them toward two adjoining armchairs on either side of a small fireplace. The office was spacious and seemed to communicate a sense of well-being.

Baer conveyed a very different appearance than the disheveled and frightened man whom Muller had protected on the train. He was attired in a well-tailored, double-breasted dark blue suit and a starched white shirt with gold cufflinks. A blue silk tie was adorned by a diamond stickpin. His longish graying hair was parted in the middle and his face was dominated by a strong chin and large eyebrows above intelligent gray eyes and a wide mouth. He had a stern appearance, Muller thought, but his face noticeably softened when he smiled–which he was doing now.

"As you can see, I'm recovered from the attack from which you rescued us–all except for this small plaster," he pointed to the white bandage above his right eye. "If I remember the condition you left the Nazi that beat us up, I suspect he's feeling a lot worse at the moment than I am." Baer's smile widened.

"My wife, sister-in-law, and I owe you a deep debt of gratitude," he continued. "That thug could have killed us; without your intervention, he would have certainly have badly injured us. It was a near thing and we thank you most sincerely." Reaching into his suit pocket he extracted a thick envelope which he proffered to Muller.

"As a banker, I'm accustomed to expressing my thanks not just verbally but financially too."

Muller lifted his hands and shook his head. "Mr. Baer, I'm pleased to accept your verbal thank you. But, please, no gift. Actually, I was protecting myself as much as you. That bruiser would have come after me next. So, my reaction was as much about launching a strong defense as it was about helping you and your family. Let's just leave it that we were provided an unusual way of getting acquainted."

Baer smiled but did not put away the envelope. "Mr. Muller, good deeds warrant appropriate rewards. I would never forgive myself if I couldn't find a way to make this small contribution to your material well-being."

Baer then looked at him with a conspiratorial air. "Maybe what I should do, is to open an account in your name at Muller & Company bank in Zurich."

Muller started. How did Baer know about his family's bank? He began to protest, but Baer interrupted him.

"Don't worry, Mr. Muller," he said, "I won't broadcast your family banking history around town. But it wasn't hard to make the connection, the banking community being as small as it is. Actually, I've met your father on a couple of occasions over the years. He and your family's bank enjoy a stellar reputation.

"In fact, Magda and her sister Harriet and I had been in Geneva visiting with one of your competitors, Banque Pictet. We'd decided that we should safeguard some of our valuables in Switzerland. I'm sure Muller & Company offers the same services to people like us, who feel themselves and their property at risk in this–how shall I put it delicately–unsettled time in Austria. So, we were returning when the attack occurred.

"Actually," he said chuckling, "maybe we should have deposited our assets with Muller & Company instead of Pictet."

Sensing Muller's discomfort, Baer returned the envelope to his pocket. "All right, Mr. Muller. We'll put this subject in abeyance for the moment, though making a deposit in your name at Muller & Company still sounds like a good idea.

"There are other subjects that we need to discuss." Baer's expression turned serious and he spoke deliberately, as if making certain Muller was paying attention.

"You have arrived in Vienna at a very dangerous moment. Actually, it got a lot more dangerous just this morning. The Chancellor ordered the Army to raid the Nazi headquarters at dawn. They shut the place down, arrested the leaders and took away the files." Baer allowed himself a smile. "I'm confident they'll find a lot of incriminating information showing that the Nazis were planning to overthrow the government.

"The fact that the German Tourist Bureau has been serving as the Nazi headquarters here has been more or less an open secret for some time," he said, pausing to proffer Muller an Old Gold cigarette.

Muller pulled out his cigarette case. "I prefer Gitanes," he said, offering one to Baer, who took it. Muller left the case on the small table next to his chair.

"I've always liked Gitanes," Baer said casually.

A signal? Muller thought; maybe.

Still, he saw no reason to reveal to Baer that he had been tipped off to the morning raid and had watched it unfold. Let's see where this conversation is leading, he thought to himself as he flicked his lighter open and lit both cigarettes.

"It's a gutsy step by Schuschnigg," Baer went on. "I'm told he's weighing a trip to Germany to meet with Hitler. Maybe he figures this will give him a little leverage."

Baer shrugged. "It's possible," he said, seeming to argue with himself. "But it's also risky. Hitler could decide to get angry and double down on his threat to take over the country. And there's no doubt that he's dead serious about that threat. He's short of money and he desperately wants to get his hand on the 470 million Schillings in gold at the Austrian National Bank; that and our Styrian coal mines and steel industry."

Baer sat back and rubbed his hands together, looking, Muller thought, like the banker he was.

"Hitler's discovering that rearmament on the scale he's pursing it is expensive. *VERY* expensive." Baer paused for emphasis. "And when ordinary Germans can't find shoes or shirts to buy, when they face shortages of gasoline and tires for their cars and when the cheese and grains and other food they're accustomed to buying isn't available or is rationed, they get restive. *VERY* restive," he added, with a nod that connected the two statements. "Even dictators get nervous when their citizens are restive–as Germany's certainly are at the moment. So, Hitler wants to steal our wealth–so he can feed the German people and pay for his rearmament program."

This was almost the same speech his father had delivered to him back in November; smart bankers think alike, Muller thought.

He sensed Baer was about to pressure him on steps he could take as Commissioner General to deny Hitler access to the funds he controlled. He wasn't comfortable talking about that at this stage. So, he decided to change the subject.

"Will Austrians resist if Hitler follows through on his threats and actually invades?" he asked.

Baer reflected a moment, then shook his head.

"Austria is a deeply divided nation, Mr. Muller," he said. "Resisting Hitler would require submerging our factional differences and forging some kind of consensus against being absorbed into Germany. You'd think that should be possible: 'us against them'." Baer sat back in his chair and his shoulders slouched. "But the chasms that exist are too deep for that to happen, I'm afraid. There's no 'us' to rally against 'them'. Schuschnigg's Fatherland Front is absolutely wedded to its Catholic Clerical party roots and its embrace of Fascism. It's probably more fearful of domestic political opposition on the Left than it is of the Nazi threat here at home and across the border in Germany."

Seeing Muller's questioning look, Baer continued.

"This town wasn't referred to as 'Red Vienna' for nothing, Mr. Muller. That was in the twenties, to be sure, but Communist and socialist sympathies remain strong here. The Catholic Church has an enormous influence here, and the Fatherland Front, the clerical party that has held power since the War represents the Catholic outlook. They perceive the Left, not as a legitimate political opponent, but as an avowed enemy, representing Godless Communism. And they have taken repeated steps to crush it.

Baer grew animated and gripped the arms of his chair, leaning toward Muller. "Some time I'll take you to the socialist section of the city; it's called Floridsdorf, an area where the socialists were able to clear away slums and build public housing that wasn't so great, but a step up from the squalor that preceded it. The Fatherland Front viewed the project as a direct threat to its leadership and they proceeded to launch what has accurately been called a Civil War to destroy it and the leadership of the Left. They sent in the Army to attack the new community."

"The army?" said Muller in disbelief, "attacking a section of Vienna?"

"Using artillery and heavy weapons," Baer said, nodding.

"It was in February 1934. We could hear the gunfire from here, and it went on for two or three days. Hundreds were killed and wounded; others fled into the sewers. The Left was decimated and their Social Democratic Party was banned.

"It divided the nation." Baer said quietly. "Even many of us who oppose the Social Democrats and the influence of the Communists were shocked by the scale of the attack that was unleashed against them."

Muller found it hard to absorb what he'd heard. Governments don't normally mount military assaults against citizens of their largest city. This revealed an entirely new dimension of the Austrian crisis.

"Is there still a standoff between the government and the Left?" he asked, "or have the divisions healed?"

"There's been no reconciliation whatsoever," Baer responded.

"No quarter was given then and none has been given since, by either side. When you visit the area, you'll see that buildings still show the scars of the shelling, with walls collapsed and roofs shattered. People are still living there; Hell, they've no place else to go."

"The upshot of all this is that there is a whole segment of the Austrian population–workers, mainly–who view their government as the enemy. So," he asked rhetorically, "would those factory hands and laborers–working class Austrians–spring to the side of the Fatherland Front if Hitler should come marching in?

"I don't think so," Baer said, shaking his head. "And the pity of it is that they're natural allies. They can look across the border and see what's happened to Social Democrats and leftist leaders under the Nazis; they've been killed or tossed into places like Dachau. The Left here knows the same fate awaits them if Hitler takes over Austria. But there's this huge internal division that neither the Freedom Front nor the Left can bridge. So, the answer to your question, Mr. Muller, is no; I don't see the nation coming together to resist Hitler."

Baer reached for another Gitane. "Sorry," he said, "I hadn't intended to deliver a speech,"

"No, no," said Muller brandishing his lighter again. "This is fascinating. Hitler is driven to take over Austria so he can steal its wealth to overcome troubles on his home front and Austria's too divided to offer much in the way of resistance. That doesn't sound like a winning hand to me, I'm afraid."

"You're right," said Baer.

"So, what's your guess on the timing? Muller asked.

Baer sighed. "At Christmas, I told Magda that I thought we had a year. A month later, I think it's a lot less. So, Mr. Muller, if, as I suspect, your sudden appointment as the League's Commissioner General for Austria has something to do with Austria's finances, I think you might consider acting sooner rather than later."

They ground out the stubs of their cigarettes and stood to shake hands.

"I hope you will think of me as an ally, Mr. Muller," Baer said as he guided him to the door. "You're likely to need some."

"Oh, and by the way," he added. "You probably should assume that your office at the Ministry and the office of the Governor of the Austrian National Bank, who's in the same building and whom I presume you will be meeting at some point soon, are both bugged."

# CHAPTER 11

The diplomatic reception was being held at the Chancellery on the Ballhausplatz.

Muller felt his sense of self-importance rise upon entering the premises where the famed Metternich had spun his tangled diplomatic webs more than a century earlier. The reception hall was architecturally stunning; high ceilings, decorative paneling set off by doric columns placed just so, parquet floors polished to a high sheen, candles here and indirect lighting there casting a warm glow. Austrians knew how to entertain in the very best taste, Muller thought to himself; they'd been doing it for hundreds of years. But that didn't make it any less bewitching. Muller took it all in, mentally pinching himself that he was a participant in this–for him–quite surreal event.

But reality quickly intervened. Events like this were hard work, especially as Muller knew no one and proceeded to introduce himself to Consul General this and Ambassador that, feigning interest and mustering small talk; Metternich never had that problem, Muller thought to himself. He was also willing to bet that Metternich had never attended a diplomatic reception–in this storied venue or anywhere else–with a pair of brass knuckles tucked carefully away in a suit pocket.

Muller proceeded to perform the obligatory diplomatic rituals, shaking hands, occasionally exchanging cards, and gamely balancing a flute of champagne with quite elegant hors d'oeuvres that were being passed.

A man about Muller's own age came up beside him. "Mr. Muller?"

"Yes" replied Muller.

My name is Edgar Raditz, from the German embassy," then he added, "I was told you carry Gitane brand cigarettes."

"I do," said Muller pulling out his cigarette case and offering one to Raditz, who reacted a little sheepishly and shook his head.

"Actually, I don't smoke," he said. "But it seemed like a good way to begin a conversation."

A signal, for certain.

Muller laughed. "Well, I suppose it is."

"Perhaps we might move to that small table," Raditz pointed, "where we could talk quietly."

Raditz led the way to the table along the wall. He was tall and blonde–Aryan, Muller thought–with broad shoulders that he held erect. As they sat down to face one another, Muller could see he had sharp brown eyes above a slender nose and narrow lips topped by a pencil-thin mustache, very presentable, thought Muller.

Raditz reached into his suit jacket and extracted a card with his name and a telephone number. He handed it to Muller.

"No title?" asked Muller.

"I play," Raditz hesitated a moment, "a variety of roles at the embassy. A lot of coordination work," he added; "a title would be limiting."

"Fair enough," Muller replied, handing Raditz his card with its long title. "You probably know my title."

Raditz nodded. "In fact, one of the things I am to 'coordinate' is keeping you discreetly informed about matters which may be of interest to you." Raditz glanced around to satisfy himself that no one was within hearing. "Actually, one of the few advantages of these receptions is being able to carry on private conversations like the one we're having now, in full sight and right under everyone's nose."

He fixed Muller with a business-like gaze. "There are several things that you should know. One is that Hitler is very angry over the police raid on the Nazi headquarters. He told the French Ambassador that he'd have Schuschnigg's head over the incident." Raditz lifted his eyebrows in emphasis and glanced around again.

"He's planning to summon Schuschnigg to Germany for what he will present as a friendly visit between neighbors, but which he intends to use as a cudgel to beat him into submission. He's ordered Ambassador von Papen to soften him up in preparation for the meeting.

"There's also a new player who's become involved," he added. "Arthur Seyss-Inquart is an Austrian lawyer whom Schuschnigg appointed as his State Counselor a year or so ago–and whom we assume Schuschnigg believes is a loyal ally. Hitler has invited him to a private meeting at Berchtesgaden in a day or two. We assume this is part of the same game; we'll learn more when the meeting takes place. But Seyss-Inquart seems to have become a name to keep in mind."

Raditz stood and removed two champagne flutes from a waiter's tray and returned with them to the table. "Prost."

He sipped from the flute and leaned toward Muller, arms on the table, speaking quietly. "I am instructed to tell you that there are those among us that fear the Führer is proceeding recklessly and endangering our German cause and that I am one of those assigned to trying to slow the pace of events. Advising you about sensitive matters is part of my job. But we should communicate carefully." Again, Raditz looked over his shoulder. "When you call my number, you are Karl," he said. "When I call yours, I am Heinz. We will leave no messages for one another, but a call from one to the other is a signal to meet the same day at 7 PM at the Bar Clover on Handelstrasse. It's close to both of our offices. Agreed?"

Muller nodded. "Let me pass some information back to you." This time it was Muller who glanced over his shoulder to be certain they were not being overheard.

"I occasionally drop into a bar where the foreign journalists gather to drink and gossip," Muller said quietly. "One hush-hush item I learned is that when the Government raided the Nazi offices they impounded a safe containing a thick document that was signed by Rudolf Hess, Hitler's Deputy Führer. Apparently, it was written in some kind of code. But in the very next drawer of the same safe, they found the cipher. So, voila, a translation was quickly available." Muller smiled at the recollection of Nigel Hamilton guffawing at this example of German efficiency.

"Supposedly it's a bombshell, laying out a detailed plan for a German takeover. Schuschnigg's furious about it and says he's ready to put the two local Nazi leaders on trial and use the document as Exhibit A to convict them in open court and to embarrass Hitler in front of the world."

Muller paused, thinking. "If what you're saying is accurate, about a meeting being afoot, something tells me that Schuschnigg may first try to use the Hess document as leverage against Hitler."

"Food for thought," he added.

Raditz looked levelly at Muller and smiled. "Muller, I think we have the beginning of a good working relationship."

They shook hands and Raditz strode off into the crowd.

Muller continued mingling for the next half hour and was preparing to leave when he caught sight of Viktor Keinböck, the Governor of the Austrian National Bank, whom Muller recognized from photographs.

Muller approached him and stood to one side while Keinböck finished the conversation he was having with two men Muller didn't know, then stepped forward and introduced himself.

"Ah, Mr. Muller," said Keinböck. "When I returned to the office this morning after my trip, they told me that you had left several messages about wanting to meet. I'm sorry to have been away for so long, but it's finally nice to meet you here."

Muller was surprised to see what a young man Keinböck was for someone who had been Finance Minister for several years even before taking the helm of the National Bank six years ago. He must be no more than in his early 50's Muller estimated; the thick mustache above his wide mouth was still dark brown, though his hair, or what remained of it, cut short as it was, showed some grey at the temples. Muller was especially struck by Keinböck's large oval eyes beneath arched eyebrows. They seemed to radiate intelligence and poise.

"I was actually hoping that we might meet somewhere privately, and outside the Ministry," Muller said.

Keinböck looked at him with a slight smile of amusement. "Outside the Ministry is a very judicious suggestion, Mr. Muller." He didn't need to say more; it was clear he understood Muller's meaning.

"Let's plan on dinner very soon," he said before being turned away by two men on his elbow. "We have matters to discuss. Have your secretary call my office tomorrow morning and we'll fix a time." He offered Muller a small wave as he was led into the crowd.

Muller noticed a commotion in the doorway and most guests turned to look as the German Ambassador, Franz von Papen, made a grand entrance accompanied by his fashionable wife. Von Papen was a large man, made to seem even more so by a massive head, a lantern jaw, pendulous ears and eyes widely spaced on either side of a prominent nose. He was a man clearly accustomed to attention and seemed to radiate a sense of self-importance.

Striding toward a knot of diplomats at the bar, von Papen brushed past Muller without a glance.

"Sorry for that." Muller turned to see Frau von Papen's wife at his shoulder. Tall and blonde, frau von Papen was dressed in an elegantly understated gown that seemed to intensify the natural beauty of her delicate complexion and full figure. What a striking woman, Muller thought to himself. She smiled at Muller and shrugged, briefly bobbing her head, acknowledging von Papen's rudeness.

"He does that when he gets the wind in his sails–which is quite often, I'm afraid," she said, apologetically, then followed in her husband's wake, but slowly and with dignity.

Who was it, one of the journalists? –Shirer maybe– who'd commented on von Papen's wife one night at the bar when they had been gossiping about von Papen's latest machinations. None of the journalists liked him; he was a notorious schemer who played up to Hitler and his crowd even as he looked down upon them from his aristocratic pinnacle.

"But Marte's different," Shirer had said. "She can't stand them and she makes no bones about it. She remembers all too well the Night of the Long Knives back in 1934, when Hitler and his SS henchmen murdered–what was it, 50? 100? who knows–of their political enemies. Von Papen was the Deputy Chancellor then. They invaded the Chancellery and murdered three of his staff right outside his office–one of them with a pick-axe, for Christ's sake. Somehow von Papen survived. But she's never forgotten–or forgiven, so I'm told. She's also very smart; an interesting lady," Shirer had concluded.

So, he'd met the interesting lady, Muller said to himself, turning to go.

An older man with white chin whiskers fell into step with him. "Aren't you Mr. Muller," he asked, "the man who likes to smoke Gitane cigarettes?"

A busy night, Muller thought, as he acknowledged his identity and shook hands.

"My name is Otto Schultz," said the man. "Chancellor's office," he said quietly. "I'm about to leave too. Can you meet in 30 minutes at Wolfe's? It's not far; you had lunch there a few weeks ago when you were first in town.

Muller looked at the man; they'd tailed him from his office as he walked to work on his very first day?

"I'll be there in 30 minutes," he replied.

# CHAPTER 12

Muller was already seated at a small booth at the rear of Wolfe's when Schultz arrived, hung his coat on a hook and sat down opposite him.

"Thank you for accommodating me," Schultz said in a friendly tone. "I had a bit of a retinue in tow at the reception this evening. Meeting now gave me a chance to send a couple of them back to the office to work and to disentangle myself from a couple of the others whom I don't trust." He shrugged.

"It's that way, these days," he continued. "But I'm pleased to make your acquaintance, Mr. Muller. You come well-recommended. We need all the help we can muster, so it's nice to meet a new ally.

"Will you share a wiener schnitzel with me?" Schultz asked. "Those canapés at the reception are never enough, but the servings here are huge. So, splitting a schnitzel should be just about right. Yes? And a bottle of Grüner Veltliner? That should do it."

He signaled, and a waiter came immediately, whom he instructed by name.

"I eat here often, Mr. Muller. That's how I know you were here for lunch ten days or so ago. We sat close to one another that day and, having a good memory for faces, I recognized you this evening at the reception."

Muller smiled, relieved. "When you said you knew I'd had lunch here I thought that meant you'd had me tailed. I'm glad to hear that's not the case."

"Assuredly not, Mr. Muller," Schultz replied, smiling. "We're not clever enough for that, I'm afraid. But in the current atmosphere, you can't be too careful."

Schultz had an impish smile and a direct manner that was refreshing. Muller decided that he liked him.

After they were served, Schultz looked over his shoulder–by now almost instinctive, thought Muller–and began to speak in a low tone.

"You probably know by now that discussions are underway about a meeting between the Chancellor and Hitler," he said.

Muller nodded.

"The Chancellor is determined to get Hitler to back off his insistent demands to take over Austria and to reaffirm his commitment to the 1936 agreement between them that guaranteed Austrian independence," Schultz continued. "He believes he's strengthened his hand by cracking down on the Nazi organization here. Among other things, we've come into possession of some very sensitive documents that would deeply embarrass Hitler if they became public knowledge."

"The Hess document?" Muller asked.

Schultz glanced sharply at him. "You know about that?" he asked in surprise. "That's very closely-held information."

"Only that it exists and that it supposedly contains a detailed takeover plan," Muller replied.

"Well, I hope you'll keep that to yourself," Schultz said. "The document is pretty damning and it may offer us some negotiating leverage.

"We're proceeding cautiously in planning this meeting," hc continued "and taking all the proper diplomatic precautions. We'll insist upon a formal invitation in proper language, an agreed-upon agenda and a pre-negotiated communiqué to be issued at the end of the meeting containing language that we're satisfied reaffirms the 1936 agreement."

"I'm told Hitler has issued instructions to von Papen to 'soften up' Schuschnigg prior to the meeting–and that he's enlisted someone in your own ministry–Guido Schmidt–to help him," said Muller.

Schultz looked up from his plate with a big grin and took a large swallow of wine. "'Softening up' is not a term anyone who is acquainted with Chancellor Schuschnigg would ever suggest as a way to communicate with him. He is a devout Catholic; a stern and rigid man. He has almost no sense of humor and he was born without that outgoing bon homie that most politicians project. He is a very hard man; not one likely to be softened up.

"He is also very courageous," Schultz continued. "He assumed the office of Chancellor in the wake of the Nazi assassination of Dollfuss four years ago. He's fearlessly confronted the Nazi threat and has kept his boot on the neck of the Left. He has the Heimwehr Fascist militia that he can use when political muscle is required and the Army is an unwavering ally.

"This is one tough man, Mr. Muller," Schultz said. He shook his head, finishing the last of his meal and putting down his knife and fork, then looked directly at Muller.

"But he's not, unfortunately, the most astute political strategist and he isn't very good at anticipating other people's agendas. His narrow-mindedness is both an asset and a weakness."

"Do you worry about Schmidt–who's apparently been recruited to push Hitler's agenda?" Muller asked.

"Guido Schmidt is an egotistical young man whose sole objective in life is to advance the interests of Guido Schmidt," said Schultz dismissively. "His wife is hugely wealthy, which accounts for his ministerial appointment in the government and which gives him a lot of freedom to operate. Her family's wealth comes from textile manufacturing, incidentally, and some of us have noted that there are factories just over the border in Germany that look ripe for plucking in the event of a German takeover.

"So, it's pretty clear that he stands to benefit financially in the event Hitler succeeds in his plan. And it's obvious that he sees himself as a suitable replacement for Schuschnigg if that were to happen.

"So, yes, Mr. Muller, we worry about Guido Schmidt. And he's deeply involved in preparations for this meeting that's being planned. If you tell me Hitler is passing instructions to him–which, frankly, wouldn't surprise me–that's a further cause for worry."

Muller offered them both Gitanes and lit them.

"I was also told that a man named Arthur Seyss-Inquart has been invited to meet with Hitler in Berchtesgaden in a day or two," said Muller. "What's that about?"

Schultz sighed and took a deep drag on his cigarette. "A bit of wild card, actually," he replied. "He's a fairly prominent local lawyer but doesn't have much of a political history. Schuschnigg was introduced to him less than a year ago. They are both deeply committed Catholics and they apparently bonded over that shared conviction. Schuschnigg tends to assume that, like any good Catholic, Seyss-Inquart will be faithful to the Clerical Party and the agenda of the Fatherland Front–a pillar of which is resistance to Nazi influence.

"So, Schuschnigg appointed him State Counselor," Schultz said. "And now suddenly he's hobnobbing with Hitler?" Schultz shook his head. "We'd suspected something like that, but having you confirm it is helpful. That kind of behavior is a source of concern to some of us. But–and this worries us too–apparently not to Schuschnigg; he seems oblivious."

Schultz's shoulders seemed to slump a little. "As I told you, we're trying to be very careful in preparing this meeting. I hope other people's agendas don't undermine that." Schultz stubbed out his cigarette and finished the last of his wine. "I'll try to keep you informed."

They exchanged telephone numbers and ways to communicate discreetly.

"I'll get the check," said Schultz as he put on his coat and strode to the entrance.

Muller decided to sit a little longer and reflect on the busy evening he'd had.

He watched Schultz as he chatted at the Café's doorway with Wolfe, the owner. Suddenly he noticed a large man wearing a cloth cap get up from his bar stool, walk rapidly to the front window of the café. Looking out, the man flared his lighter, then pocketed it and walked quickly to the doorway, following close on Schultz's heels.

Muller tensed. That was some kind of signal the man had given.

Shit! Someone's after Schultz.

He sprang to his feet and hurried to the front of the café, pausing only long enough to grasp Wolfe's arm.

"Mr. Wolfe, get some of your men to follow me as fast as you can," he hissed. "That guy who just walked out is after Schultz. We need to help him. Quickly!" he said over his shoulder as he flung open the Café door.

At first he didn't see anything in the gloom. Then glancing to his right, he saw Schultz in the grasp of the man from the Café. He had Schultz in a hammerlock, his elbow under Schultz's chin and was dragging him toward a car parked just up the street. The car put its headlights on and Muller could see the shadow of a second man running toward them.

Muller had time to slip on only one brass knuckle as he stepped toward Schultz's assailant.

"Let him go," Muller shouted. But the man paid no heed and continued dragging Schultz, whose arms and legs were flailing in a vain effort to free himself. The man's back was to Muller so he punched him as hard as could in the kidney.

The man cried out in pain and staggered, losing his grip on Schultz, who tumbled to the pavement.

"Schultz, get back inside," Muller yelled.

The second man was now upon them and lunged at Schultz. Muller tackled him at the waist and the two of them fell to the pavement, rolling over one other as they grappled. From the corner of his eye Muller caught a glimpse of people running toward them from the Café entrance. One large man in a white chef's uniform carried a wooden rolling pin. He began pummeling Muller's assailant with it, shouting "Let him go you son of a bitch."

As the man tried to fend off the blows, he relinquished his grip on Muller who freed himself and sprang to his feet. He saw the man whom he'd punched doubled over, his face contorted in pain, with two Café waiters surrounding him, one brandishing a meat cleaver and the other a long kitchen knife.

The Chef proceeded to take charge of the other man. "Face down and spread eagle," he shouted.

"Do you hear me?" He yelled at the man, delivering a kick in the ribs for emphasis. "Spread eagle or I'll beat your head into a mashed potato." He aimed a vicious blow with the roller which the man barely avoided.

"Okay, okay," he said, rolling on his stomach and spreading his arms and legs as ordered. "Just quit hitting me."

Muller glanced toward the waiting car, but the driver, seeing what was happening, gunned it and disappeared around a corner.

Muller tucked the brass knuckle back in his suit pocket. He didn't want to have to explain it. As he did so, he noticed smears of blood on his hands and sleeve and realized his nose was bleeding profusely.

The staff now had the situation well under control. Muller walked back into the Café, applied a nearby napkin to his nose and sat with his head back to stanch the flow of blood.

Schultz ran to his side. "Are you hurt, Muller?" he asked anxiously.

"Just a bloody nose," Muller said through the napkin. "The guy must have hit me when we fell; I'll be fine."

"Well, I certainly thank you for rescuing me," Schultz said. "Those goons were going to take me out, I'm sure. Another body found overnight in the Danube," he said with a snort. "Someone doesn't like the advice I'm giving to the Chancellor, I guess."

Muller began to remove the napkin from his nose, which seemed to have stopped bleeding. A waiter came up to them with a damp towel and Schultz took it, wiping the blood off Muller's cheek and neck.

"That's looks a little better," he said. "But stay seated a few more minutes so it doesn't start bleeding again. Looks like the Police are here. I'll step outside to have a word with them and come right back."

Muller laid his head back again and closed his eyes. His nose throbbed and he could feel a bruise on his leg.

The other patrons of the Café had all been watching events unfold. One of them came over and offered Muller a glass of water, which he gratefully accepted. "That was a nice job you did," he said. "You know, I was sitting here with my wife and our friends. I saw that guy come in and look around before he took a seat at the bar. He was dressed wrong; didn't look like he belonged here, if you know what I mean. Then he sprang up when that guy walked out and made a signal with his lighter. I saw the lighter from where I was sitting, sir. It had a big Nazi swastika decoration on it. So, I think you can probably assume he was one of them."

"We've got to crush them, Goddammit," he added.

"Thanks for telling me," Muller replied, "and for the water."

As he was about to stand, Schultz returned, trailed by a burly Policeman, and waved him back into his chair.

"Stay seated, Mr. Muller. This is Ober-Lieutenant Truber. He runs the precinct here."

The policeman pulled up a chair next to Muller. "You certainly did a job on those two fellows, Mr. Muller," he said.

"That one guy's shitting blood; he's going to hurt for a while. Which is fine! The guy deserved it."

"His lighter apparently has a Nazi symbol," Muller said. "A customer here told me he saw it."

"We have it," Truber replied. "We'll find out who sent them. They're not talking just yet. But they will."

An hour later, after taking their statements, Truber assigned separate policemen to drive Schultz and Muller home.

As they stood to leave, Schultz looked up at Muller, who was a head taller. "I'm very much in your debt, Mr. Muller. I will be certain that we remain in very close touch."

# CHAPTER 13

At his office a few days later, Frau Metzinger informed Muller that someone named Heinz had telephoned but left no message. Muller thanked her for the message.

So, Raditz from the German embassy, he said to himself; that meant a meeting at Bar Clover on Handelstrasse at 7 PM.

Muller had to wait about ten minutes before Raditz approached his table and sat next to him.

"It appears that you weren't followed," Raditz said. "I spent the last few minutes double-checking. That's good."

Then he signaled a waiter. "I'm in need of something strong," he said to Muller. "Join me in a double whiskey and soda?" Muller nodded. "Two, then," Raditz said to the waiter.

Raditz rubbed his eyes before turning his gaze on Muller.

"What I'm about to relate is scarcely to be believed," he began, "but it's true and, frankly, a little scary. Yesterday Hitler fired von Neurath, our Foreign Minister–and my boss, by the way–and replaced him with that toad von Ribbentrop and, even more startling, he's gotten rid of his two highest-ranking Army commanders and put himself in control of both the Army and the Defense Ministry. He's removed any constraints on his power to order the Army into Austria at any moment of his choosing. How's that for openers, Mr. Muller?"

Their drinks arrived and he clinked his glass against Muller's. "Prost!"

"What in the world happened?" Muller asked.

"Part of it–maybe most of it, who knows–goes back to a meeting in November," Raditz began. "Hitler got all of the top German leadership together and directed them to prepare plans for war in Eastern Europe in 1938, or latest 1939. He told them he was going to expand Germany into Austria, Czechoslovakia and Poland to fulfill his determination to gain new territory–lebensraum, as he calls it–and he said he would use the army if he couldn't achieve his objectives diplomatically.

"He told them that the French and British wouldn't lift a finger to stop him and that he was determined to act. He then demanded that all those assembled at the meeting pledge their full support for his plan without any reservations."

Raditz paused and took a very large swallow from his drink.

"Well, much to Hitler's annoyance, there were a lot of objections," he continued. "Von Neurath disputed Hitler's political analysis, warning that the French would surely react. Both General von Fritsch, who was Commander-in-Chief of the Army, and General von Blomberg, who was Defense Minister, told him in no uncertain terms that the Wehrmacht was simply unprepared for war that soon. Not enough equipment, petrol, tires, ammunition, weaponry, etc. Even with all the rearmament steps taken during the past couple of years, they told him, the military wasn't ready.

"Hitler was apparently furious, so he went to work with Göring and Himmler to remove the naysayers. And here," Raditz paused to signal for another round of drinks, "is where the story gets really juicy."

Muller lit a Gitane, and remembering that Raditz didn't smoke, didn't offer him one. "Tell me," he said expectantly.

"So, Blomberg first," Raditz said. "He's a widower and about a year ago he proceeded to marry his secretary. Scandalous, of course," said Raditz, rolling his eyes, "but everyone swallowed hard and they went ahead–apparently even Hitler and Göring attended the ceremony in a show of support.

"But not long afterward, the Berlin police chief let it be known that the new Mrs. Blomberg had a long record as a prostitute and a model for pornographic photographs. Well!" said Raditz. "Last week, they decided to trot out the evidence and confront Blomberg. 'Either resign or we'll ruin you.' So he resigned on January 27. They waited to announce it until yesterday, February 4.

"That's when they got Fritsch, the Army commander. They accused him of being a homosexual and even produced a witness. Fritsch went ballistic, denying everything and demanding an Honor Trial. But Hitler forced him to submit his resignation too.

"Then he proceeded to appoint himself to fill both vacancies." Raditz mimicked wiping his hands clean of any opposition. "No more military interference with the Führer's wishes. He's now in total control of the German armed forces.

"Removal of von Neurath for Ribbentrop was almost an afterthought," he added. "Von Neurath has no political base in the Party; he was a hold-over from Weimar that Hitler kept in power only so long as he was useful. Von Neurath's disagreement at the November meeting rendered him expendable, so out he goes, replaced by Ribbentrop who–I guarantee you–will never, ever, contradict Hitler or utter even a syllable of disagreement with him."

"So, a clean sweep," said Muller as he absorbed the news.

"It's almost enough to make me take up smoking," said Raditz with a grim smile. "Oh, and I nearly forgot," he added. "He fired von Papen too; but that cat has nine lives. By coincidence he was already traveling to Berchtesgaden to discuss preparations for the meeting with Schuschnigg, which Hitler had been stalling."

"We now know why," Raditz said as an aside. "Anyway, he persuaded Hitler to let him remain in office, but Hitler ordered him to speed up planning for the meeting and to make sure it happens very soon."

Muller absorbed the information Raditz had delivered. He fingered his glass, circling the rings of moisture it made on the table, staring into the middle distance.

"I'm thinking about Hitler's occupation of the Rhineland," he finally said in a pensive tone. "It was almost exactly two years ago."

"I remember it very well," Raditz replied. "A lot of us believed at the time that Hitler had acted rashly. The French could have retaken it with scarcely any effort and simply swept him from power."

Muller nodded. "We were told that General Blomberg–the same guy you said Hitler just fired–was adamantly opposed, saying they would be helpless to prevent the French from overpowering the tiny force that Hitler was insisting that he order into the Rhineland. Göring was convinced it would be a fiasco too, and he frantically tried to talk Hitler out if it. But Hitler ignored them both, dispatched a dozen or so under-manned battalions across the bridge at Cologne and proceeded to occupy the entire territory of the Rhineland.

Muller became animated as he recounted the story. "As he had predicted, neither the French nor the British–certainly not the League of Nations–did anything about it. Not a shot was fired. In a single day, he gained full control of what was the industrial heartland of Germany–which he has now, of course, converted into the arsenal of German rearmament."

Then he paused and sighed. "I was in Danzig at the time. My boss, the League's High Commissioner for Danzig, was very alarmed by the event–in part because we could see Danzig as a potential next target for Hitler to decide to occupy; a small City State in what had formerly been Germany that was strategically located and enjoyed protection by the League under the Treaty of Versailles. Danzig was–and remains–highly vulnerable."

"Ultimately, Hitler decided not to invade–at least he hasn't done so yet," Muller smirked as he spoke. "But what struck us both at the time was the spectacle of the leader of a great nation like Germany seemingly able to do whatever he wanted, without any apparent constraints. He could override his military leadership, ignore objections of even his closest advisors, like Göring, and simply roll the dice, gambling that sending the army into the Rhineland wouldn't provoke a war with France.

"At the time, we thought to ourselves, 'how do you deal with a leader like that?'" Muller shook his head.

"What you're reporting to me now takes this anomaly another step further, Mr. Raditz; Hitler's simply eliminated any potential military check on his ambitions by putting himself in charge of the armed forces. There aren't any more senior military leaders now; they're all his subordinates.

Muller looked up and fixed Raditz with a steely gaze.

"Is there no one left in Germany who can stand up to this man?"

Raditz fidgeted with his drink, glanced away, clearly discomfited. Finally he spoke.

"There are some of us in Germany who share your misgivings," he said quietly.

The two men sat in silence for some time.

Finally, Raditz broke the spell.

"Actually, there's another anniversary coming up too," he said with a weak smile.

"Oh? What is it?" Muller asked.

"Kellogg-Briand," Raditz replied. "It was signed ten years ago this summer. A professor of mine sent me a note about it earlier this week reminding me. He said it might offer a solution to our current problems."

"I assume he was joking," Muller said.

Raditz nodded. "It's what passes for candid political speech in Germany today."

The Kellogg-Briand Pact; Muller remembered it well from his days at Cambridge. It had been an article of faith among pacifists–but had broad appeal to a war-weary public too.

"It was the shortest agreement in diplomatic history," he said. "If my memory is right, only two articles."

Raditz grinned. "That's right. Article One outlawed war as an instrument of national policy and Article Two said that all disputes among nations must be settled by peaceful means. That was it.

"And it was signed by more than sixty nations" he added.

"Including Germany, right?" said Muller.

"Yes." Raditz nodded.

"Well then; that's our solution," said Muller smiling broadly and clapping his hands. "Mr. Raditz, you simply have to take yourself over to the Chancellery in Berlin and hand Hitler a copy of the Kellogg-Briand Pact. 'Germany signed this agreement a decade ago Mr. Hitler, so you have to abandon your policy of threatening to invade Austria.'

"That'll do it," Muller went on, standing and making a deep mocking bow toward Raditz. "He'll thank you profusely, kiss you on both cheeks and immediately go on the radio to announce a new policy of harmony and good will toward Austria.

"Hurrah!" He lifted his hands in triumph.

Muller looked about himself to see men in the bar staring at him and quickly sat down again, sheepishly, but still grinning.

"I'll get right on it, Mr. Muller" Raditz was laughing too.

The two men sat a moment in shared amusement at the preposterous image of presenting Hitler with a copy of the agreement.

"It's pretty hard to believe that the world's leading statesmen actually agreed to sign to such a meaningless document," Muller said quietly. "What were they thinking?"

Raditz nodded. "I don't expect there'll be much of a celebration at the ten year anniversary this summer," he said. "Meantime, Hitler's recent actions have put the Austrian kettle on to boil.

Raditz stood. "Whatever is going to happen is probably going to happen sooner rather than later. If I were you, Mr. Muller, I'd plan accordingly."

# CHAPTER 14

Muller sought out Schultz, from the Chancellor's office, and passed him the information he'd been given by Raditz about Hitler's decisions. Schultz nodded dejectedly.

"We'd pieced most of that together from news reports and our own sources," he said. "To me, the most worrisome aspect is Hitler's move to take control of the Army. It was common knowledge that Fritsch and Blomberg were not keen on deploying their brand-new *Wehrmacht,*" he said. "They're both professional army officers and come from a tradition that views the Army as a military weapon to be used only as a last resort. Hitler, however, sees everything through the lens of his own ideology. The Army is just another tool in the arsenal he's prepared to use in order to impose his will.

"The decision to just sack the two of them still came as a real surprise; we'd had no hint that something like that was in the works. And what you're telling me now–that Hitler blackmailed them into stepping down–is truly shocking.

"What a way to treat the highest-ranking members of the German military," he mused. "And how will that action influence the behavior of other German officers who might think of telling Hitler things he doesn't want to hear?"

Schultz ran his hands through his hair, absorbing what Muller had told him.

Finally, he squared his shoulders. "What all this says to me is that Hitler's going to threaten the Chancellor with invasion if he doesn't surrender Austria's independence," Schultz paused, "but I can't persuade Schuschnigg of the risk. Schuschnigg's a traditionalist; he just can't fathom tactics that involve threatening war.

"Plus, both von Papen and Schmidt are saying all the right things to him," Schultz added, "promising a constructive meeting, even accepting our wording in documents setting out the meeting agenda and the text of a final communiqué confirming Austrian independence. According to them, the meeting will be some kind of love fest.

"All of which reinforces my suspicions," he added. "But it's precisely what Schuschnigg wants to hear.

"So, we'll see who's right, Mr. Muller," Schultz concluded. "The meeting will take place within ten days."

# CHAPTER 15

Muller was alarmed. This crisis was accelerating faster than he'd expected. Viktor Keinböck, the Governor of the Austrian National Bank, was dragging his feet and still had not fixed a date for them to meet. Keinböck was the key to Muller's planning on how to protect Austrian bank reserves in the event of a German takeover; somehow, he needed to unlock that door–urgently, in light of Raditz' warning.

Concluding he was out of other options, Muller made an appointment to see Friederich Baer again.

Baer agreed to meet that very afternoon and greeted him warmly.

"It's very nice to see you again, Mr. Muller," he said, grasping Muller's hand. "I was planning to contact you, but you beat me to it. So welcome."

"Oh, and by the way," he added with a smile and a conspiratorial look, "I understand that you performed yet another courageous rescue operation, saving our friend Otto Schultz from being abducted at Café Wolfe the other night. Well done. Brass knuckles come in handy again?" he asked impishly.

Muller shook his head admiringly. "You do have excellent sources of information, Mr. Baer," he said. "We were able to keep the story out of the papers and it was being closely held. But yes, I did use the brass knuckles again, or rather only one of them," he said a little sheepishly.

"Well, one seems to have done the trick according to what I'm told, Mr. Muller," Baer responded. "I guess we're going to have to enlarge the size of that account we're going to open in your name at Muller & Co. in Zurich." He chuckled at Muller's look of discomfort. "If we continue to delay setting it up, maybe we'll have reasons for making the sum even larger."

"We'll have to see, won't we?" Baer said laughing. "But I'm sure you have other things on your mind that you want to discuss, so please proceed."

Muller thanked him. "Mr. Baer, when we met here the last time–what was it, three weeks or so ago?–you told me that you were convinced that Hitler would follow through on his threat to take over Austria because he wanted to steal its wealth."

Baer nodded. "I still feel that way."

"You also speculated that my appointment as Commissioner General of the League might have something to do with Austrian finances and you volunteered to become an ally. I'd like to take you up on that offer, Mr. Baer," Muller said. "I need some help.

"But," Muller continued, "I need to warn you. If my plan comes to fruition and you are found to have taken part in it, you and your family would be in grave danger of arrest by German authorities."

Baer gazed at Muller levelly. "Thank you for warning me, Mr. Muller. But as I told you the last time, my family and I have transferred most of our portable wealth to Banque Pictet in Geneva. I have also procured living accommodations there and we have Swiss residency visas in hand. Magda and I and the rest of our family are ready to leave at a moment's notice if it comes to that.

"The reality is that the Nazis already have ample reason to put me on their list. So, I see little additional risk in taking on a role in your plan–whatever it is–to help protect Austria's wealth."

Muller nodded. "All right; let's begin.

"You already know that Austria is obligated on the 25-year loan from the consortium of foreign banks in the amount of roughly 570 million Austrian Schillings. That's public knowledge," Muller said.

Baer nodded. "Payable in 1959."

Muller continued. "My plan is to arrange for repayment of that loan amount in the moments before Austria is annexed by Germany and before Austria's funds pass into the hands of the Germans. That way the money won't be there for Hitler to steal; it will be back the hands of the lenders–the banks–who will make very sure Hitler can't get at it."

Baer's gaze was piercing. "And how do you plan to accomplish that, Mr. Muller?"

"The key to making the repayment is an order from Viktor Keinböck, the Governor of the Austrian National Bank. He has to initiate the process," Muller paused. "And I've now been here for three weeks and I haven't been able even to meet with him, let alone try to persuade him to participate in what I'm sure you'll agree, is a scheme that would infuriate Hitler.

"And that's why I've come here to see you, Mr. Baer. I want to enlist your help in getting Keinböck to buy into this operation."

Muller paused, his heart beating loudly in his ears. There it was; he'd revealed his plan. He had to trust his instinct that Baer would not betray him. He covered his nervousness by reaching for his cigarette case.

Baer sat back in his wingchair, then quickly leaned forward to accept the Gitane that Muller proffered and his light. He fixed Muller with a steady gaze.

"That's the very reason I was about to contact you again, Mr. Muller," he said. "Keinböck assumes there's some kind of plan is afoot, but he doesn't know you and feels he has no reason to trust you. So, he asked me to find out what's going on and to advise him on how to proceed. Your visit this afternoon anticipated my request for a meeting."

Baer took a long drag of his Gitane and tapped the ash into the nearby ashtray.

"Viktor Keinböck is a very cautious man, Mr. Muller," Baer continued. "He's risen quickly–he was only in his early thirties when he was named Finance Minister in 1922, right after the war. He found a way to remain in that position through all the political and economic upheavals that followed. Then, four years ago, Schuschnigg appointed him to head the central bank. Keinböck has seen a lot of water pass under the bridge; he is not a man who is disposed to act rashly,"

Baer and Muller stubbed out their cigarettes.

"Would he entertain a plan to protect Austria's wealth and deny it to the Germans?" asked Muller.

"Mr. Muller, I've known Keinböck for many years," Baer replied. "He is very much a creature of the Catholic hierarchy that has dominated Austrian politics since the War. I have every reason to believe that he considers himself an Austrian patriot and that he'd be prepared to defend its interests. I told you he was appointed to head the central bank by Schuschnigg. He's in fact very much like Schuschnigg; severe and conservative.

"So, I don't know if he'd be prepared to buy off on the plan you just described. But the fact he asked me to find out what you're up to tells me that he's worried by what he's seeing–worried enough that I'm confident that I can bring the two of you together for a meeting.

"But he's suspicious," Baer went on. "Your predecessor as Commissioner General became a flaming Nazi sympathizer; so much so that he resigned to go head up the Nazi Party in the

Netherlands. The League did nothing about replacing him for a year. Then suddenly you were appointed as the new Commissioner General. No one knows anything about you. You don't come from the Secretariat; you're neither a banker nor an economist.

"Then you show up here and begin making inquiries about Keinböck–including requests for one-on-one meetings." Baer shrugged. "As I say, he's cautious; he suspects that you have an agenda, but he's not sure it's one he wants to be involved with."

Baer smiled. "I told him I was the one that warned you about both of your offices being bugged. He said he'd wondered how a new arrival like you knew that.

"I also told him that you'd probably saved my life on the train," Baer added. "He was impressed. My guess is that he's by now learned that you rescued Otto Schultz too. That will definitely be a plus, as he knows Schultz from his relationship with Schuschnigg."

Baer added, "I haven't told him that your family owns Muller & Co.; that's just between us–unless he figures it out on his own.

"Let me try to broker a meeting between the two of you as soon as possible." Baer concluded. "I'll host it here so neither of you has to take responsibility for it. Agreed?"

Muller nodded. "Thank you, Mr. Baer," he said. "That's what I hoped this meeting would accomplish."

## CHAPTER 16

Baer was as good as his word. He arranged the meeting with Keinböck the very next day at 5 PM in his office.

Muller was the first to arrive. He was ushered into a well-appointed conference room with a highly-polished round table beneath a decorative hanging light and three comfortable conference-style chairs arranged around it. There was a pad of paper before each place, along with a sharp pencil and a glass ashtray.

Through the open doorway, Muller saw Keinböck arrive. He was guided into the conference room and the two men were shaking hands when Baer entered from a side door and greeted them both. A waiter trailed him, carrying a large pitcher of water. He filled three crystal glasses which he positioned alongside the three notepads, placed the pitcher in the center of the table, then retreated.

"Just water to start our meeting," Baer said. "Champagne is on ice in the event we have cause to celebrate later." He smiled and gestured to Muller and Keinböck to be seated, taking the third chair himself. "Thank you both for coming," he said. "I'm pleased to serve as an intermediary to bring you both together.

"Viktor," Baer said, turning toward the banker, "I've known you for most of your professional life. I know you will approach this discussion with the integrity that I've come to expect.

"Mr. Muller" he said turning this time toward Muller, "I've known you a much shorter period of time. But three weeks ago, you saved my life. I'm prepared to treat that as a very serious down payment of good faith."

Keinböck spoke up. "I'm also reliably informed that you rescued Otto Schultz from being abducted just a week ago too. I thank you for that intervention as well; Schultz's a friend and a valuable member of the Chancellor's senior staff."

Keinböck then smiled gravely and added, "In addition to any other qualifications you may possess, Mr. Muller–of which I'm sure there are many–you have certainly arrived in town with a well-deserved reputation as a guardian angel of some kind."

Muller felt himself redden. "That's nice of you to say, Mr. Keinböck. It's not a role I'm accustomed to playing. So, let's put it aside, if we may."

Muller turned to Baer. "Thank you for organizing and hosting this meeting, Mr. Baer. As the newest in town, perhaps I should begin."

Without awaiting their reactions, he continued.

"Let me state at the outset that I am acutely aware that my qualifications and experience in the field of finance are far outweighed by your own. So, I feel rather presumptuous in offering the suggestions I propose to place before you this afternoon. But we live in a strange time, when regular order sometimes gets upset. This appears to be one of those occasions."

Muller reached into his suit pocket to extract his cigarette case, and offered his Gitanes. "Would anyone care to share one of these?" he asked.

"I'm just back from London," Keinböck said, "and I have some Pall Malls I can offer." They all accepted and Muller flared his lighter for them.

"I was appointed Commissioner General for Austria by the League Council in early December," Muller continued. "I did not seek the appointment nor have a hand in the appointment process. But I was duly sworn in and now occupy that position. Frankly, you gentlemen know much more about the duties of the Commissioner General's position than I do. I am focused on one fairly narrow aspect of his role: the authority the Commissioner General is entitled to exercise over the revenues collected by the Austrian Customs Bureau and those generated by taxes on the sale of tobacco."

"Which we are all now evading by smoking English cigarettes," Baer observed with an indulgent smile.

Muller acknowledged the point and went on.

"As you know, the actions of the Commissioner General are directed by what's called a Control Group. This is composed of officials appointed by finance ministries of the four nations that are guarantors of the 570 million AUS loan: France, Britain, Czechoslovakia and Italy. As you probably also know, the Control Group has not met since the loan closed in 1936, over two years ago. The directives they adopted at that time remain in effect and define the authority of my office with respect to the use and disposition of the Customs and tobacco revenues."

Muller stubbed out his butt and took a quick sip of water. "Those revenues are deposited in your bank, Mr. Keinböck."

Keinböck nodded. "They are held in accounts for payment as directed by your office, Mr. Muller."

"Correct." Muller replied. "And the Control Board directives essentially instruct the Commissioner General–that is to say, me–to use those funds to make quarterly debt service payments to the lenders, as required by the terms of the loan."

"That's right," said Keinböck. "You send the directive to us to make the payments and we execute them by telex bank transfers."

"But what is the Commissioner General supposed to do in the event Austria is faced with being taken over by another nation, say, by Germany, for example?" asked Muller. "In that event, Austria would cease to exist; it would simply be absorbed into Germany.

"Debt service payments are made in advance, empowering the borrower to continue to enjoy the benefits of the loan during the forthcoming quarter, until a new payment is due. But if Austria were to disappear, it would no longer exist as a borrower nor enjoy the loan benefits.

"What is the Commissioner General's responsibility if that eventuality were to occur?" he asked, looking at Keinböck and Baer.

Neither man responded.

"Let me offer a hypothetical answer," Muller said. "Let's suppose for a moment that the Commissioner General were to conclude that, if the sovereign nation of Austria were on the brink of destruction, his authority obliged him to declare that the quarterly debt service should not be paid and he therefore gave formal notice that he was refusing to order the bank to make the quarterly payment."

Muller paused to let Keinböck and Baer consider what he was suggesting.

Then he continued.

"I expect you will agree that refusal to make the required quarterly debt service payment would constitute an act of default under the terms of the loan. If that's right, and I think it is," Muller went on, "then the borrower–Austria–would be in default and–acting through its central banking authority, the Austrian National Bank–it would be obliged to repay the lenders the full-face amount of the loan."

Muller paused again for emphasis before continuing. "What I'm suggesting, therefore, is that in that situation, the Austrian National Bank would have full legal authority–indeed, arguably, a legal *duty*–to pay back the full 570 million AUS loan to the lenders–even if that meant essentially emptying the National

Bank's vault–and leaving next to nothing there for the occupying power to seize."

Muller's statement was met with silence.

He waited for someone to respond.

After several moments, Keinböck turned to face Muller, his hands clutching the edge of the table and his eyes narrowed to slits. "Utterly preposterous!"

"Sir," said Muller, "Mr. Baer is convinced that Hitler is determined to take over Austria in order to steal its wealth." He turned to Baer. "You stand by that position, am I correct?"

"Yes," Baer replied.

Turning back to Keinböck, Muller spoke forcefully. "Chancellor Schuschnigg is scheduled to meet with Chancellor Hitler in Berchtesgaden within the week. Hitler has told the French Ambassador he will have Schuschnigg's head. Ambassador von Papen and your own Minister Schmidt have been instructed to 'soften up' Schuschnigg for the meeting. And most important, Hitler has taken personal command of the German Army and thereby empowered himself to unleash his military forces. There is a very real possibility that Schuschnigg will be confronted with a demand to surrender Austria to Germany or face a German invasion."

Hunching his shoulders, with his arms on the table, Muller leaned forward toward Keinböck, and looked at him directly.

"The scenario I just suggested a moment ago–Austria swallowed up by Germany and ceasing to exist as a nation–could occur within a matter of only a few days or weeks," he said. "This is not a hypothetical conversation."

Keinböck returned Muller's gaze. "Utterly preposterous," he repeated.

Then he turned to Baer.

"Friederich, would you be good enough to excuse yourself? Mr. Muller is wildly erroneous. I need to acquaint him with some truths better spoken privately."

"Of course; I remain available if I'm needed." Baer stood and left the room.

Keinböck offered Muller another Pall Mall which he accepted.

"Maybe being dismissed from our conversation will offer our friend Baer some measure of deniability if he is ever interrogated about this meeting," said Keinböck, exhaling a cloud of smoke. At least we can hope so", he added.

"As I've said twice," Keinböck continued, returning to the thread of their conversation, "your remarks are utterly preposterous. At least at one time they were," he added. "But no longer I'm afraid.

"I have similar intelligence about the forthcoming meeting," he said. "Our mutual friend Otto Schultz fears that the Chancellor, as he is prone to do, is approaching the conference with misplaced confidence, listening to what he wants to hear, rather than weighing the risks he may confront.

"We may, indeed, Mr. Muller, be faced with precisely the terrible scenario you just sketched. And I have been obliged to ask myself what I should do if that should come to pass. I'm afraid I must confess that I haven't been able to decide."

Keinböck paused and pushed back his chair. "Do you suppose our friend Baer has anything stronger than water to offer us?" He stood and began opening drawers in the cabinet behind them.

"Ah. Here we are," he said, triumphantly holding up a full bottle of Dewar's Scotch. He proceeded to open it and poured them each a large slug.

"Prost." They clinked glasses.

Keinböck looked directly at Muller. "You realize, of course, that your plan would mean a death sentence from Hitler."

Muller nodded. "I said the same thing to Mr. Baer."

"No League of Nations immunity, Mr. Muller," Keinböck added. "You'd just disappear."

"Not a happy prospect. But yes, I understand." Muller replied.

"Me too; I'm afraid we're in the same boat, Mr. Muller."

They paused to consider what lay ahead.

Keinböck finally broke the silence.

"I like the idea of trying to empty the vault if the Germans take us over," he said. "I hadn't thought about triggering a default on the loan and using our gold and currency reserves to pay off the lenders. They're all big commercial banks–Barclays, Banque de Paris and so on–eleven of them all told, if I remember right. The loans were syndicated globally, so J.P. Morgan and Guarantee Trust Company in New York will be involved, and probably some British Commonwealth banks too. There's not a chance those bankers would let go of any funds we were to pay them. Hitler could yell and scream all he wants; the bankers won't return a pfennig. So that part of your plan would certainly work," he said.

"Taking the steps to actually trigger a default is a little trickier than you suggested," he went on. "Among other things, we'd need to have in our hands a formal declaration of default and a demand for immediate payment if I am to make a transfer of funds. There's more work to be done there."

Muller elected not to interrupt and describe his solution to that issue.

"There is also the problem of how to physically accomplish a transfer of funds out of our bank to the creditors," Keinböck continued. "I've been thinking about that problem wholly separate and apart from what you just suggested. And I haven't come up with a solution," he added.

Keinböck paused and poured them both some more whiskey.

"Let's suppose Hitler decides to occupy Austria," he continued. "One of the first places he'll seize is the Bank. If I'm still there, sitting at the telex machine transferring funds, they'll either shoot me on the spot or cart me off to one of those camps. Neither alternative is very palatable, I'm afraid.

"I've tried to think about what my escape route could be," he said and shook his head. "I'm afraid I haven't found one yet.

"Remember, if I'm going to transfer the money, it has to be at the last possible moment," he said. "I can't bankrupt the country before an occupation actually takes place. What if by some miracle, the occupation fails or gets called off. If the money's already gone, then Austria's saved but dead broke. That's not an acceptable outcome either.

"So, it's a last-minute event; I think about that, then find myself going back to wondering how to escape."

Keinböck turned to face Muller directly.

"If we were doing this together, you'd face the same risks too, Mr. Muller," he said, pouring out the last of the whiskey.

"Prost, again!' Keinböck leaned forward and clinked Muller's glass.

"We need to give this proposition more thought," he said, and downed the rest of his drink. Muller followed suit and they walked out into the winter evening.

"I'll be in contact," Keinböck said as they parted ways.

# CHAPTER 17

Muller decided to stop at the Café Louvre before returning to the hotel. He was hungry and he found it amusing to sit with the journalists as they gossiped and compared notes. It was a good way to get caught up on the latest rumors–which sometimes turned out to be accurate–and he'd found he was always welcome when he bought a round or two.

As usual, they were grouped around a booth toward the back of the café along the wall.

Shirer greeted him and pulled out a chair, motioning for him to sit. Hamilton and Boothby were arguing as usual and the couple from the *New York Herald*–he'd learned they were Martha and Henry Fodor–were engaged in separate discussions with several newcomers whom Muller assumed he'd be introduced to later.

Hamilton turned to greet him, asking if he'd heard why Hitler was keeping himself cooped up in his lair at Berchtesgaden and refusing to be disturbed by affairs of state.

Muller shook his head, looking puzzled.

"Well," said Hamilton, obviously enjoying himself, "It appears that he's pinned a big street map of Vienna to his wall and he's brought in a draftsman's table where he spends hours designing architectural monstrosities which he'll build to replace the current 'decadent' baroque and classical look of the city. It'll be a way to celebrate his triumphal return to Austria as its conqueror."

Hamilton mimicked the Hitler salute as he roared with laughter and the others joined in.

"I thought you were going to say he was too busy being fitted with a new uniform to celebrate his promotion from lowly corporal to Commander-in-Chief of the German armed forces," said Shirer.

"Well that too," Hamilton responded. "He even made Göring into a Field Marshal; that certainly merits a new uniform for Fat Hermann too."

"They could go to the same tailor," Boothby chimed in.

"Just so long as he's not a Jew," added Hamilton, guffawing.

"Oops," he said, glancing at Fodor. "Sorry, Henry; No slur intended."

Fodor waved him away. "Ordinary Austrians are more annoying than you every day."

They all reached for their new drinks as the waiter put his tray on the table to serve them.

"On a more serious note," said Shirer, "Hitler's military shakeup is a big deal–and scary." He paused, shaking his head reflectively, refilling his pipe. "Von Fritsch and von Blomberg were the architects of rebuilding the *Reichswehr*–that tiny force

Germany was permitted to retain under the Versailles Treaty–into the *Wehrmacht*, that's now threatening to invade Austria with tens of thousands of soldiers under arms. The fact that Hitler sacked them–both professional soldiers, and neither one shy about reminding Hitler that he is not one–is a bad sign for anyone hoping to keep Hitler's hands off Austria."

Hamilton then chimed in again. "I was told that Hess' secret plan–the one we're not supposed to know anything about–involved getting von Papen to organize a big demonstration in front of the German Trade Bureau, then having someone up on the roof of the Opera House across the street shoot him as he addressed the crowd. Hitler could then use von Papen's murder as an excuse to march into Austria."

"Someone has to restore order, right?" said Martha Fodor.

Hamilton responded by bowing in her direction with a smile. "At least it would have gotten rid of von Papen; there's that to say for it," he added with a laugh.

Shirer rose and slapped some schillings on the table. "CBS has me off to Ljubljana to broadcast a concert by some Goddamn children's choir. I've got to catch the train. They won't find time for me to broadcast news about what's happening here, but there's always an audience for children singing. Shit."

He shrugged into his coat and strode out of the Café.

There was a pause, which Muller took advantage of to order another round.

"I've filed my story on this, so none of you can steal it," said Henry Fodor. "But I had a meeting today with Ernst Sailer."

"The leader of the Social Democrats?" asked Hamilton, glancing sharply at Fodor. "He's in exile in Czechoslovakia. The Party here has a price on his head."

"That's the guy," Fodor said. "And you're right; after Schuschnigg and his Clerical Fascists banned the Social Democrats in '34, they set up shop across the border–well protected by Czech left wing parties that are legal there. They've got a weekly newspaper they smuggle back here and they're financed by money coming from labor organizations around Europe."

"And from Moscow, too," Hamilton interrupted. "There's always been a big Communist influence in that crowd."

Fodor nodded. "I'm sure of it. There's no love lost in the Kremlin for Schuschnigg's Clerical–Fascist government here. But what's interesting is that the leadership of the Left is coming to view Hitler as more of a threat than the government. It's common knowledge that the Social Democrats have kept a resistance movement alive here despite the government's continuing efforts to crush them. There are entire neighborhoods in the working-class sections of the city where socialism is the dominant influence. There's a left wing underground movement that stays out of sight but is biding its time."

"Right," said Hamilton, interrupting again. "But what they're waiting for is the Comintern Revolution. Their enemy is Schuschnigg's government–his Clerical Fascist Party and the

Fatherland Front; they're not just hostile to one another, they're at war!

"That's been a fact of life in this country for years," Hamilton continued, his voice rising. "You can't tell me that Ernst Sailer–or any of the other so-called leaders of the Left–is thinking about supporting Schuschnigg. It's preposterous," he said, downing his drink and looking around for another.

Fodor finished his drink too before responding. "These guys have set up a system that allows them to travel back and forth pretty easily between Vienna and their exile headquarters in Czechoslovakia. Sailer told me that keeps them very much abreast of what's going on here and what their supporters are thinking."

"And they're saying they're frightened about what would happen to them if the Germans were to take over and impose Nazi rule?" asked Muller.

Fodor nodded. "They're acutely aware that the Nazis destroyed the Social Democrats in Germany–and that they did it a lot more brutally than the Government has acted here–bad as that's been. Death squads, concentration camps, forced labor, military conscription; that's what they see ahead from a Nazi takeover.

"So, they're trying to make contact with the government," he concluded as the new round of drinks appeared.

"And the Government has told them to piss off," Hamilton said. "Right?"

"So far," Fodor nodded.

Hamilton sighed and slumped against the back of the booth.

"That's such a good example of why this country is so fucked up and so frustrating to cover," he said quietly. "The last time there was a real election here, the Left wound up winning nearly half the vote. Christ, if the Government and the Left found a way to live together, they'd be absolutely invincible. They could shut down the Nazi sympathizers in a heartbeat. But they've never been able to do that. Each side views the other as a deadly enemy and they've spent most of the last 20 years looking for ways to destroy one another."

Hamilton looked at Fodor. "Nice try, old boy," he said. "I hope your readers love your story. But it'll never happen. Not in this lifetime."

Fodor shrugged and everyone took a large swallow from their glasses to digest what they'd heard.

Muller stood up to leave. "Mr. Fodor," he asked, "did Sailer tell you anything about the underground network the socialists have set up to travel back and forth to Czechoslovakia?"

"Not a word," Fodor replied. "Why do you ask?"

"Just wondering," said Muller, adding several schilling notes for the drinks tab.

Back at his hotel, Muller placed the white paper on his windowsill and when he met Franz the next evening he told him to do two things: first get a message to their friend in Geneva to be alert and ready to act, possibly in only a matter of days or weeks; second, to see what he could find out about the socialist network of routes into Czechoslovakia.

# CHAPTER 18

It was Saturday and Muller decided he needed a break, so after breakfast he tossed his tennis gear and racket into a canvas bag and walked the few blocks to Kaiserplatz to catch the tram out to the Sportshalle. He'd tried to sign up on the tennis ladder but hadn't gotten any calls. So, he thought he might be able to pick up a game, or at least get in a vigorous rally if he showed up in person.

A disinterested attendant shrugged when Muller inquired about the ladder. "I don't know how that works," he said yawning and returning to the magazine he was leafing through. So, Muller proceeded to the locker room and changed. He approached the pro, who promised to try and find him a game, but didn't seem to make much progress. Muller was able to get on a court a couple of times and participate in warm up drills, but each time the missing player showed up. He was getting discouraged sitting in the lounge above the courts.

He picked up a discarded newspaper from Innsbruck, and reading its description of a pro-Nazi demonstration didn't improve his mood. Apparently, the police had broken up the march, but not before a major fight had broken out resulting in burning cars and Jewish stores being vandalized–"which was understandable," according to the paper since the Jewish owners had become so "insufferable" in their behavior.

Muller sighed. Innsbruck was near where the attack on the train had taken place; it was becoming notorious as a hotbed of Nazi sympathizers.

Then he glanced up and saw the pro standing on the far court waving him to come down.

Muller jogged around the other courts to where the pro was standing.

"Can you fill in for a mixed doubles match?" he asked. "They're good enough to play with you and lost their fourth."

"Certainly," Muller responded with a smile.

"Come on, then," said the pro, leading him over to a threesome and doing the introductions.

"Horst," said a large black-haired man with a prominent brow; "my wife Ursula," gesturing to the tiny blonde next to him. She smiled and shook Muller's hand.

"And I'm Steffi Farber," said a dark-haired woman who had been crouched looking for something in her bag and now stood to greet him. Muller took in her almost perfectly oval face with large brown eyes beneath arched eyebrows.

"I'm Paul Muller," he responded noticing the strength of her grip as they shook hands. "I came hoping to find a game."

"Well, you've got one," Steffi said with a smile that showed off very white teeth. "We hope you're ready; these games usually degenerate into a grudge match." She had dark hair with curls that seemed to cascade over her left ear. "My regular partner got called to the Emergency Room this morning to sew up and stitch and set broken bones from another one of those militia fights last night. So, you're in luck, especially if we beat these two."

They hit a few warm ups and Muller immediately saw that they were experienced players. Good; this should be fun, he thought.

They won the racket spin for serve and Steffi tossed the balls to Muller.

"You begin, Paul; I want to see what you've got," she said, moving into the forecourt. Muller aced Horst to his forehand side then tested Ursula's backhand. She whipped a low shot back that caught Muller at the ankles and he mis-hit into the net.

Okay, he thought; game on.

Back and forth they went for the full hour they were allotted. Steffi was very quick and showed off a deft drop shot for a couple of winners. No small talk, just tactical comments–'stay back'; 'I've got it'–and the occasional, 'Good shot' or 'Oops, sorry'.

They won the first set 7-5 and were tied at 6 when time ran out.

The four of them came to the net and congratulated one another, perspiring a little too much to hug.

"Is there a place I can buy us a beer after we change?" asked Muller. "I'd like to do that as a thank you–and a gracious winner," he said laughing.

"Sure," said Steffi, "there's a place near the tram stop. Let's meet in the lounge after we change."

Muller and Horst chatted amiably as they showered and dressed. He was a Postal worker, he said, and his wife taught kindergarten.

"You're a better player than Marc," he said to Muller, adding "Marc's the doctor who couldn't make it today." He laughed. "Steffi is usually all over him because he misses shots and gets out of position. She's really outspoken and not shy about expressing herself. By the end of the match, he's usually pretty pissed off. I guess they're colleagues at the hospital, but she's on his case.

"Anyway, none of that today with you, Muller," he laughed. "She had to scramble to keep up with you. That was good. Maybe she'll dump him as her partner and persuade you to take his place."

"I don't know about that," Muller replied noncommittally. But it might be fun he thought; Steffi was a good player, and she was quite attractive too.

The nearby café was nearly empty as they sat down together. Horst and Ursula said they were just staying a moment and shared a bottle of mineral water.

"I'm up for a nice mug of beer and a schnitzel for lunch," said Muller. "Will you join me?" he said turning to Steffi.

"Absolutely," she replied. "I need that beer and didn't have much breakfast."

The four of them briefly recapped high points–and low–of their match before Horst and Ursula departed.

"Prost," said Muller tipping Steffi's mug with his own. "That was fun. And we did win," he added.

Unexpectedly, Steffi stood, leaned across the table and kissed him on the cheek. "I told you good things would happen if we did," she said, laughing impishly. "What could possibly be better than that?"

"We probably shouldn't go there," Muller replied with a grin. Steffi reddened a little but smiled back at him.

Their wiener schnitzels arrived and they dug in.

"You're at one of the hospitals?" he asked.

Steffi nodded. "St. Cecelia's," she said. "I'm an operating room nurse," she added, "at least that's what my title is; I've completed all the course work and I could be a surgeon except they won't permit *a woman* to become licensed. So, I do everything that the male surgeons do–and most of the time better–but they always finish up the incisions and sign the paperwork as the attending physician, saying a polite 'thank you nurse Farber' from their lofty positions.

"It really is annoying," she said, "and there's nothing I can do about it. I complain, I talk back to them and point out their mistakes–that just makes them all the more determined to keep me down.

"Like today," she went on, "there was a big clash overnight between two of the militias and there were a couple of dozen serious injuries. But rather than call me in to shoulder part of the work, Marc–that's the player who didn't show up today–told me this was man's work and sent me on my way.

"Well screw them!" she said defiantly. Then glancing at Muller, she added, "This is when I'm always told I should apologize for my bad manners in speaking out of turn. Well screw that too; I've got nothing to apologize for. If you're offended, you're free to leave; I'll pay the bill. But I don't back down," she said. "Ever."

She lifted her chin.

This time it was Muller who stood and leaned over to kiss Steffi on the cheek. "Bravo," he said, applauding and signaling for two more beers as he resumed his seat. "I have a sister who is cut from the same cloth. She's now a physicist in Chicago. When I visited her last year, she complained about the same thing, with the same 'screw you' attitude."

"So, I'm comfortable and see no need to go anywhere," he said offering Steffi a Gitane and a light.

"And what about you? What do you do?" Steffi asked.

Muller responded, describing his role in a very general manner and deflecting her inquiry.

They continued chatting together, through another beer and several cigarettes, conversing easily and laughing together.

"You know," he said, "one of my disappointments is having been in Vienna now for over a month–the birthplace of Mozart and home to so much glorious music–and I've not been able to find time to attend any concert. I asked the concierge at my hotel last evening to get me a ticket tonight for either the opera or the symphony. No luck; both sold out."

Steffi looked at him with a bemused expression. "I tried to do exactly the same thing and met exactly the same result. So, this has to be fate." She smiled, "And entitles me to do what polite, well-mannered young women are not supposed to do."

"And what's that?" Muller asked cocking his head and smiling back at her.

"Invite you to dine with me this evening at my apartment," she said. "My butcher told me he has some fine fresh spring lamb. In addition to being a great surgeon and a highly competitive tennis player, you'll find I'm a really good cook."

Muller laughed and readily accepted, and promptly at 7:30 PM he rang the entry bell at Steffi's apartment on Tigergasse, just off Kaiserplatz, carrying two bottles of 1934 Chateau Lynch-Bages Bordeaux.

Steffi was dressed in a gold lamé blouse with a high collar and a floor-length, faintly patterned dark blue skirt. Her dark curls were once again piled around her left ear and she was wearing pink lipstick. She looked very glamorous, Muller thought, and told her so. She curtsied with a smile of acknowledgement and took charge of the wine.

As he walked into the spacious and warmly-decorated apartment, Muller heard the unmistakable strains of violins and spied a handsome gramophone on a table in the corner.

"Mendelssohn," he said, pausing a moment, listening, "the Scottish Symphony. One of my very favorites," he said. "What a splendid welcome."

Steffi handed him a chilled bottle of Grunter Veltliner and an opener. "White wine before your red," she said, smiling. "I'm glad you liked my selection. I've got quite a large music collection and splurged on a good gramophone so I can enjoy it."

"You know Mendelssohn's music is banned in Germany," he said.

Steffi nodded, "Clearly Jewish music," she said. "Pieces like *"Elijah* or *The Christmas Oratorio*; very subversive." She rolled her eyes.

"I was in a choir in Danzig that was ordered not to sing *Hark the Herald Angels Sing,*" Muller said, shaking his head.

Steffi led him to a cabinet where she stored several dozen record albums. To Muller, it was like finding himself in a candy store and he sat down on the rug and began pulling one album after another out of the shelves, exclaiming in wonder: "Chopin's nocturnes, Schuman, oh and you even have the requiems," he said excitedly. "Ah, here's the Brahms, and the Faure–and the Mozart–the very best. We need to put this on for dinner," he said. "Not sad at all, just magisterial music."

Steffi left him to finish preparing the meal as Muller happily explored the collection.

The dinner was as good as Steffi had promised; the lamb done just right, pink and tender, accompanied by red cabbage and dumplings. The Bordeaux flowed and they laughed and giggled as Muller stood to change the record stacker on the gramophone holder after the records dropped and the arm with the needle returned to its slot.

Pushing back his chair as Steffi cleared the dinner plates, Muller placed a Strauss waltz on the turntable, whirled Steffi into his arms and they spun around the living room. Holding Steffi close, Muller suddenly felt himself getting a very large erection, which proceeded to stiffen as Steffi pressed against him, then kissed him passionately, her tongue seeking out his.

They clung together, then Steffi disengaged and led him quickly toward the bedroom, where they tumbled onto the bed and began fumbling with one another's clothing. She threw herself on top of him and they made love, climaxing quickly, then started over, this time more slowly, but intensely, gasping and crying out.

Much later, Muller got up to use the toilet. When he returned, he saw that Steffi was holding a bowl of whipped cream.

"I'd planned to serve this with dessert," she said moving toward him as he became aroused again. "But now I have a much better place to use it."

They finally awoke the next morning, tangled in the bedclothes and one another. Steffi rose and began walking toward the bathroom. "I have a great big shower, with a lot of hot water," she said mischievously, smiling back at him.

"Ow!" she said stumbling as she stepped on Muller's suitcoat as it lay on the floor.

"What have you got in here, Paul," she said, squatting to reach into the suit pocket. She blanched as she extracted the brass knuckles.

"My God," she said, dropping them and putting a hand over her mouth, glancing first at the weapons then at Muller. "Are these what I think they are?" Steffi looked stricken.

"They're brass knuckles," said Muller. "I carry them for protection. Sorry if they're upsetting."

"My God," she repeated.

He rose to kneel beside her and put his arm around her shoulder, hugging her tightly. "Go start the shower," he whispered.

But the mood had broken.

They showered and embraced, then dried themselves, Steffi putting on a housecoat while Muller began collecting articles of clothing and getting dressed.

"Let me run to the corner and bring back coffee and some pastry," he said. Steffi nodded silently.

When Muller returned, Steffi was subdued and looked downcast. Muller found two cups, poured them both coffee from the container and handed her a pastry as they sat at the kitchen table.

She put her hand on his and when she looked at him, he could see that she had been crying.

"Is there something I can do?" he asked.

She shook her head. "It's just that it was such a wonderful time yesterday and last night. No Nazi threats, no brawlers to stitch up–Paul, you've only been here a month; you have no idea of the anxiety and stress that we live with. Every day is a struggle: my battles with the surgeons and the hierarchy at the hospital; the political face-offs between the Clerical-Fascists and everyone else; the street violence that never seems to let up; and overhanging it all, Hitler threatening to overrun our country. Everyone eyes one another suspiciously–which side are you on? Am I at risk doing business with you–or even talking to you?

"People don't trust one another anymore; what passes for normalcy is a struggle for survival. It's unnerving–and exhausting."

She lifted her head; fixed Muller with a smile and took his hands into hers. "And then there was yesterday. Two people met–serendipitously–on a tennis court and proceeded to have a wonderful day–and night–of laughter, song, wine, and fun in bed. It was an escape–a flight of fancy that separated us from the daily grind; it buried the tensions we're forced to endure. It was magical."

"Then I stepped on your *brass knuckles*," she fairly spat the words, "and it punctured the balloon."

"I'm not blaming you," she said tightening her grip on his hands. "I'm sure you have to protect yourself. I realize I don't quite know why."

"I can explain," Muller interrupted.

"It doesn't matter," Steffi cut him off. "Everyone has to protect themselves. God knows, I see broken bodies every day of people who couldn't and suffered the consequences.

"No; it's just that stepping on those weapons–after having just made love to the man who would wield them, and do so for reasons I realize I know nothing about–pricked the balloon, and I came crashing back down to reality, and to all the uncertainty and anxiety that define life in Vienna today." She sighed.

"It's very depressing." she said quietly, reaching for his packet of Gitanes, accepting Muller's light and inhaling deeply.

"Would you like me to leave?" asked Muller.

"No," she replied. "Not yet; not until you've made love to me again."

# CHAPTER 19

Muller was pensive as he returned to his hotel. Steffi was right; yesterday had been a magical release from the pressures he was feeling too. Could they rekindle that atmosphere together again? He wanted to and sensed Steffi did too. They'd agreed to see each other again next week. Maybe the situation here will be better by then, he thought to himself; that might help.

The concierge handed him his key and a note saying that someone named Heinz had called and left a message "three hours early."

Raditz wanted to meet at 4 PM instead of 7 at Café Clover.

The afternoon had turned chilly and rainy so the café was crowded. Raditz had taken a table in a small alcove near the bar where they could speak without being overheard. He appeared disheveled; unshaven and wearing a wrinkled shirt with no necktie. Two large drinks were on the table.

"I took the liberty of ordering large whiskies for both of us," he said as Muller seated himself. "We'll need them."

He fixed Muller with a grim look. "I think von Ribbentrop is out to have my head," he said. "My sources remain good for now, but I might be recalled to Berlin at any moment, so I moved up our meeting time as a precaution. I'm afraid the news is bad and I wanted to be sure to get it into your hands before I get pushed aside.

"You should light up, Mr. Muller, and drink up too, while I tell you an even more bizarre tale than the one I related last time."

Muller did so.

"Schuschnigg traveled to Berchtesgaden yesterday to meet with Hitler," Raditz said. "Total secrecy; there was no announcement of any kind. The Chancellery told reporters he'd taken a day off to ski.

"Some ski trip!" Raditz sneered.

"He took a special train early in the morning to Salzburg, then switched to a car, with only a small security contingent along as an escort. When they got to the border, a big German Horch limousine was waiting for him–along with Guido Schmidt and Franz von Papen in the backseat to accompany him the rest of the way. The German border guards refused entry to his security detail and replaced them with a large escort consisting of members of the Austrian Legion–those are Austrian Nazis that Schuschnigg ordered deported to Germany for illegal activity," he added. "They all detest Schuschnigg and assigning them as his escort was an insult that set the tone for what was to come.

"When they arrived around noontime, Hitler made Schuschnigg cool his heels for thirty minutes, then summoned him to his office. Hitler never stood to greet him or offer him a seat. With his own staff around him–including Schmidt and von Papen–Hitler proceeded to launch into a furious tirade and dressed down the Chancellor of Austria like he was some kind of errant schoolboy."

Raditz pulled some papers from a pocket. "One of our foreign ministry staff members was the note-taker and I have a copy of some shorthand notes of what Hitler said."

He looked at Muller. "I've read it several times and I can still scarcely believe it," he said. He put on small glasses and began to read.

*"How have you dared all these years to torture* my *people*–my *German people in Austria? God has made me Führer and ruler of every man and woman of German blood in every country on earth. You shall bow to my will as all the rest of the world shall bow, or I will break you. I demand obedience from you and shall enforce it, if necessary with my armies. You have played your last card, Herr Schuschnigg, and you will accept and sign here, at once, before you leave this house, the terms that I have prepared for your surrender, or I will issue the order to march into Austria immediately."*

Raditz removed his glasses and folded the notes, putting them back in his pocket. "There's more, I'm told, but you get the idea–it was just a tirade.

"At some point, Hitler apparently flung a document containing eleven demands in Schuschnigg's face repeating, 'You will sign this before you leave today'. Then he ordered Schuschnigg into the next room where General von Reichenau, commander of what he called the Armies of Austrian Occupation, showed him the strategic plan to invade and garrison Austria. After that, they sat down to a lunch–which was apparently consumed in total silence. Hitler never spoke a word and no one else dared to break the silence." Raditz shook his head, looking at Muller with a wan smile.

"Very peculiar," he added; "almost medieval.

"I'm told Hitler even ordered Schuschnigg not to smoke; 'No one smokes in my presence without my permission' or words to that effect.

"Anyway, they proceeded to pressure Schuschnigg all afternoon," Raditz continued, "Schmidt and von Papen piling on too. Finally, he accepted three of Hitler's key demands. He refused to agree to the others, telling Hitler they posed constitutional issues that were beyond his authority. And he insisted that in return for his concessions, Hitler should issue a declaration reaffirming confirming his 1936 statement recognizing Austrian sovereignty and independence.

"Hitler pocketed Schuschnigg's concessions and told him they must be put into effect no later than Wednesday–three days hence; in effect, an ultimatum. Then he told Schuschnigg he would deliver a speech to the Reichstag and the German nation on the following

Sunday where he would 'set the record straight on Austria'. Then he turned on his heel and abruptly walked out. End of meeting. Schuschnigg arrived back in Vienna on his special train around 3 AM this morning."

Raditz shifted in his seat, clearly uncomfortable with the message he was delivering. He nervously ran his hand across his lips before resuming.

"We're told that all this is being kept under strict wraps by the Austrian Government," Raditz warned, "so almost no one else here knows about it. The Chancellor's office issued a bland upbeat communiqué this morning reporting only that a constructive meeting between Hitler and Schuschnigg had taken place, but without offering any details. That set off wild speculation in the press. What will happen next is anybody's guess."

Raditz ordered two more whiskies, looked at Muller with a wan smile and spread his hands wide. "And that, Mr. Muller, is the story of this so-called conference."

Muller sat back in his chair, his head spinning. Finally, he said, "You're confident that what you've told me is an accurate account of what happened?"

"Yes," Raditz replied; "Unfortunately."

"Can you tell me what demands Schuschnigg accepted?" Muller asked.

"Yeah, and they're pretty bad," Raditz said. "Those Austrian Legion Nazis that Schuschnigg kicked out of the country? He has to let them back in. That's a couple of thousand rabid Nazis who will be returning to Austria–a lot of them with scores to settle. He also had to agree to make Schmidt Foreign Minister. So, you can kiss goodbye any diplomatic initiative to try and relieve the situation.

"Finally–and this is the big one–he had to agree to turn over the Interior and Security Ministry to an Austrian Nazi sympathizer acceptable to Hitler. So that means all law enforcement in Austria will be subject to Nazi veto, effectively removing any legal constraints on Nazi activity of any kind here."

"Did they agree on who this new minister would be?" Muller asked.

"Apparently after being hounded on this point, Schuschnigg told Hitler that he would appoint Arthur Seyss-Inquart. You'll remember I reported to you earlier that Hitler had invited Seyss-Inquart to meet with him, so he clearly knows the man. But he feigned ignorance and insisted on receiving assurances from Schuschnigg that Seyss-Inquart would be submissive to his–Hitler's that is–orders."

"Seyss-Inquart," Muller mused, "Schuschnigg's devout Catholic friend and Nazi sympathizer. Do you suppose Schuschnigg thinks he can exercise some restraint on Seyss-Inquart?"

Raditz shrugged. "Maybe, but I wouldn't bet on it."

"This is meant to be formally agreed and announced by Wednesday?" Muller asked.

Raditz nodded.

"And if the Austrians don't cave in by then, Hitler will send in his troops? Is that the plan?" Muller's voice rose.

Raditz nodded. "It looks that way," he said quietly, putting his finger to his lips.

Muller slumped back in his seat. He finished the last of his drink. "I've never heard of any meeting between government leaders that remotely resembles what you've described," he said glumly. "Couldn't Schuschnigg have just walked out?"

"I'm sure he thought that would trigger an immediate invasion," Raditz replied.

Muller nodded. "And he probably decided not to go toe–to–toe and trade insults for the same reason.

"God," Muller exclaimed, shaking his head in wonder. "Can you imagine what the atmosphere must have been like in that room? You're the Chancellor of Austria paying a visit in response to a formal invitation from the German Chancellor; the agenda is agreed upon and all the documents have been prepared in advance–then suddenly the script goes out the window and you're confronted by a wild man, claiming to be some kind of Teutonic Messiah, accusing you of torturing his people and ordering you to capitulate or face immediate invasion."

Muller paused. "How does anyone prepare for an ordeal like that?" He sighed deeply, and turned to face Raditz. "And you, Raditz? What will happen to you if you're ordered back to Berlin?"

Raditz hesitated, running his left hand over the stubble on this cheek before responding. "I'm not entirely certain," he said, glancing at Muller hesitantly. "I'm viewed within the Ministry as one of von Neurath's strongest allies; that's not going to endear me to von Ribbentrop–whom I despise."

After pausing and twirling his glass, Raditz went on. "Those of us whom I described in our first conversation as wanting to temper Hitler's agenda have certainly been weakened by all this. And if he succeeds in swallowing Austria, can Czechoslovakia be far behind? He's making the same claims to represent the Sudeten Germans living there as he's making about German-Austrians living here. And Poland? You know that history very well; most of what was carved out for the Poles at Versailles was formerly Germany. So, he's making claims there, too."

Raditz looked at Muller. "Do I really want to go back to the Ministry in Berlin facing that prospect? It's caused me to scratch my head a lot recently, and now, given the news that I just shared with you..." He shook his head, then added, "Hitler seems utterly confident that the French and the British will let him get away with whatever he decides to do in Eastern Europe. But what if he's wrong?"

Raditz looked at Muller with a stern expression. "What if the French decide to call his bluff and send that huge army of theirs across the frontier? They could march straight to Berlin. Hitler's new *Wehrmacht* would be flattened like a pesky mosquito. Do I want to be a part of that scenario?"

Raditz stood and placed a schilling bill on the table. "I'm trying to decide what I should do. I'll try to let you know when I figure it out," he said, putting on his coat.

Muller stood too, and they shook hands as Raditz took his leave.

Muller sat back down and ordered a mug of beer. He didn't need another whiskey. He ran back in his mind what Raditz had told him.

Schuschnigg had clearly miscalculated. His assumption that he had gained leverage over Hitler by shutting down the Nazi office in Vienna and arresting the Party leaders last month had proven to be completely wrong. Hitler had lured him to his headquarters, using false pledges of harmony and good will, and then he'd just gone for the jugular: either you surrender Austria to me or I'll send in the Army.

Poor Schuschnigg, Muller thought to himself; he'd never seen it coming.

And the manner in which Hitler delivered his ultimatum, Muller mused; Schuschnigg surely must have thought he was confronting a madman when Hitler flew into his tantrum.

And, in the end, he'd capitulated. The concessions he finally made effectively undermined Austrian sovereignty by delivering law enforcement and foreign policy into the hands of Nazi turncoats who answered to Hitler.

As Muller reflected, he found it hard to see how Schuschnigg could survive in office.

What to do, Muller wondered. Was this really the end game that he and Keinböck had talked about preparing for?

He decided to stop at the Café Louvre on the way back to his hotel to see what he could learn.

The usual gathering of journalists was clustered in its customary booth near the back and, despite the Government's news blackout, they had most of the story about Schuschnigg's abortive journey.

Nigel Hamilton, as usual, was the loudest voice. "Christ, if Hitler's going to pull his madman act, Schuschnigg has to tell people about it; he can't just slink back to Vienna and go silent. Bill Shirer can put him on the radio and let him broadcast his story to the world.

"'Let me tell you what this lunatic Hitler said to me yesterday,'" Hamilton mimicked Schuschnigg. "'He fancies himself the leader of all Germans everywhere and they must obey him. And, by the way, if they won't, he says he'll send in the army. *Sieg Heil.*'" Hamilton put two fingers on his upper lip representing Hitler's mustache and threw out his right arm in the Nazi salute, bringing it down as a fist that banged the table, to a scattering of laughter and applause.

"Hamilton, you're a goner when Hitler arrives in town," crowed Boothby. "Dachau's too good for you; only a firing squad will do."

Hamilton turned to Henry Fodor. "Speaking of that, Fodor, how long are you and Martha going to stick around? Jews don't do so well in Nazi regimes–especially if they're nosy reporters."

Fodor shrugged. "It's already pretty unwelcoming for us here. How much worse can it get?"

"Oh, a lot worse," said Shirer. "Your press credentials won't do much good."

Fodor smiled. "We'll see. Maybe Hitler won't come after all."

"That doesn't sound like what he told our friend Schuschnigg yesterday." Hamilton said. "And goddamn it, why is Schuschnigg just clamming up about it?" He turned to Muller. "You've heard that Hitler apparently put on a madman act for Schuschnigg and read him the riot act?"

Muller nodded. "I've never heard of anything like it before."

Shirer pointed his pipe at them. "If Schuschnigg had any imagination, he'd fly to Paris, get Chamberlain and Mussolini there too, and tell them what happened. If he won't go public and tell his story to the world, at the very least he should get the heads of government around a table and let them know the kind of unstable maniac Hitler revealed himself to be. They all seem determined to give Hitler what he wants; well, they ought to know that he's really an unhinged menace and they'd better begin thinking about putting the brakes on him."

Shirer drew on his pipe before going on. "But of course, he won't do anything of the kind. He's a conservative, a staunch

Catholic and a hidebound traditionalist. He'd be incapable of even conceiving a daring diplomatic thrust like that."

"He's also holding a pretty weak hand," Boothby interjected. "Hitler's got 66 million Germans to Schuschnigg's 7 million Austrians; he's got a big army while Austria has almost none; and while Schuschnigg's Fatherland Front flexes its political muscle all the time, it's got strong enemies on both the right and the left, waiting for it to stumble. A hard time to be bold," he concluded, shaking his head.

"But at least if he'd go public and tell the story of what happened, he'd strengthen his hand here in Austria," said Hamilton. "There are a lot of Austrians who may not be big fans of Schuschnigg, but who would react very angrily to being insulted by Hitler. With all their internal divisions, most Austrians have a strong sense of patriotism."

Shirer got up to leave. "But he won't do that. He's not made of that kind of stuff."

Muller decided to leave alongside Shirer. He needed to put a piece of white paper on his hotel room windowsill.

# CHAPTER 20

Viktor Keinböck was amenable to Muller's suggestion that they stroll over to the Danube riverbank and find a bench where they could sit and speak without being eavesdropped.

It was a cloudy, chilly afternoon and they both put on gloves, pulled down their hats and turned up their coat collars as they seated themselves gazing at the swift-flowing, muddy river.

"Not very inviting today is it, Mr. Muller," Keinböck said. "Rather like the events we're dealing with; fast moving and not very clear." He sighed. "I assume you've heard the rumors that Hitler treated Schuschnigg with utter contempt and demanded that he sign documents that would have terminated Austrian statehood."

"It sounds very threatening," Muller replied.

Keinböck nodded. "Someone could certainly make the case that Austrian independence effectively ends once the law enforcement and foreign affairs ministries are under German control. But for now, at least, the country is continuing to manage its affairs. The market's open, shops are doing business, people are at work, there are no riots in the street; on the surface, it appears that nothing's changed. Of course, things *have* changed," he added; "just not enough to warrant taking steps to bankrupt the country."

"The fact that the Government has stayed mum on all this for three days now strikes me as a mistake," Muller replied. "Everyone seems to know the story. What's to be lost in making a clean breast of things?"

Keinböck smiled. "That's not how we do things here. Also, Schuschnigg's playing for time–trying to mount a rear-guard action. I'm told that's why he hasn't made a speech or gone on the radio to explain things. He hopes to keep control and, believe it or not, he's expecting Hitler to reconfirm his commitment to Austrian independence in the speech he's scheduled to deliver next Sunday."

"And you, Mr. Keinböck," Muller asked, "do you share his confidence?"

Keinböck sighed. "No. I don't rule it out, but like our friend Mr. Baer, I'm persuaded Hitler needs to steal Austria's wealth, and that it's only a matter of time before he just goes ahead and does it. And that, Mr. Muller, is why we need to keep discussing our plan."

Even sitting on the remote riverbank bench, Keinböck instinctively looked over his shoulder before continuing.

"I've done the math," he said. "The 570 million AUS loan amounts to roughly 350,000 ounces of gold. Our total gold reserves are about 400,000 ounces. Almost all of that is stored at the Bank of England in London. We only have about 3,000 ounces here in the Bank's vault. So, what I'd need to do, if I decide to pay off the loan, is to make a transfer of our gold on the books of the Bank of England."

"How would that work, exactly?" asked Muller.

"Let me explain the process as I've figured it out," Keinböck replied. "Most of the world's entire stock of gold is stored in the vaults of the Bank of England. Bullion is very heavy–a seventeen-inch cube weighs about a ton–so it's hard to transport and very expensive; insurance costs are prohibitive. So, years ago, the world's central banks agreed to an elaborate system of 'earmarking', where national gold stocks are physically divided into separate national stacks in the big Bank of England vault and identified by white name tags. This stack is French, this one's American, and so on. And every day a group of men descends into the vault to load bullion bars onto a cart with rubber tires and wheel them from one stack to another, adding or subtracting bars and affixing the white name tags, to reflect the prior day's transactions.

"The gold never leaves the vault," Keinböck went on, "but what was Austrian gold one day will be in someone else's stack the next day, if there's been a sale."

Muller nodded. "I can understand that, but how can Austrian sovereign gold be transferred to the accounts of all those commercial lenders you spoke about?"

"That issue could have posed a problem, but we're in luck," said Keinböck with a smile. "In our case–I checked the loan document to confirm this–the manager for the syndicate of bank lenders is none other than the Bank of England, wearing its commercial hat. So, I can simply send a telex to our designated gold account manager at the Bank of England, directing him to transfer 350,000 ounces of our sovereign gold to the Bank of England, acting in its central banking role, along with instructions to convey it to the Bank of England's commercial side, for the account of the lenders' syndicate."

"So, the Bank of England acts as both a central bank and in a commercial role–in this case as the syndicate manager for commercial lenders?" Muller asked.

"That's one of the reasons the Bank of England is such a powerful financial institution," said Keinböck nodding. "Once our gold is transferred to the Bank of England, it will flow through the Bank to the syndicate and then directly into the accounts of the lenders–and as we discussed earlier, once they have it, they won't let Hitler get his hands on any of it."

"Moreover," Keinböck said, "this procedure also means that I only have to send one telex to effectuate the transaction; if the Bank here is under siege by the Germans when we're trying to make the transfer, that could become important.

"So, Mr. Muller, I've satisfied myself that, at least in theory, a transaction of the kind we've been discussing could be accomplished."

Then he turned his body on the bench, leaning forward to face Muller directly, and fixed him with a stern look. "But I want to stress to you that I'm a long way from being ready to pull the trigger on any of this. Austrian sovereignty has not yet ended; there is an Austrian government in office conducting the affairs of state. I have no plausible authority–and absolutely no intention–of acting on this plan unless and until Austria is on the very brink of extinction. And we are not at that stage, Mr. Muller. Are we clear on that?"

"Yes sir," Muller replied. He didn't give voice to the thought that it was probably only a matter of days until they would be at that stage.

# CHAPTER 21

Otto Schultz looked exhausted when he and Muller were finally able to meet later in the week at Café Wolfe.

"We've had cabinet meetings virtually around the clock since Schuschnigg returned early Sunday morning," he said. "I assume you saw the statement that we issued in the wee hours of Wednesday morning announcing the new cabinet appointments."

"I did," Muller nodded.

"Despite the insistence of his entire cabinet and advisors, including me, Schuschnigg refused even to entertain the idea of repudiating the concessions he'd made to Hitler, even though he was clearly acting under duress," Schultz continued

"Schuschnigg is a very stubborn man, Mr. Muller." Schultz accepted a Gitane and a light from Muller. "We've spoken before about his unbending personality–his firm conviction that he is pursuing the right policies; it's probably rooted in his devout faith. But for whatever reason, he just wasn't rattled by Hitler ranting and raving at him. He even told me that he'd been faintly amused by the whole show; that it revealed Hitler as being weak and forced to throw a tantrum to cover it up."

Schultz looked at Muller with a faint smile. "He seems to have taken everything in stride and remains confident that he will prevail and preserve Austria's independence."

"But the new cabinet appointments will surely make that very difficult to do," said Muller.

Schultz paused. "Schuschnigg is persuaded that he and Seyss-Inquart can work together and preserve the status quo. They've had intensive discussions about that during the cabinet meetings over the past few days. Seyss-Inquart eventually promised Schuschnigg that he would continue the practice of forbidding overt Nazi activity and he re-appointed the current police chief with instructions to carry out that mandate."

Schultz ran his hands through his hair. "I don't know, Mr. Muller." The fatigue was evident in his sagging shoulders. "Maybe he and Seyss-Inquart can actually keep things together.

"I remain pessimistic," he added. "But when I said a moment ago that Schuschnigg was unfazed by Hitler's behavior at the meeting, I meant it."

"So why did he make the concessions then?" Muller asked.

"I think he decided they were the right tactic for the moment," Schultz responded. "He concluded that he could control Seyss-Inquart, so he agreed to appoint him to the Interior and Security Ministry and get Hitler off his back on that issue. Giving the Foreign Ministry to Schmidt was even less of a concern.

Schuschnigg has always taken the lead personally on foreign policy initiatives; Schmidt's a lightweight and Schuschnigg knew that he could shoulder him aside anytime it became necessary."

"Besides," Schultz added, "Schuschnigg had tried to call Mussolini to ask for help even before he left for Germany. He was told that *Il Duce* was on the slopes somewhere in the Dolomites skiing and was indisposed–no doubt working on the tan on that bald head of his," Schultz smirked. "The French and the British had already signaled their indifference. So, Schuschnigg knew going into the meeting that foreign support was off the table, for the time being anyway. So, he let Schmidt have the Foreign Ministry," Schultz said shrugging. "That was just throwing a bone–to Schmidt as well as to Hitler."

Muller eyed Schultz, waiting to continue until the waiter had set down their plates. He was tired of sausage and sauerkraut and had ordered chopped liver with pickled onions.

"So, what happens next?" Muller asked. "He's made the new appointments but he hasn't explained to the country what they mean or told them what to expect."

"We wait for Hitler's speech on Sunday night," said Schultz. "Schuschnigg expects Hitler to reconfirm Austria's independence. He's kept his part of the bargain; he expects Hitler to do the same."

"Will he?" asked Muller.

"We'll see, won't we," said Schultz, his mouth full of chopped liver.

# CHAPTER 22

To Muller, the City of Vienna seemed to tiptoe through the wait for Hitler's speech on Sunday night. The mood was unsettled and on trams or seated in cafés–even walking in crowds–he heard snippets of whispers and observed exchanges of glances as people compared notes or shared concerns in whispers or low tones. It was so odd, he thought, that the Government had announced the cabinet changes but no storyline to accompany them. Confusion was rampant. He'd been told by the journalists that their pro-Nazi sources feared the moment was lost and that Hitler had decided to postpone his threatened takeover. On the other side, pro-Government supporters waited, fearing the worst.

It was a kind of collective exercise in holding one's breath, he decided.

To break the spell, Muller had agreed to meet Steffi again for tennis on Saturday morning. This time there was no pretense about Marc not showing up; Muller was the fourth. Once again, they played a vigorous match and when their time expired, he and Steffi again commanded a narrow lead. This time Ursula and Horst joined them for lunch and they spoke mainly of tennis, avoiding any reference to politics or Hitler's much anticipated speech.

That evening, he'd reserved a table for the two of them at Gerstner's, one of Vienna's most inviting gasthaus taverns. The hotel concierge had highly recommended it and had reserved a booth for two in what was called the Haklplatz, a small, warmly-lit room with a dark wood decor, painted scenes on wood panels and the mounted head of a large, fierce-looking boar on one wall.

Steffi arrived promptly at 8 PM and expressed delight. "I haven't been here in years," she exclaimed. "I used to come with my parents when I was a girl; it was a favorite."

Muller ordered a bottle of dry Riesling and they began exploring the menu.

"The concierge told me I could order a meal that was similar to the one Emperor Franz Josef would consume every Sunday," Muller said. "Tafelspitz–a special cut of beef boiled in bouillon."

Steffi laughed, "Of course; that's what I used to order here, and all the trimming too–let's see; right, here they are," she said checking the menu, "sautéed potatoes, nutmeg-scented creamed spinach and crushed apple sauce spiked with horseradish."

The waiter took their order and complimented their choices.

"Are your parents still alive?" Muller inquired.

"My father died two years ago," Steffi replied. "He was an engineer and designed machinery for the Austrian Railway system. He and his brother, Uncle Miklas, started the company before the war. Uncle Miklas died in the Spanish flu epidemic in 1920 when I was young, but Father carried on the business. When he died of a heart attack, our attorneys sold it and my mother and I came into quite a bit of money. That's how I'm able to afford my nice apartment–and that fancy gramophone you liked so well." She flashed Muller a smile.

"And your mother?"

Steffi made a face. "Not long after Father died, Mama decided to take the waters at Karlsbad. While she was there, she met a Swedish Baron." Her eyes crinkled. "Paul, you know the Swedes make such a thing about how democratic and egalitarian they are; well, let me tell you, Barons abound there–a title, no money, but a keen eye for a wealthy widow. Not long afterward, Mama decamped for some island near Stockholm where, I assume, she and her Baron are living happily together–off her money."

Steffi twirled her wine glass. "Actually, I thought recently about the possibility of going there–if war were to break out. But now, I've decided not to leave," she said, smiling. "Things have suddenly changed for the better at the hospital. Jewish doctors are leaving to flee the country and the nuns who run the place can't wait to get rid of the rest of them. They've always disliked having to tolerate Jews and now–with the Nazis waiting in the wings–they see the chance to clean house. So, between those leaving to emigrate and those being pushed out, suddenly there are big opportunities for promotion–even for a woman!" Steffi grinned and tossed her head for emphasis.

"Nurse Farber now is going to become Surgeon Farber, fully licensed and assigned a surgical practice," Steffi's smile grew wider. "Too bad for the Jews, I guess, but that's their problem. I'm glad to see them go. For me, it's the opportunity I've been fighting for all these years. Living under Nazi rule–if that's what it finally comes down to–is a small price to pay as far as I'm concerned. So whereas, just a week ago I was thinking I might have to sail off to Stockholm, now I'm all set to stay here and do the surgical practice I've dreamed of for so long."

"Prost!" She clinked her wine glass with his.

At that moment, a team of three waiters, all costumed with the emperor's red and white sash appeared at their table, presented the tafelspitz with well-practiced flourish, and invited Muller and Steffi to enjoy 'the favorite meal of the Hapsburg Emperor'–which they proceeded to do with enthusiasm.

# CHAPTER 23

The next morning, when Muller returned to his hotel, he was surprised to find the streets largely deserted. Generally, on Sundays there were marches and rallies by contending forces, which sometimes deteriorated into pushing matches and fights. But today, there was none of that. Everyone's still holding their breath, he decided.

Actually, he welcomed the comparative quiet. He was sleepy and planned a late morning nap to compensate for a night of very vigorous love-making. Steffi seemed energized by her newly-promised promotion and they had recaptured the sensual escape they'd found a week earlier. Muller had made certain to shed his jacket in a location where Steffi would not step on his brass knuckles again when she got out of bed.

Since it was a cold morning, he decided to stop at a café to warm himself and take another coffee. Continuing to reflect on the evening, his mind returned to the conversation over dinner and Steffi's dismissive remarks about the Jews that were being removed from positions at the hospital. He'd been caught up in the moment of their romantic evening and he hadn't reacted to her remarks. But recollecting them now, they gnawed at him. Her attitude was hardly unique; anti-Semitism was rife in Austria–and was formally enshrined in law in Germany. But he'd always found the casual acceptance of that kind of attitude distasteful, and it lowered his respect for Steffi as he thought about what she'd said.

He could understand her determination to be accepted as a qualified surgeon. But the big hurdle she'd faced was being a woman–and she fiercely opposed being excluded just because of that factor, even though she met all the other qualifications. How did she suppose the Jewish doctors felt about being dismissed just because they were Jews?

He recollected sitting in warm sunshine around a swimming pool in Hollywood a year earlier at a Warner Brothers Studio party. His cousin had married a studio executive–a Jew–and he'd stayed with them, Elise, Sam and their two children, for nearly a month during his travels in the US. That afternoon, the two of them had been conversing, lying on adjoining chaise lounges sipping drinks with small umbrellas, and he'd asked Elise if she'd had any issues adjusting to life in sunny California. She'd responded by snapping at him angrily.

"You mean living here among all these Jews? Well, I like it just fine, and why shouldn't I?"

Muller remembered he'd sat up to face his cousin. "Elise, I meant the weather, for goodness sake. It's a little different climate here than it is in Switzerland."

Elise had been silent a moment, then shook her head as if collecting herself.

"I'm sorry, Paul; I shouldn't have reacted that way," she'd said. "I guess I'm a little defensive about living here with Sam and this movie crowd that's mainly comprised of Jews. I shouldn't be," she'd added; "it's like any community–some good, some not so good, some gems, some bad apples–but no different. Except we're viewed as more glamorous, which I guess we are, but also as Jewish–which is why the stars that are Jews have all taken good American–Christian, that is–names.

"So, when someone asks even an innocent question, as you did a moment ago, we tend to go into a crouch. I'm afraid it's a fact of life."

Muller finished his coffee and left a coin, buttoning up his coat to go back outside to the cold Vienna morning.

It certainly was a fact of life here in Vienna. But he still didn't like it.

When he got back to the hotel, he found an empty envelope awaiting him. Time enough to get some sleep before beginning the careful routine of getting to the meeting with Franz.

When he finally set out from the hotel a little after 6 PM, he saw crews at work mounting public address speakers at several busy street corners. Hitler's speech was scheduled for 8:30 PM; the Government had obviously decided to broadcast it to the streets, and, early as he was, he still saw knots of men beginning to gather near the speakers.

Franz's message at the meeting at Heinrichshof was cautious. He had made preliminary contact with the Social Democratic resistance, he said, but they were very reluctant to take any step that could jeopardize their current system for smuggling people across the border.

"They use vessels on the Danube and road or rail traffic between Vienna and Bratislava, which are all heavily-traveled commercial corridors for Austrian exports to Czechoslovakia," Franz said. "The system's lubricated by a discreet arrangement of bribes, camouflaged as commercial payments, that work well enough, but they don't want to overload it with any high-visibility escapes. They also made plain that any offer to help they might make would come with a very high price tag."

Muller had expected that. "Ask them if they'll consider taking payment in gold."

Franz cocked his head, looking puzzled.

"We're dealing with the Austrian National Bank, Franz," Muller reminded him. "Central Banks have gold, some of which can become portable."

Muller didn't say more, but he had been thinking about raising with Keinböck the possibility of stealing some of the gold and bearer-bond securities in the vault at the central bank, in addition to raiding Austrian gold at the Bank of England.

Muller had grave doubts that the socialist people-smuggling system would work as an escape route for Keinböck and him. There would be a high risk of betrayal; none of the leftist leaders had any incentive to do favors for a senior member of a Government that relentlessly persecuted them. Still, greed had its uses; if the socialists thought they could obtain payment in gold, they might put scruples aside. It was worth testing.

Muller had brought a forged Swiss passport with him from Geneva, hidden in the false bottom of his trunk. He also had several blank versions that could be doctored for Keinböck by someone skilled in that dark practice. Franz said he had a candidate in mind that knew the business. Muller made a note to have an early conversation with Keinböck and stood up to leave. Franz motioned him to resume his place.

"One more thing. Just before I came over for this meeting I received an urgent signal."

Franz didn't need to say who the signal was from.

"He wants you to go to London as soon as possible to assess the possibility that Eden will replace Chamberlain as Prime Minister and bring pressure on Hitler to lay off Austria."

Muller reacted with surprise. "Did he say what information he has suggesting that's going to happen?"

Franz shook his head. "He said you know how to find out what's going on there. I'm to report back your agreement to take this on."

Muller took a deep breath. The pace of events here was quickening; departing even for a few days could jeopardize the plans they were laying. But if the events Hausamann had hinted at were to come about, that could fundamentally change the whole situation. So, he could understand why Hausamann wanted him to go–the unstated message was 'try to make it happen.'

"Tell him I'll make arrangements as promptly as possible."

They departed the meeting separately and Muller headed back to his hotel. He wanted to be able to listen to Hitler's speech without interruption and he'd arranged with the concierge to get access to a radio in the Hotel's large top floor suite that was unoccupied at the moment. He stopped to pick up bread and cheese along with a bottle of red table wine and by 8:30 PM was sitting at a table in the large suite with the Telefunken, in its handsome brown wooden cabinet, on a bench next to him. Reception was good on a clear night, and adjusting the dial with the round knob, Muller found himself able to hear clearly.

As speakers preceding Hitler warmed up the crowd for the main event, Muller half-listened and mused about Hausamann's instruction to visit London. Eden replacing Chamberlain and confronting Hitler on his campaign to absorb Austria? Muller thought that sounded unlikely. Eden had been one of the architects of Britain's appeasement policy toward Hitler, after all. Muller had witnessed firsthand Eden's willingness to concede issues to Hitler when Eden was acting on behalf of the League of Nations. He recalled his frustration as Eden repeatedly blocked or delayed action at the League to strengthen the Free City of Danzig, all in the vain hope of inducing Hitler to make a broad European peace agreement.

Muller knew that Eden had become distrustful of Hitler, but was Eden really preparing to seize power in Britain and confront him? Muller had not followed British political developments closely since departing Danzig over a year earlier, but he had a pretty good idea of how to get caught up quickly.

As Muller began planning his next steps, Hitler finally began to speak. Muller listened intently but with mounting disappointment.

As was typical, Hitler spoke at length and repeatedly returned to well-worn, and, for the faithful, much beloved, attacks on Jews, Bolsheviks and Communists. His familiar denunciations of the Treaty of Versailles and the unfair reparations imposed upon Germany were greeted with outbursts of cheers and applause from his Nazi audience, causing Hitler to pause and let the cries of "*Seig Heil*" echo in the chamber where he was delivering the speech. All this was quite tedious and Muller found himself pacing in front of the Hotel's windows where, from this twelfth floor vantage point, he could see across to the Prater, where the Riesenrad, the giant wheel, was lit up and slowly rotating. The streets below seemed deserted, except for a small crowd off to his left, lounging around one of the loudspeakers.

When was Hitler going to speak of Austria, Muller wondered, as he continued to drone–well, not drone–shout on. Then, finally, after a pause, Hitler launched an attack on two states that he declared were engaged in "torturing millions of Germans"–an unmistakable reference to Austria and Czechoslovakia. Germans were being deprived of political rights and "the general right of racial self-determination as Germans." It was intolerable; Hitler went on, for a world power like Germany to stand idle while,"...co-racials are subjected to continuous suffering because of their sympathy for the German race and its ideology." Ideology as embodied in the Nazi Party and the leadership of its Führer, Muller mused as he continued to listen.

"We must end this unnecessary and unacceptable torture," Hitler declared. "We will assert our power to overcome this outrage. Our mighty fist is ready to strike those who would deny us."

His audience roared approval.

And moments later, the speech ended. Not a word about Austrian sovereignty or his commitment to Austrian independence.

Muller reflected. Hitler had had flung down the gauntlet and made clear his determination to impose a solution on his own terms. He had raised the political stakes yet again and brandished the threat of invasion.

Muller sighed and resumed pacing at the windows, sipping the last of the wine. But now when he gazed out, the streets were no longer deserted; they were suddenly crowded with people. He raised the window and he could hear the shouts.

*Seig Heil! SEIG HEIL!*

*Ein Volk, Ein Reich, Ein Führer! Seig Heil*

The shouting and chants reverberated in the night air.

Muller elected not to leave the hotel but instead stayed at the windows watching the crowds surge and listening to the shouting and snatches of the *Horst Wessel Lied,* the co-national anthem of Nazi Germany. Finally, he finished the wine and went down to his room, where his efforts to sleep were interrupted by periodic crescendos of noise from the street below.

How must Schuschnigg feel? Muller wondered. Betrayed again and humiliated; but probably not yet broken, Muller surmised.

He turned out to be right.

# CHAPTER 24

The next morning, Schuschnigg issued a proclamation banning political meetings or demonstrations. Seyss-Inquart took to the air waves at noon and quietly, in measured tones, admonished Austrians of all political persuasions to remain calm and avoid any disorder. Listening to the speech on the radio in his office, Muller thought Seyss-Inquart sounded reasonable and even-tempered; he was struck by the contrast with Hitler's bombastic delivery. Did this portend that Seyss-Inquart really would keep the promise he'd made to Schuschnigg to hold the Nazis in check?

Muller had beaten Frau Metzinger to the office that morning But as soon as she arrived, he'd directed her to send an urgent telex to RCS Stevenson at the British Foreign Ministry. Stevenson was the top civil servant in Whitehall advising Eden on League of Nations affairs. He had been the official responsible for Muller's appointment in 1934 as Secretary to Sean Lester, the League's High Commissioner for Danzig. At various times during the ensuing two years, Stevenson had been both an ally and an adversary, as Lester and Muller had sought, and generally failed, to persuade Eden, who was in charge of the League's Danzig policies, to strengthen the High Commissioner's hand against repeated challenges mounted by Nazis in Germany and locally in Danzig itself.

Although Eden repeatedly declined to act, Muller had cemented a relationship with Stevenson. They had quarreled and annoyed one another, but close interaction on delicate diplomatic strategy had cemented connections between them; they were both professionals and had come to respect one another.

Muller reflected. Would Stevenson respond to a request to meet with Eden to take up the Austrian issue? Muller decided to give it a try. He dictated the text of the message to Frau Metzinger.

'The Commissioner General of the League of Nations for Austria formally requests a meeting with the Minister to discuss matters related to Austria. Paul Muller, Commissioner General.'

Then he dictated a second message. 'Stevenson, Would appreciate your help. Muller'. He instructed Frau Metzinger to send the two telexes about a minute apart.

Muller descended the grand marble staircase to the cavernous first floor offices of the Austrian National Bank and left a message with Keinböck's secretary that he would be taking a brief stroll to the banks of the Danube at 1 PM and asking Keinböck to join him "for a brief cigarette break" which wouldn't interfere with his other meetings.

"If this is to be just a cigarette break, then we need more of those long Pall Malls I got in London instead of your short

Gitanes," Keinböck said with a smile as he sat down next to Muller on the bench and accepted his light. "Too bad I ran out."

Muller grinned back at him. "Just ask for more from London; I'm sure they'll deliver a case; anything for Appeasement. You've heard Chamberlain's new nickname?"

Keinböck shook his head.

"Neville j'aime Berlin," Muller said. "Ha! A good fit, I'd say."

Keinböck barked a sharp laugh. "A good fit indeed."

"So, a quick item of business during your break," said Muller. "We need to prepare a new passport for you. Whatever route out of here we choose after pulling off our project, assuming we do it, will not be accomplished using your current passport. You're going to need a new identity. I need you for a couple of hours one evening very soon to go underground with me to visit a dark artist who does these things."

Keinböck looked levelly at Muller, weighing the message, then nodded. "Thursday at 8 PM?"

"Done," said Muller. "Meet here and bring passport photos. I'll arrange things, probably, including a really bad meal while we wait."

"End of cigarette break," said Keinböck, standing and striding back to the Palace.

When Muller returned to his office, Frau Metzinger handed him a telex flimsy. It read, 'Come ASAP Stevenson'.

"I called the Travel Section," she said. There's an Air France flight that leaves Vienna at 4PM today for Paris and a connection to London that will get you there by 8:30 this evening; you gain an hour with British time."

"Very good, Frau Metzinger," Muller said. "Please book the flight and make a reservation for me at the Hotel Dorchester. And reply to Stevenson with my flight information, asking him to pick me up at the airfield."

# CHAPTER 25

Muller's flight was in one of the new Air France Bloch 220 twin-engine aircraft that had a sleek aerodynamic design. It carried 16 passengers but as Muller boarded, he saw it was only half full. The three-hour flight was remarkably smooth, and the pretty Air France stewardess served a surprisingly tasty meal, accompanied by a Montrachet and a 1928 Cote des Nuits. They landed on time at Le Bourgeot, just north of Paris, and Muller was hustled aboard the connecting flight to London. It was the much smaller Bloch 120, with overhead wings and twin engines. It carried ten passengers and was full.

Muller told himself night flights were routine these days; but he had to confess to being a little nervous. He was still more accustomed to traveling by rail. And sure enough, once airborne, his misgivings seemed warranted. Over the English Channel the small aircraft was buffeted by strong winds that sent it into steep rises followed by sudden, heart-stopping drops. Passengers were vomiting into small bags and the smell along with the violent gyrations made Muller wish he was on a smooth train ride instead of bouncing around in a small plane bucking a windstorm over the icy Channel.

But less than an hour later, they landed without incident at Croydon Aerodrome near London. As Muller walked down the aircraft steps with a sense of relief, he spied a black BMC touring car parked alongside the terminal building and RCS Stevenson leaning against a fender.

Muller recovered his valise from the plane's cargo bin and strode over to the car where Stevenson greeted him with a warm handshake. They chatted amiably as Muller placed his suitcase in the boot and slipped into the passenger seat next to Stevenson.

"I decided to drive out myself," he said. "Fewer sets of ears to listen in, unless this car's wired–which I don't think it is."

"So," he continued, "Mr. Commissioner General; am I expected to genuflect?"

"One knee obeisance will suffice," said Muller grinning. "But only for thirty seconds, for you, as one of my most loyal subjects."

"Eminence," Stevenson responded, bowing over the steering wheel. "But I can still beat his grace on the tennis court."

"Don't be so sure," said Muller. "I have newfound authority for my first serves."

They chuckled together.

"I suppose congratulations are in order," Stevenson said as he accelerated out of the aerodrome. "I saw the announcement when I was in Geneva for the December League Council meetings.

Neither Eden nor I go there as much now," he added, "for obvious reasons."

Muller nodded. "The League certainly has a threadbare appearance now. It's disappointing."

"Then why take on this new assignment?" Stevenson asked. "International finance was never your specialty".

"It was time for me to get back in the game," Muller responded. "You know how disillusioned I was the way Danzig turned out–sent packing by the Nazis after being sold out by the League–including by your boss."

"Don't go blaming Eden for everything," Stevenson replied sharply.

"No, not everything," said Muller, "but enough. Anyway, I had to get away. I spent nearly a year traveling, most of it in America, where I could put the experience behind me. Americans have no interest whatever in what's happening in Europe; they've got plenty of other things they prefer to worry about.

"But when I returned to Switzerland late last year, I realized the problems we worried about together at the League had only worsened. Soon after, I was offered this position and, given the seriousness of the predicament Austria is facing, I accepted and moved to Vienna to begin the job in early January."

"And now you're turning to Eden for help?" Stevenson said, glancing across at Muller.

"Well there aren't many other places to look," Muller relied "Italy was Austria's strongest ally after the Germans mounted that failed coup attempt in 1934. But now, Mussolini's changed sides. All the members of the League lined up against him and imposed sanctions on Italy when he invaded Abyssinia. Germany wasn't part of the League and didn't follow suit. And he and Hitler seem to be eying some kind of diplomatic embrace.

"When the Austrian Chancellor called him a couple of weeks ago to seek support, he was told *Il Duce* was off skiing and wasn't available.

"The French?" Muller continued. "They seem to be completely paralyzed politically, and with Ministers changing every month or two, we don't even know who to talk to at the Quai d'Orsay.

"So that leaves Britain," Muller concluded. "Your ambassador in Vienna is, how shall I put it diplomatically…"

"Drunk most of the time?" Stevenson interjected.

"Well, that too," Muller replied. "He's certainly not a reliable intermediary.

"So, what to do?" Muller went on. "Nearly everyone I'm dealing with thinks Britain is so committed to its policy of appeasement toward Hitler that there's no prospect you'd intervene and align yourselves with Austria against his crude takeover attempt. But I thought it was worth taking a stab at finding out if that premise is mistaken. So here I am."

Stevenson swung the car into the entry for the Dorchester and handed the keys to the doorman telling him he'd return for the car in an hour or so. Muller went to the reception desk to sign the registry and turn over his passport. Then he joined Stevenson in the hushed bar, where only a few balding heads were visible above high-backed, overstuffed chairs.

Finding a quiet booth, they both ordered tall glasses of Johnny Walker and soda. When the waiter returned with their drinks, they clinked glasses and each took a long sip.

Stevenson turned to face Muller directly.

"I assumed most of that when I responded to your message," he said. "And I recommended that you come as quickly as possible, because if there's to be any prospect of the kind of help you're looking for, now is the best time to raise it. Eden's at sword's points with Chamberlain over his interference in foreign policy matters that are supposed to be Eden's bailiwick. He's the Foreign Secretary, after all; but Chamberlain keeps undermining him. It's gotten so bad that Eden's at the point of resigning; if he does, he has the influence to bring down the government and become Prime Minister himself.

It's no sure thing," Stevenson continued. "Chamberlain's a powerful leader and absolutely convinced that he's the only man smart enough to face down Hitler. But Eden is the most popular politician in the House. If he decides to call in all of his chits and mount a no-holds-barred campaign, he could win."

Muller paused and let what Stevenson had said sink in.

"Will he do that, do you think?" he asked.

Stevenson smiled enigmatically. "As you well know, Muller, that's always the question with Eden. Will he throw caution to the winds and lead his troops out of the trenches to win the day, or will he shrink from the battle and let the opportunity slip away?

"I really don't know the answer," he concluded, draining the last of his drink.

"But our feckless strategy toward Austria is one more piece of evidence that British policy needs to change and Chamberlain must go. I've set up meetings for you tomorrow to help make that case."

# CHAPTER 26

The next morning, Muller was guided to a seat near the window in the Dorchester's understated breakfast dining room. He ordered an English breakfast of eggs, bacon and toast with marmalade and asked the waiter to bring him a copy of the *Daily Telegraph.* He scanned the paper, searching for any news from Austria, hoping to find Nigel Hamilton's byline. And sure enough he found a small story in which Hamilton reported the continuing standoff between the Government and supporters of Hitler's demands. Muller took note of the news that Schuschnigg planned a major evening speech before parliament in two days' time. Quickly calculating the travel time and loss of the hour upon leaving London, Muller decided he needed to be on a plane before noon the next day if he were to get back to Vienna in time for the speech–which he decided was imperative.

He quickly penned a note and handed it to the waiter, instructing him to take it across the lobby to the concierge, who could make the arrangements.

As he sipped a second cup of coffee, his eye was caught by an article in the paper reporting on a communiqué issued by the Foreign Affairs Committee of the House on the subject of the Prime Minister's policy toward Hitler. It quoted the Committee Chairman, Paul Emrys-Evans as endorsing Chamberlain's approach, but in what Muller read to be rather muted tones.

'While alternative approaches deserve to be considered,' the article quoted the Chairman as saying, 'it cannot be said that the Prime Minister's policy warrants disparagement by this Committee.' It then went on to quote David Margesson, whom it identified as the Chief Tory Parliamentary Whip as expressing 'satisfaction' with the communiqué.

Muller smiled to himself. It was pretty obvious that the Chairman and the Whip had found anodyne language to mask a disagreement. That was the way things were done when the parties weren't ready to go to the mat. But if what Stevenson had told him last evening was accurate, maybe the day wasn't far off when the diplomatic gloves would be removed.

He tucked the thought away as he finished the last of his coffee and strolled across the lobby to the concierge desk. A British Airways flight departing the next day at 10:30 AM to Berlin would connect to a Lufthansa flight arriving in Vienna at 6:40 in the evening. Assuming it was on time, that would leave him ample time to get to Schuschnigg's speech. He told the concierge to make the arrangements.

Stevenson had instructed Muller to meet him at Westminster Palace at 11:00 AM. Muller hadn't been in London for over three years, and he found himself enjoying the short taxi ride around Hyde Park Corner, past Buckingham Palace and alongside St. James Park to the Thames where Big Ben stood watch over the Houses of Parliament at Westminster Palace.

Alighting from the taxi, he spotted Stevenson, near the entrance.

"I'm going to introduce you to a man named Jim Wilson," Stevenson said, after they'd greeted one another. "He's Eden's Parliamentary Secretary, and along with Bobbety Cranborne, the most influential figure in Eden's political orbit. The question of Eden's resignation is political–and what you want to tell him about Austria will hopefully influence his political judgment. So, I thought Wilson was the man to see. I've briefed him about your experience and assured him that you're reliable and can keep your mouth shut. So, you should feel comfortable speaking candidly with him.

Muller nodded. "Thanks Stevenson," he said. "I'll do that. But who's this 'Bobbety Cranmore'?"

Stevenson smiled. "Pay no attention to that silly nickname, Muller. He's a Cecil. That name probably won't mean anything to you as a Swiss, but Cecils have held influential positions in Britain ever since his ancestor, Robert Cecil, was spymaster for Queen Elizabeth in the seventeenth century. Cranborne is an influential member of parliament, he's one of Eden's deputies in the Foreign

Ministry and he's a determined opponent of appeasement–and of Chamberlain, too.

"If Eden decides to take on Chamberlain, it will be because these two men have lodged the steel in his spine."

Stevenson steered Muller into Westminster and guided him along a corridor to a doorway. "This is the Strangers' Bar," he said. "It's where members and staff can meet members of the public – 'strangers'–as the Commons doesn't have offices for members."

Stevenson rapped on the door which opened and an overweight, balding man in full Morning Coat attire asked how he could assist them.

"We have an appointment with Mr. P. I. Wilson, Mr. Eden's Parliamentary Secretary," said Stevenson.

The man gestured for them to enter. "You're expected," he said.

Before them was a long rectangular room with a small bar along one wall and clusters of small armchairs arranged in no particular order leading to a bank of tall Tudor style windows in the rear. It had the look of a men's club, which, Muller immediately realized, was precisely the objective.

A tall man with a high forehead and dark hair slicked down on either side of a center part approached them. He greeted Stevenson, then after introductions, shook hands with Muller.

"Welcome, Mr. Muller," he said with a broad smile. "Stevenson has spoken well of you. I look forward to learning what information you can impart about the situation in Austria, which is of considerable interest to us."

Stevenson excused himself and told Muller he'd leave a message at the hotel about dinner that evening.

Wilson led the way toward two leather-clad chairs close to the windows, which Muller could now see overlooked the Thames. Wilson was friendly and garrulous as they took their seats and awaited the tea they had ordered.

Muller smiled. "I lived in Britain while attending Cambridge and my mother's English, so I've been visiting here since boyhood. But I cannot for the life of me understand the British penchant for offbeat given names. Stevenson's a 'Ralph', but insists on going by his initials, 'RCS', and I gather you're initials are 'P. I.' but you go by 'Jim'."

Muller shook his head. "I can't find the logic."

"No logic," Wilson replied chuckling. "In my case, for reasons never persuasively explained to me I was named 'Polonius Ignatius'. You can imagine how well that was greeted at boarding school; I still have a lot of scar tissue to show for it," he said, inspecting his knuckles.

"So, I became 'Jim'," he said, "even though as adults we'll address one another as 'Mr. Muller' and 'Mr. Wilson'." He shrugged, smiling. "This is a subject entirely too complicated for us to solve today. Let's move onto something simpler, like saving Austria from Hitler."

Muller offered Wilson a Gitane from his cigarette case, which Wilson accepted with alacrity. "European cigarettes are hard to find here," he said, drawing deeply and exhaling smoke with a grin.

"Stevenson told me you've had some experience dealing with Eden in connection with the Danzig problem," Wilson said. "I'd be interested in your impressions."

Seeing Muller hesitate, Wilson smiled. "I won't be offended if you're critical; he's a difficult man to work with–brilliant and insightful, but also stubborn and sometimes insensitive. So please feel free to speak candidly."

"Thanks," said Muller. "I *was* critical of Eden's actions. Please understand that I was a junior player at the time–Secretary to Sean Lester who was the League's High Commissioner in Danzig and who was Eden's principal point of interface. I'm sure you recall that Eden was Britain's Minister for League of Nations Affairs at the time and was assigned responsibility by the League for overseeing the League's mandate to protect Danzig, which had been established in the Treaty of Versailles.

"From the time Lester assumed his post in early 1934 until he and I were forced out in the fall of 1936, Danzig–and the office of the League's High Commissioner–were under siege by Nazi Germany and by a locally-elected Nazi party.

Muller didn't want to lecture, but he saw Wilson nodding attentively.

"During that period, we repeatedly sought support from the League Council in Geneva, but on each occasion, Eden, as the League Council's leader, blocked action and forced us to try and maintain the status quo, until we were finally betrayed by the Polish Foreign Minister and run out of town by the Nazi government."

Muller stubbed out his cigarette in the ash tray and sipped the last of his tea.

"We understood why he was doing it," Muller continued, keeping his voice neutral and speaking calmly. "Eden and Stevenson kept us fully informed. The plan was to avoid rocking the boat with Hitler on Danzig so Eden could pursue the larger goals of his appeasement policy. He was prepared to make whatever concessions were necessary to persuade Hitler to accept a broad agreement to keep the peace in Europe.

"Appeasement was Eden's policy, Mr. Wilson," Muller said. "It was his idea and he was its foremost proponent. Danzig was small potatoes in his world; a marginal irritant, and our pleas to rap Hitler's knuckles over claims of Nazi misbehavior in that small, far-off city had to be subordinated to his grander plans for peace in Europe.

"I'm afraid I'm beginning to sound bitter," Muller said apologetically, "and I don't mean to. Eden was engaged in high stakes diplomacy. If he had pulled it off and persuaded Hitler to stabilize Europe and end his threats, he would have achieved a major triumph and his tactical plan of appeasement would have been hailed as brilliant. We understood all that at the time and accepted it–grudgingly perhaps, but fully recognizing what was at stake."

Muller paused, and decided to plunge on. Wilson needed to understand where he stood.

"But the problem was–and continues to be–that Hitler hasn't bought into Eden's plan. He hasn't entered into any agreement and he hasn't moderated his behavior; if anything, he's become even more bellicose. He's taken the concessions that appeasement offered him and proceeded to up the ante. So, when I hear that Chamberlain and Eden are in disagreement about Britain's policy of appeasement toward Hitler–the policy that Eden sired and pursued relentlessly over several years–you'll understand why I find myself more than a little confused."

Muller paused a little sheepishly as Wilson reached for another Gitane. "I didn't mean to make a speech like that. But I guess I had to get it off my chest," he concluded and flashed his lighter.

Wilson smiled. "Don't apologize," he said. "I greatly appreciate your candor. And so, would Eden, incidentally, because he feels much the same way, now. He acknowledges his authorship of appeasement, but he's clear-eyed enough to recognize that it hasn't worked out the way he intended–and he's grown very mistrustful of Hitler. He's concluded that even if Hitler were to enter into a Europe-wide peace plan at this point, he'd never live up to it and wouldn't hesitate a moment to violate it if he thought that would be to his benefit.

"Eden's still committed to finding some peaceful way to the ease the growing tensions with Hitler, though; he's not ready to get into an armaments race with Germany, for example. But he's come to the conclusion that appeasement isn't sufficient."

"I haven't seen anything to suggest that Eden has disavowed appeasement or has proposed some alternative approach," interrupted Muller.

"It's a little more complicated than that, Mr. Muller. Let me try to offer you some context," Wilson said glancing around to be sure there were no nearby eavesdroppers. Muller was amused; people don't want to be overheard, even here in London–especially not in Westminster Palace itself, he thought to himself.

"At the time, you and Lester were dealing with Eden, Stanley Baldwin was Prime Minister," said Wilson. "But he retired at the end of May in 1937 and was succeeded by Neville Chamberlain, who is a very different kettle of fish. Whereas Baldwin was low key and a conciliatory leader, Chamberlain, by contrast, is disciplined, opinionated and determined to impose his will on the House. He is intolerant of dissent and he's assembled a team of whips under a Chief named David Margesson to enforce discipline and punish any member of the House he perceives as opposing him. It's a very different environment here now from the one Eden was operating in when you knew him."

"I saw an article in the paper today that mentioned this fellow Margesson," said Muller. "I'd never heard of him, but the article said that he and the Chair of a House committee had come to agreement on the language of some communiqué regarding British policy toward Hitler; I read it as implying that Margesson had forced some modification of the communiqué, and I wondered what that meant."

"Ha!" said Wilson sharply; "a perfect example of what I was describing. Paul Emrys-Evans is Chair of the Foreign Affairs Committee of the House and has become disillusioned by the government's appeasement policy. When he drafted the communiqué you read about in the paper, he expressed his misgivings and was sharply critical, accusing Chamberlain of doubling down on appeasement even as its inadequacy becomes more evident. Margesson found out about it and jumped all over him, threatening to strip him of his Chairmanship and make his life in the House a nightmare. Emrys-Evans decided to back off for the moment and he amended the communiqué with grudging acceptance before issuing it publicly. But he's furious and he'll back Eden to the hilt if he challenges Chamberlain."

Wilson paused; Muller gained the impression he was weighing how candid to be. Then Wilson, evidently deciding to cast off caution, leaned forward and looked directly in to Muller's eyes.

"It's that way it is on nearly every issue," he said evenly, but Muller could hear the barely suppressed anger; "Chamberlain demands total loyalty and won't brook dissent. It doesn't help that he's also a perfectly charmless human being. He has no sense of humor, refuses to mingle with the members in the smoking room and uses a small, tight coterie of whips to enforce Party discipline. I was approached early on by a shadowy outsider–who's not even a member of the House, but whom he's installed in an office next door to his–who tried to recruit me to spy on Eden.

"That's the kind of atmosphere we're operating in, Mr. Muller" Wilson said, lifting his hands in frustration. "It's very tense.

"And it's especially so in foreign affairs. Chamberlain has convinced himself that he is the only man in the government fit to conduct the nation's foreign policy. None of us knows where that attitude came from. He's not well-traveled and has no foreign policy expertise or experience. He's never met either Hitler or Mussolini, for example. But he's determined to exert total control over that vital portfolio.

"As you might expect, Mr. Muller, that attitude has put him in direct conflict with Anthony Eden, who is Foreign Secretary and has been the chief architect of British foreign policy for several years. On a host of issues, Chamberlain has sought not just to bypass Eden and the Ministry, but to pursue solutions that we–along with a growing number of other Tory members–believe are just plain wrong.

"So that is why, as Stevenson told you, Eden is on the verge of resigning from the Ministry and mounting a campaign to topple Chamberlain and replace him as Prime Minister."

Wilson then sat back in his chair, having shown his cards.

"Tell me how the information I can provide about the Austrian crisis can help," said Muller.

Wilson replied without hesitation. "In our view, refusing to support Austria against Hitler's aggressive designs offers yet another example of Chamberlain's foreign policy errors. He's issued direct orders that it is the government's policy to avoid criticizing Hitler on any subject–and that extends to Hitler's threatened takeover of Austria. As far as Chamberlain's concerned, Austria's a long way away and it's a small country that's not very important. They all speak German there anyway, so why make a fuss over it?"

Just then, a slender, balding man wearing a bright red tie approached them. Wilson immediately stood to greet him and Muller followed suit.

"Mr. Muller, may I introduce the Honorable Member, Robert Cranborne."

"Bobbety," said Cranborne, "I'm more comfortable that way." He pulled up a chair without more ado, seated himself and motioned for Wilson and Muller to resume their seats.

"We're glad you came to see us, Mr. Muller," Cranborne said. He spoke rapidly and radiated a sense of restless energy.

"We need to get Eden briefed up on what's happening with Austria so we can use it to go after Chamberlain," he said.

"I'd hoped to meet Eden and tell him directly," Muller said.

Cranborne nodded. "We're setting that up for later this afternoon. But we'd like you to inform us too, to ensure there's no slip up or misunderstanding. We're reasonably familiar with the basic story. We get good reporting from *The Daily Telegraph.* What we're really looking for is the kind of insight that the press doesn't report."

"*The Daily Telegraph* reporter, Nigel Hamilton, has become a friend," Muller said. "He's a good reporter, so the stories you've read should provide a pretty accurate picture."

"Nigel Hamilton," Cranborne chuckled with a smile; "too loud, too pushy, drinks to excess–and yes–a good reporter.

"So, what do you have for us, Mr. Muller?"

"You're probably familiar with the Government's raid on the Brown House in January," Muller began.

Cranborne nodded. "They arrested the local Nazi Party leaders and confiscated the files," he said. "Did they find anything?"

Muller described the Rudolph Hess dossier which laid out a blueprint for a demonstration that would explode out of control and lead to the murder of Franz von Papen as a pretext for Hitler to restore order and take over the country.

Wilson was taking notes.

Cranborne crinkled his eyes. "Von Papen," he muttered; "a snake that one."

"Schuschnigg threatened to make everything public and try the local Nazis for planning to overthrow the Government," Muller went on. "He thought it would give him leverage on Hitler, but he completely miscalculated.

"Instead, Hitler laid a trap," Muller went on. "He invited Schuschnigg to visit him at Berchtesgaden, promising to reconfirm Austrian sovereignty and defuse the crisis. But it was all a ruse. When Schuschnigg got there, Hitler blew up at him and demanded that he agree to a list of non-negotiable demands to submit to German rule.

"This is one of the key points that I want to convey to Minister Eden," Muller continued. "Hitler completely lost control and became unhinged, raging at the Chancellor of a neighboring country like some kind of Teutonic madman. 'I am the acknowledged leader of all Germans everywhere.' 'I will bend all of you to my will', 'I will force my enemies to submit to me'." Muller paused.

"The man behaved like he was insane." He looked at Cranborne and Wilson. "Leaders of the democracies need to understand that they are not confronting some conventional national leader who occasionally behaves like a crank. This man is dangerously unbalanced."

Cranborne looked at Muller with a level gaze. "Some of us have come to the same conclusion," he said quietly. "The problem is that sometimes the man is not crazy insane; instead, he's crazy like a fox."

Cranborne paused, reflecting. "You're right," he said, "Eden needs to hear this. It's another reason he should summon up the courage to unseat Chamberlain."

The meeting continued for another thirty minutes as Muller described the treachery of Seyss-Inquart and the new Foreign Minister Guido Schmidt and the strength of the Nazi movement in regional Austrian cities. He also reported on the hints at possible restoration of relations between the Fatherland Front and the Socialist Left.

"An anti-Nazi coalition between the government and Austrian workers parties could fundamentally alter the state of play if it were to come about," Muller said. "But it faces long odds; the divisions between them are still very deep and time is running out."

Wilson and Cranborne exchanged glances, nodding at one another.

"This has been very helpful, Mr. Muller," said Wilson, sliding his notes into a folio.

"It would be nice if we got some of this insight from our friends at MI-6," said Cranborne with a sarcastic expression. "But we don't, so we're pleased to get it from you."

"If you can meet me at the Foreign Office at 4PM this afternoon, Mr. Muller, I'll arrange for you to have a conversation with Eden. I'm confident he'll be pleased to meet with you."

Muller smiled. "I certainly hope so; I'll be there."

# CHAPTER 27

Muller was surprised to find the British Foreign Office appearing rather scruffy. The corridors weren't well lit and the liner rugs appeared threadbare. The Grand Staircase retained its architectural splendor, but Muller thought the decorative domed canopy looked faded; some of the inlaid tiles were chipped and the large chandelier hanging beneath it, above the staircase, had a few bulbs out.

Still, it was a grand building; a symbol of the far-flung British Empire and home, not just to the Foreign Office, but also the Commonwealth Office, the India Office and the Home Office. A large structure built in the classical style, it remained, after all these years, a center of British global power and influence.

Ushered into the Foreign Secretary's suite, Muller was struck by the larger than life full-length portraits of prominent predecessors: Palmerston, Asquith and two more he didn't recognize and he was too far away to be able to read their names at the bottom of the gold leaf frames. After only few moments, one of the attendants motioned them to enter the Foreign Secretary's office.

Wilson gestured Muller to precede him.

The room that he entered seemed smaller than what Muller had expected, perhaps because it was dwarfed by the high ceilings and the tall bookcases that lined the walls. But he didn't have time to reflect on his surroundings, as Anthony Eden rose from behind his desk and strode to greet him, smiling, his hand outstretched.

"Mr. Muller," he said as they shook hands. "What a pleasure to renew our acquaintance. Welcome."

He led Muller toward a grouping of handsome armchairs around a small table to the left of a fireplace where a peat fire glowed warmly.

Muller was struck again, as he always had been in Eden's presence, by his striking appearance: tall, graceful, mustache and hair framing a perfectly-proportioned face, and an effortless carriage; he remained a commanding figure, and Muller found himself feeling a case of the butterflies.

But Eden soon put him at ease.

"All of us admired the way you were able to buttress Commissioner Lester in those difficult sessions we had in Geneva facing off against that odious Nazi leader from Danzig–Greiser, wasn't that his name?" Eden continued, nodding in response to his own question. "It was uncomfortable having to accommodate a man so undignified and unreliable."

Then he cocked his head at Muller, "And Stevenson has always said that you were the one behind that newspaper story by the woman reporter, published on the very day the Council was taking up the issue of declaring the 1935 Nazi election in Danzig to be a fraud. I was frantically trying to stop the Council from acting and this newspaper article arrived on the desks of all the Council members laying out the very persuasive arguments on why I was wrong and imploring the Council to act. Stevenson said you set the whole thing up."

Eden smiled, recollecting the incident. "Well?" he said encouraging Muller to respond.

"He gives me too much credit, Minister," Muller said, wishing he could find a way to change the subject.

"That doesn't sound like a denial to me, Mr. Muller" Eden said laughing and tapping the table for effect.

"And it nearly worked, too," he added. "In fact, now, with the benefit of hindsight, I wish it *had* worked and that the Council had thrown out those Nazi rascals, forcing a new election in Danzig–which you and your supporters contended they would lose, am I remembering correctly?"

"That's right, sir," Muller replied, "They had become deeply unpopular."

Eden sighed.

"That would have been a well-deserved comeuppance for Herr Hitler," he said. Then, shaking his head as if to clear away memories of past mistakes, turned to face Muller.

"But let us speak of more contemporary matters, Mr. Muller," he said. "Bobbety Cranborne told me the details of your account of Hitler's unhinged behavior in his meeting with the Austrian Chancellor. It's very disturbing information. And not entirely surprising, I suppose. I've met with Hitler a half dozen times and while I never encountered anything resembling the tirade you described, I certainly found him to be volatile and a bit erratic."

He paused and Muller suppressed a smile, confident that no one–not even a man as rash as Hitler–could summon the will to tongue-lash the dignified and imperious Anthony Eden; it was inconceivable.

"Our very capable ambassador in Germany reports incidents of this kind of manic behavior," Eden continued, "and certainly in the newsreels of Hitler's speeches, we've seen him get so worked up as to apparently lose control, and begin shouting and even spitting into the microphone." He shook his head.

"But no one can plausibly argue that Hitler's has to be removed from office because he's some kind of modern Caligula or Ivan the Terrible. This is the twentieth century, Mr. Muller; we no longer permit monsters to take power. Hitler may not fit our definition of a suitable leader for a county so powerful as Germany. But that doesn't provide justification for us to mount a campaign deliberately aimed at toppling him from office.

"I take your point that Hitler crossed a line with Schuschnigg; it's a concern we need to factor into our analysis as we try to manage events," Eden said; "duly noted, with thanks. But Bobbety told me you have some additional issues you wanted to raise with me. Let's move on to those."

Muller nodded to himself as he prepared to respond. He'd made his case, raised the warning flag on Hitler's behavior and Eden had acknowledged it. He decided it was time to turn to the subject of Austria's finances.

"Thank you, Minister," he said. "I want to call your attention to the serious financial consequences that would ensue if Hitler were to take over Austria. There are two points actually. The first relates directly to my responsibilities as the League's Commissioner General for Austria. You may remember that the League was instrumental in arranging a new loan to Austria. It repaid the Bank of England's emergency loan in the wake of the run on Creditanstalt and refinanced the underlying loan, extending the term until 1959. The total amount was 577M Austrian schillings."

Eden nodded. "I remember it, but not the details," he said.

"The League arranged for the loan to be guaranteed by Britain, France, Czechoslovakia and Italy," Muller continued. "If Austria were to default on that loan, the guarantors–which include your government, Minister–would be responsible for repaying the private commercial lenders.

"Here's my concern, sir. If Hitler takes over Austria, he is very likely to repudiate the loan, and Britain and the other guarantors will be left holding the bag."

"I hardly think that's likely, Mr. Muller," Eden replied. "If Hitler were to repudiate its debts, Germany would lose access to the capital markets, and that would put a serious crimp in Hitler's re-armament program. Germany has a strong interest in preserving its credit standing, so it seems to me that the risk that you pose isn't realistic."

"But Minister, with all due respect, Germany would not be repudiating a German obligation," Muller responded. "It would simply be permitting a loan made to Austria–a country that would no longer exist–to lapse. It's not a *German* credit; it's *Austrian*. I'm sure bankers will make the arguments you suggested, Minister, but the loan documents nowhere impose any obligation on Germany. And don't forget, the banks want access to German lending as much as Germany wants access to their credit; German borrowing is a great business for the banks. Are they likely to cut Germany off, just because the Austrian loan lapses–when repayment is guaranteed by four credit-worthy nations?

"I would argue that the more likely outcome is that, if Germany lets the loan lapse–which I would fully expect it to do in the event of a takeover–the lending banks will go through the motions of objecting, then turn to Britain and the other guarantors for payment and proceed to make new loans to Germany. So, Hitler will get to have his cake and eat it too. He'll get to keep the loan proceeds–and probably direct them into his re-armament program–while the four government guarantors pay off the lenders.

Muller spread his hands and looked at Eden with a small smile. "It looks like too good a deal for him to pass up."

Muller decided to plunge on. "And Minister," he added, "it would probably be awkward politically for the government to explain to British taxpayers why it has to use their money to pay off an Austrian loan, but didn't take steps to prevent Hitler from seizing Austria in the first place."

A look of irritation crossed Eden's face; it was clear he did not appreciate being lectured about the political consequences of the government's current hands-off policy toward Austria–even if it were Chamberlain's policy, not his

"That will suffice, Mr. Muller," he said stiffly. "You have a second point?"

Muller understood that the meeting was about to end and that he was being instructed to be brief.

"Yes, Minister," he said. "Most of Austria's gold reserves are located here, in the vaults at the Bank of England. If Hitler were to seize Austria, he would certainly try to take the gold too. I am authorized by the League to inquire if there is a plan by the British government to freeze the Austrian gold account."

"And on what grounds would the government be justified to take such a step?" Eden asked, still irritated.

"Overthrowing the duly-constituted government of a neighboring state would certainly violate the League's covenant, Minister," Muller replied, "and even though Germany has resigned from the League and is no longer a member, Austria remains a member. The League seems powerless to prevent Germany from illegally seizing control of Austria's government. But League officials are wondering if the British government will act to prevent Germany from also stealing Austria's gold."

Eden glared at Muller for several very long moments. Then, he stood and smiled thinly. Muller stood as well; the meeting was clearly over. Eden offered Muller a perfunctory handshake and turned to Wilson.

"Jim, you can see Mr. Muller out, then return for a word."

As they reached the door, Wilson whispered, "Wait for me in the anteroom."

Muller found a seat beneath the large portrait of Lord Palmerston.

Well, he thought, I got to make my points. But Eden clearly hadn't liked what he was hearing, and his chilly reaction wasn't reassuring. He certainly hadn't given the impression of a man preparing to seize the initiative and fling down the gauntlet at Chamberlain; it seemed to Muller more as if Eden just wanted the problems to go away.

Moments later, Jim Wilson reappeared from Eden's office.

"I'll see you out," he said. "Sorry Eden was a little rude at the end."

"He certainly didn't seem to welcome my comments," Muller said, shrugging into his coat.

"No, but he understood them well enough," said Wilson as they left the Foreign Secretary's suite and began strolling down the corridor toward the marble staircase.

"He told me to prepare a minute and remind him to raise the issues with Sir John Simon–he's the Chancellor of the Exchequer," Wilson explained. "He's very tightly aligned with the Prime Minister in his commitment to the government's appeasement policy; Sir John will certainly be a bellwether on Chamberlain's likely reaction to the points you raised."

"I didn't sense Eden had an immediate urge to storm the barricades," Muller said.

Wilson shrugged. "Eden keeps his own counsel," he said; "Bobbety and I will be meeting with him to help him decide on his next steps. Frankly, I think you provided him another persuasive set of arguments for why he needs to replace Chamberlain.

At the head of the stairway, he turned and shook hands with Muller.

"We'll see, won't we?" he said. "Thank you for coming over."

# CHAPTER 28

Muller rehashed the meeting that evening over dinner with Stevenson in the almost deserted dining room of the hotel. Liveried waiters stood idle in the glittering space that was lit by candles and a large chandelier.

Stevenson listened to Muller's account, without interrupting.

"He's a hard man to read, Muller," Stevenson said finally. "But I'd say you touched a nerve from the abrupt way he brought the meeting to a close. That's not normal behavior for Eden; he's usually polite to a fault."

Stevenson took a large swallow of the claret they were drinking with a dinner of turbot, overcooked and dry, a regular feature of English food preparation that Muller did not miss. Turbot had just come into season and should be served just underdone and juicy. He had never understood why British chefs, seemingly uniformly, could take a perfectly good piece of fresh fish–it wasn't confined to turbot–and proceed to cook the flavor right out of it; it happened all the time. Muller chewed the tasteless meal and forced himself to concentrate on what Stevenson was saying about Eden's reaction to their meeting.

"He's really at the end of his rope with Chamberlain and that may have made him testier than usual, When I returned to Whitehall after introducing you to Wilson, the two of them had another dust-up over colonial policy, of all things."

Muller looked at him quizzically.

"Right," Stevenson said; "not a subject much in the news these days, but somehow Chamberlain's concluded that he can curry favor with Hitler by finding a way to return African colonies to Germany–recognition of German prestige and all that; very much a Chamberlain kind of thing, and it's really irritating to Eden."

"I don't understand," said Muller.

Stevenson sighed. "It is a little obscure, but it's a commentary on the times and Chamberlain's willingness to interfere in matters that are normally left to the Foreign Office. You probably know that the Versailles Treaty stripped Germany of it African colonies," Stevenson continued. Muller shook his head. Stevenson smiled.

"You Swiss don't think in colonial terms like we do, Muller," he said. "It was actually quite a big deal at the time. We took over German East Africa and renamed it Tanganyika while the South Africans took control of South-West Africa. Germans have always griped about being mistreated this way, so Chamberlain decided he should find some formula to satisfy them. But there's a problem; Tanganyika has become a very valuable colony for us. It's a huge exporter of foodstuff to the Empire, so the Colonial Office won't hear of getting rid of it, and the South Africans have turned South-West Africa into a gold mine–literally; it's become a huge mining asset for them.

"So, Chamberlain realized he had to find some other African territory to offer Hitler. He proceeded to look at the map and settled on a central African region along the Zambezi that he believed he could persuade the Belgians and the Portuguese to part with."

Seeing Muller watching him with a look of disbelief, Stevenson paused, pointing his fork in Muller's direction for emphasis. "I'm not making this up, Muller," he said.

"If you say so, Stevenson," Muller said in a patronizing tone; "it sounds like a harebrained scheme to me. But Eden went along with it?"

"No," replied Stevenson, "and that's the point. Eden thought it was foolishness because he was convinced that the Belgians and Portuguese were no more ready to surrender colonial territory to Germany than we were. But he insisted that if Chamberlain wanted to pursue this policy, he should at least extract some kind of *quid pro quo* from Hitler; knowing Eden as you do, you won't be surprised to learn that the *quid* Eden demanded for Chamberlain's colonial *quo*, was a commitment from Hitler on European disarmament.

"Chamberlain wouldn't hear of it," Stevenson said. "For him, the goal in handing colonies back to Germany–someone else's colonies, by the way, but no matter–was to make a unilateral gesture of good will; a symbolic act of generosity that would encourage Hitler to respond in kind and initiate German policies that would reduce tensions and increase harmony."

"Stevenson, are you pulling my leg?" Muller said chuckling.

"Maybe I exaggerate slightly as a tribute to the claret," Stevenson replied, "but not much. Chamberlain's decided that Hitler is a gentleman and will respond to gentlemanly policies on our part.

"Eden profoundly disagrees," he continued. "They had a sharp disagreement this afternoon when Eden objected to Chamberlain unleashing that mean-spirited Whip Margesson to browbeat the Members into obedient support for his policy.

"Neither man is willing to back down. Eden will surely resign in protest; the only question is whether he'll take the fight to Chamberlain and seek to unseat him."

"And will he?" Muller asked again.

Stevenson raised his long-stemmed glass and clinked it with Muller's, then finished the last of the claret.

"I certainly hope so."

# CHAPTER 29

Muller ordered a car the next morning to take him to his flight and learned to his surprise that British Airways had moved its operation from Croydon Aerodrome to the smaller Heston Airfield situated to the west of London.

Muller inquired about the change from his driver.

"Croydon has the reputation of being the most modern air terminal in Europe. That's where I arrived the other night from Paris Le Bourget on Air France," he said. "So why is British Airways flying out of Heston?

"Croydon's gotten so busy, sir," came the reply. "Imperial Air uses it to fly to its far-off destinations in the empire and all the European carriers use it, like your Air France flight. They like the new terminal building and the control tower. British Airways has Heston pretty much to itself, and they claim it doesn't have as many fog delays.

"Me? I prefer Croydon, sir; higher fare to get out there." The driver glanced back at Muller in the rear-view mirror with a grin.

They arrived soon enough, pulling up before a cluster of low, non-descript buildings. After paying his fare, Muller entered the nearest doorway and saw a sign pointing him down a corridor toward the British Airways departure gates. It was not crowded, with only a handful of people seated in uncomfortable chairs. Muller presented his ticket and passport.

"We'll board in thirty minutes, sir," said the uniformed attendant.

Muller glanced out the window and saw a De Havilland DH 86, a workhorse twin-engine 12-seat aircraft that retained the biplane twin wing structure. It had a reassuring, solid look to it, he thought.

They boarded on time, the plane nearly full, with only two empty seats, and took off smoothly, the loud engines causing the aircraft to vibrate and drowning out any possibility of conversation. Muller waited apprehensively for the turbulence he'd experienced over the Channel to appear, but the flight was smooth. Muller could look below and see several small vessels casting wakes in the sea, then the French coast suddenly appeared, and they were flying over the French countryside dotted with farmhouses and small villages.

Muller was new to flying and was enjoying gazing down from his window seat. Suddenly, he started and sat forward, trying to get a better view. The trenches; he could make them out clearly, broken up here and there by farmers and villages reclaiming the land. But there was no mistaking the scar that remained distinct and served as a reminder of the terrible fighting that had occurred right below him less than 20 years ago.

As the plane flew on toward the German border, Muller sat back thinking; was it conceivable that another war was near? He hadn't reached a conclusion when he dozed off.

Arrival at Berlin's Tempelhof Airport was uneventful. During the approach, Muller could see the vast construction project underway to build a huge new terminal building. He had read about this new Albert Speer-designed super-building that was meant to symbolize Nazi Germany's strength and superiority. It certainly looked impressive, he decided.

The passenger terminal still in use was a much more modest affair, a low building made of brick siding that resembled a railroad station more than it did an airport–though it did have a glassed-in control tower that was apparently a recent addition.

Muller de-planed and followed the signs for connecting flights. He entered a room for Lufthansa transit passengers and joined a line leading to a ticket window manned by a single attendant. When Muller reached the head of the line and handed over his ticket and passport, the pasty-faced attendant glanced at him, then picked up the receiver of the black telephone next to him, dialed a number and spoke briefly. The he handed Muller's papers back to him.

"Go to that office on the left and wait," he said officiously, pointing to a door.

What's this about, Muller wondered. But he did as he was told and entered a small windowless office with a table, two chairs and no other furnishings. He shut the door behind him and heard a click. He tried to turn the door handle. It was locked.

Annoyed, Muller sat in the chair on one side of the table and lit a Gitane. No ashtray. That's their problem, he decided.

Minutes passed and Muller grew increasingly impatient. Grinding out his butt on the floor, he stood and tried the door again, rattling the handle and rapping the wood surface with his knuckles. Nothing happened. He returned to his seat, then stood and began pacing.

What the Hell was going on? He had a connecting flight to get back to Vienna.

Finally, the door opened and a stocky man with short hair and a thick neck, wearing a telltale long black leather overcoat entered the room, closing the door firmly behind him; Gestapo. Muller annoyance was tempered by momentary uncertainty.

"What's the meaning of this?" he said angrily. "Why am I being detained and locked in this room?"

The man looked at Muller coldly and sat down in the chair behind the table.

"Sit down and give me your papers." For a big man, he had a curiously high voice. "Now," he added, slapping his hand on the table.

Muller stood, gazing at the man, his hands on his hips. Then he placed his ticket and passport carefully on the table and took the other seat, lighting another Gitane.

"Smoking is not permitted in this room," the man said sharply.

"I don't see any sign," Muller replied, exhaling.

"I'm telling you," the man said firmly. "Put it out."

Muller took another drag, then ground out the rest with his heel.

"Are you going to tell me what this is about?" he demanded, glaring at the man.

"All in good time," the man responded. "I would remind you that you are here as a visitor to the German *Reich* and you are subject to its rules," he added, paging though Muller's passport and glancing at the ticket.

"I am in Berlin as a transit passenger who is ticketed on an international flight between London and Vienna," Muller retorted.

"But you *are* in Berlin, and therefore within the German *Reich*," the man said.

Then he looked up from the papers. "Why were you in London?"

"I am a diplomat and am entitled to diplomatic immunity," Muller said angrily. "You have no business asking me that question and I have no obligation to respond to it. Kindly give me back my papers and let me get to my connecting flight."

"You are an employee of the League of Nations, of which my government is not a member and which it rightly counts as an oppressor. So, don't presume to lecture me," the man said angrily.

"This passport says you're posted to Vienna. Why were you in London?"

"That's none of your business," Muller said standing up and reaching for his papers. "I have a plane to catch; kindly permit me to do so."

The man stood and faced Muller, unsmiling. He placed Muller's papers in a side pocket of his overcoat.

"We know exactly who you are, Mr. Muller, and what you're doing." He moved to just a few feet from Muller, looking him in the eye. Muller could clearly see the scar tissue on the man's oft-broken nose and bright pink scar on his neck. The man put his finger on Muller's chest in a menacing matter.

"You will remain here," he said. "The German *Reich* will decide when and how you will depart."

With that, the man rapped once on the door and it immediately swung open, then closed as he exited.

Muller slumped into the chair and lit a Gitane. What–or who–had triggered what was an obviously deliberate act of detention? And what were his choices? Muller's mind raced. For now, he was a prisoner in a windowless room with a locked door. There weren't many available options.

Suddenly, the door opened and a uniformed Lufthansa attendant entered holding Muller's passport and ticket. He wore a wide apologetic smile.

"Mr. Muller, we're so sorry. There was a terrible mistake; please come with me and I'll see you aboard your connecting flight right away," and he led Muller out of the room, through the Transit Room, guiding him by the elbow along a corridor toward the Lufthansa departure gates.

The attendant kept up a prattle of apologies for the 'mix-up' and 'misunderstanding'. Muller ignored what he was saying and concentrated on getting to the gate so he could board his flight and get out of Berlin. Moments later they arrived at a gate marked with sign saying 'Vienna', but the desk was unmanned. The attendant opened the door and led Muller toward a Fokker aircraft whose engines were already running, the propellers idling. The loading door was still open and the attendant motioned Muller to board, handing him his ticket and passport.

Muller entered the aircraft and the stewardess pointed to a vacant seat two rows ahead on the right. As Muller seated himself, the door was closed and the plane began taxiing. He sank back into his seat, sliding his papers into his breast pocket and folding his legs over his valise. Gripping the armrests, he tensed for the takeoff, then, as the plane became airborne, he shut his eyes and willed himself to relax.

# CHAPTER 30

Muller's flight arrived in Vienna right on time and upon deplaning, he took a taxi to his hotel. The efficient Frau Metzinger had left a message informing him that the Chancellor's speech that evening would be delivered before the full Parliament and that the entire diplomatic corps had been invited. She had put his pass in the envelope, which Muller slipped into his pocket. Glancing at his watch, he decided to leave at once to ensure getting a seat.

Successfully working his way through what was an unusually large and enthusiastic crowd, Muller found an aisle seat in the Diplomatic gallery and he glanced around at the spectacle that was unfolding before him.

The public gallery was already fully taken up by members of the Fatherland Front who were applauding and whistling. Outside Muller could hear other Party members chanting and shouting.

*"Oesterreich, Oesterreich*

*"Red-White-Red*

*"Schuschnigg, Schuschnigg!"*

The enthusiasm seemed to grow and became contagious as Party members and parliamentarians in the chamber began chanting in unison and stamping their feet.

*'Kurt-von-Schusch-nigg*

*'Kurt-von-Schusch-nigg*

*'Oes-ter-reich*

*'Oes-ter-reich*

The Nazis aren't the only ones that can stage rallies, Muller thought. The Fatherland Front was pulling out all the stops and the cheers and applause grew louder still as Schuschnigg appeared at the back of the chamber. He made his way down the aisle toward the podium, which was decorated with banks of fresh tulips arranged in the red-white-red national symbol, and as he mounted the steps of the podium, a large Austrian banner was unfurled from the ceiling and slowly lowered into position above him.

*"Schuschnigg!*

*"Oesterreich!*

The cheering went on until finally, Schuschnigg, hands raised, succeeded in quieting the crowd. He stood erect, projecting strength and confidence.

"We stand here tonight to reconfirm our unshakable allegiance to the free, Christian, Federal Republic of Austria," he said in a loud, firm voice.

The chamber erupted in cheers and chants.

Muller looked about him; this was a very genuine outpouring of emotion–even passion–he thought. He'd seen propaganda rallies before, enthusiasm whipped up and enforced by party discipline; but this seemed different. There was a sense of spontaneity, a release of pent-up enthusiasm that seemed quite genuine.

Schuschnigg was finally able to resume his speech, and he too seemed caught up in the moment. He recounted Austria's miraculous recovery from the shattering defeat in the War and the days of hunger and hardship that followed, and he enumerated popular economic and social achievements that the Government had delivered, hailing the abundance of goods and jobs that citizens enjoyed. Muller read into these remarks a calculated dig at Hitler whose rearmament program had caused shortages and meager choices for many Germans.

He then went on to address the current crisis. "We have given abundant proof of our goodwill and good faith. We expect our German neighbors to act in the same spirit and to follow through on the reassurances given by their Führer that measures will be taken to prevent any interference in Austria's internal affairs. Illegal behavior by any Party–including especially the Nazi Party–will not be tolerated by my Government."

Schuschnigg paused as cheers erupted, then continued to growing applause.

"We have gone to the very limit in our concessions and we must now call a halt and say, this far but not further.'" The crowd roared. "The Lord God will not desert our country," he concluded: "Our victory is assured. Until death! Red-White-Red! Oesterreich!"

As Schuschnigg stepped down from the podium, his audience stood and greeted him with frenzied applause and cheering that was echoed in the street outside.

It was quite a performance, Muller thought, as members of the diplomatic corps turned to one another in acknowledging what had been an extraordinary event. Everyone knew that Schuschnigg, who was ordinarily a dull, pedantic speaker, had somehow tapped a deep well of patriotic emotion that swept up his supporters with unexpected passion. Where would it lead, Muller wondered.

By now it had become almost a routine for Muller to stop by the Café Louvre before returning to the hotel, and he did so again after leaving the Parliament building. Most of the journalists were finishing up their stories or filing them at the nearby Western Union office. Nigel Hamilton, however, had completed his job and had a large mug of beer before him as Muller sat down next to him in the usual booth.

Muller had come to respect the deep knowledge and insight that Hamilton possessed. He was often boorish in his behavior–too loud and brash for Muller's taste. But there was no mistaking his intellect and he had a seemingly endless list of excellent sources who passed him very good information. Tonight, he seemed uncharacteristically withdrawn.

"I expect everyone will be gushing over Schuschnigg's performance," Hamilton said dismissively. "And they'll miss the real story."

Muller looked at Hamilton inquisitively. "Well, actually it *was* a remarkable speech," he said. "Tell me what I'm missing."

Hamilton fixed him with a level gaze. "While Schuschnigg was speaking here in Vienna and reaffirming Austrian independence, the Austrian provinces were taken over by the Austrian Nazis. *That's* the real story," he fairly spat out the words. "In Graz, an hour before the speech, 20,000 local Nazis took over the main square and occupied the town hall. They tore down the Austrian flag and proceeded to rip it to shreds before they ran the swastika up the flagpole. Then they cut the wires to the PA system so no one heard Schuschnigg at all. They were in full uniform and staged a full Nazi-style rally–with no interference from the police. Same story in Klagenfurt and Salzburg and Linz."

Hamilton ordered another beer. "It's the new strategy. Overwhelm the Government outside Vienna. And Seyss-Inquart is right in the middle of it...at Hitler's direction. Listen, I'm taking a train out to Graz tomorrow. You can come along if you like. My source tells me that'll be the place to be."

Muller said yes and they agreed to meet at the East Banhof the next afternoon in time to catch the 14:37 limited to Graz.

Muller strolled slowly back to his hotel. He hadn't felt comfortable sharing the story of his Tempelhof detention with Hamilton. The more he'd thought about it, the more he'd become convinced that what had occurred was a warning directed at him personally. It was the Nazi Government's way of informing him that they had him in their sights and that they were prepared to punish him if they concluded he went too far in opposing them.

Muller had accepted the premise that going about his job of passing warnings along to the Austrian government–not to mention plotting to dispose of Austrian gold–was risky. But the danger had seemed far off–like a dark cloud on the horizon. Now it looked as though someone in the Nazi hierarchy had decided to single him out; they'd found out he was transiting Germany and they'd sent that scar-faced Gestapo heavy to deliver a very personal message that he was the target on a potential hit-list.

It was a disconcerting realization. But the more he thought about it, the more annoyed he became. He'd never liked being threatened, especially if the intent was to deter him from doing something he had decided was the right course of action–as in this case, helping Austria resist Hitler's loathsome embrace.

Listening tonight to Schuschnigg's courageous words and seeing the enthusiastic reaction of his Austrian audience, Muller felt re-energized to continue his mission.

And on that upbeat note, he turned off his bedside lamp.

# CHAPTER 31

The next day at the East Banhof, Muller offered to buy tickets for them both and Hamilton accepted, specifying first class, even though there was only a single first-class coach attached to the train.

"You'll see why," Hamilton said.

A few minutes later, after they'd mounted the steps to their compartment, a delegation of what were obviously Government officials strode along the platform to the first-class coach. In the midst of the group of men was a slight, somewhat stooped man, who walked with a limp.

"Seyss-Inquart," Hamilton hissed quietly.

Muller glanced nonchalantly out their compartment window to avoid calling attention to himself. Seyss-Inquart was in deep conversation with another man and was facing directly toward Muller. He had a bland appearance, except for large horn-rimmed glasses; a high forehead and dark hair, but no distinguishing features. He looks like the solicitor he was said to be, Muller thought; plain and unimpressive.

As the train prepared to depart, the knot of officials separated and the traveling party, including Seyss-Inquart, mounted the steps to the next compartment.

"Maybe he'll come next door and offer his neighbor an interview," Muller said teasingly.

Hamilton snorted. "Not that one. A real cold fish, he is." Hamilton leaned in toward Muller. "Schuschnigg is sending him out to Graz to calm the Nazis and restore order. My source tells me it's going to be a lot different than that."

Hamilton winked and put his finger to his lips. "We'll see," he said finally, settling his head on a pillow and closing his eyes.

While Hamilton slept soundly, Muller gazed at the passing countryside as the train headed south. He'd been able to pass word to Otto Schultz that he was traveling to Graz and Schultz had responded that Seyss-Inquart was being dispatched there to settle things down. Now Hamilton's source was predicting that Seyss-Inquart would betray the Chancellor; Muller felt uneasy about what was about to transpire.

Ninety minutes later, the train pulled into a small village and stopped. A large black Horch limousine was parked alongside the narrow platform, flanked by two police cars. A train porter brought a stepstool which he placed beneath the compartment door to help the Government delegation disembark. Muller watched as Seyss-Inquart limped to the Horch and stepped inside. Special arrangements were evidently being made to prepare for the Minister's visit to Graz, Muller thought to himself. He wondered why arrival at the railroad station wasn't deemed satisfactory. The cars carrying Seyss-Inquart and his delegation drove off.

The train lingered at the small village station for a moment before slowly pulling out. As it did so, Muller saw a sign on the wall of the station that read 'Judenburg'. *Jewtown?* Muller said to himself. He poked Hamilton and pointed it out.

Hamilton sniggered. "Austria loves her Jews."

A few minutes later, the train pulled into Graz. To Muller's surprise, he saw Brown-Shirted storm troopers lounging on the platform and more uniformed personnel inside the station; several civilians openly wore red Nazi Party armbands with the white patch encircling a black swastika. Policemen were also present, but gave no indication of having even the slightest interest in this illegal display of Nazi Party affiliation. And as he stepped outside the station, Muller caught sight of Nazi swastika flags hanging from several building flagstaffs, though he looked up and saw the Austrian flag flying above the train station.

Well; this is different, he thought.

Hamilton's contact had told him to go to the Park Hotel and await instructions. So, the two of them walked to the hotel, which was situated just beyond the broad plaza that, as was the custom, stretched in front of the train station. They turned the corner and Muller stiffened when he saw what a large sign identified as the Park Hotel. The entire façade of the building was draped with Nazi red, black and white banners. Uniformed SS and Brown-Shirted dispatch riders were guarding their motorcycles pulled up in front and more uniformed personnel were stationed at the doorway. It seemed evident that this was some kind of Nazi Party headquarters.

Muller and Hamilton exchanged glances, and strode to the entrance. They were politely asked for their papers by a slight, sallow-faced man in a suit that was a size too big, a Nazi badge prominently displayed on his lapel.

Hamilton looked the man over and told him he had no business asking for their papers in a public hotel lobby. Muller could see Hamilton bristle at being accosted; he was having none of it and said so in his customarily loud tones. Two burly Storm Troopers in full Brown Shirt uniform appeared at the elbow of the functionary and glared threateningly.

At that moment, a slim man with brown hair and a thin mustache rose from a chair in the lobby and walked up to them. He was dressed in civilian attire; a dark suit, neatly pressed white shirt and a blue tie. He carried an unmistakable air of authority.

"Mr. Hamilton," he said, dismissing the others with a glance. "Welcome. We've been waiting for you. My name is Ludwig Frisch. I'm the Fatherland Front Director here; we hope you had a pleasant journey from Vienna." Frisch took Hamilton by the elbow and began steering him back toward the doorway, Muller following in their wake.

"Actually, we have you set up at the Hotel Grand on the Plaza, just around the corner and next to the telegraph office, so it will be easier for you to file your stories."

Frisch smiled engagingly and looked back at Muller. "And you are?" he inquired.

"An observer," Muller replied.

"Ah," said Frisch in a neutral tone.

"He's with me," said Hamilton impatiently stopping and turning back to the Park Hotel lobby. "What's going on here, Frisch?" he said. "These aren't Fatherland Front symbols I'm looking at. You seem to have missed what your party leader and Chancellor said the other night in parliament about keeping Nazi displays out of Austria. And who told you I was coming to Graz?" Hamilton's tone was testy.

"Just follow me," said Frisch soothingly. "I'll explain everything when we get to the other hotel."

"Up yours, Frisch," Hamilton said loudly; "I'm not going anywhere until I see Seyss-Inquart and his cohorts make their grand entrance here."

"What makes you think the Minister's coming here?" Frisch said nonchalantly.

But, as if on cue, the Horch limousine pulled up to the hotel entrance.

Hamilton smirked at Frisch. "Don't play me for the fool," he said, positioning himself for a good view of what would happen.

The hotel lobby seemed to spring to life as men snapped to attention, forming a corridor in front of Seyss-Inquart as he limped to the doorway. Hamilton and Muller were elbowed aside as a delegation of boys and girls wearing Hitler Youth and Hitler

Maidens uniforms were steered toward the doorway, bowing and curtseying toward their visitor and offering him spring flowers–not, Muller noted, red-white-red Austrian tulips.

At the far end of the lobby, a figure in a formal SS uniform–black with red and white piping and highly polished tall boots–stepped toward where Seyss-Inquart was receiving the gifts, drew himself up to attention and thrust out his right arm. "*Heil Hitler*", he exclaimed, and the others in the lobby responded in kind–except Seyss-Inquart, Muller noticed, whose hands were holding the big bouquets. Then, recovering, he handed the flowers to an aide standing behind him, took several steps in the direction of the SS officer and delivered the Heil Hitler greeting before walking up to him, clapping him on the shoulder and guiding him toward the elevator bank where the two of them entered a car and the door quickly closed behind them.

Hamilton nudged Muller. "Let's get out of here," he hissed.

But Frisch was immediately at their elbow. "The Hotel Grand is just a block or so away," he said. "Let me escort you."

Hamilton didn't respond, but nodded, and he and Muller followed Frisch outside and around the corner.

In front of the Hotel Grand, Hamilton stopped and turned on Frisch. "Who told you to expect me?" he demanded.

"Why, an acquaintance in the Vienna press corps overheard you saying that you were traveling here, and thought to let me know," Frisch responded, smiling engagingly. "We do like to welcome journalists–especially from influential British newspapers," he added, still smiling.

"So, you're the Nazi censor?" Hamilton said, glaring at Frisch.

"Dear me," Frisch said. "That's not the term I would use at all. I like to think of myself as the facilitator that can persuade the telegraph office to transmit good stories without any delay."

"After you've approved them, of course," said Hamilton angrily. "Well, I repeat myself Frisch: up yours!" and he stalked away, with Muller following.

They walked back to the train station to find the bar and restaurant. A crew of laborers was at work erecting what appeared to be a platform in front of the station. Hamilton stopped and went over to one of the workers.

"Nazis staging a march tonight?"

The man nodded. "That's all they're good for, marching around, singing–and beating up people like me," he said matter-of-factly. "But I'm paid to build these things. They want a reviewing stand? They'll have one." He shrugged.

"Maybe it'll collapse," said Hamilton with a smirk.

The laborer guffawed. "That'd be a sight, wouldn't it? Ha!"

"So what time's the show?" Hamilton asked.

"Nine tonight." The workman went back to hammering nails.

"Let's stick around," Hamilton said to Muller as he headed for the bar. "We'll see what else is in store for us here in cheery Graz."

After numerous beers and truly bad sausages for dinner, Hamilton and Muller stepped outside to watch as the parade began.

Dignitaries took their places on the reviewing stand, Seyss-Inquart and the black-uniformed SS officer seated in front. Spotlights had been rigged on building rooftops to light up the plaza. A large crowd gathered opposite the station, leaving room in front of the reviewing stand for the marchers to file past.

What followed, Muller thought to himself, could have leapt straight from the newsreel clips of Nazi parades in Berlin. A military band came first, in full Brown-Shirt uniforms, playing martial airs and Nazi songs. They positioned themselves just beyond the reviewing stand and provided the tempo for the marchers that followed. Two SS units goose-stepped past the stand, eyes-right to take the Hitler salutes, their steel helmets gleaming in the lights. Next was a company of what appeared to be Austrian Army veterans, some in Great War uniforms. They carried brightly-lit torches and sang lustily as they passed. A squadron of motorcycles followed, the vehicles decked with Nazi banners. Uniformed riders standing on their stirrups revved their engines and saluted the stand. The crowd of onlookers cheered and Muller noticed windows opening in buildings across the way as residents broke out Nazi flags, placing them in holders or draping them from window sills.

Then the SS units returned to the plaza and drew themselves to attention, standing in formation in front of the reviewing stand.

The tall SS officer strode to the podium and exclaimed the Nazi greeting.

*"Seig Heil"* came the response in unison.

"Fellow German Austrians," the officer said into the loud speaker microphone which echoed across the plaza. "It is my honor and my pleasure to present to you Minister Arthur Seyss-Inquart, the leader of our government who is paving the way for our glorious return to the Greater German Reich."

Tumultuous cheers.

Seyss-Inquart strode to the microphone–seeming to suppress his limp–and addressed the crowd in measured tones.

"There comes a time," he said, "when the demands of history and of blood coalesce into a journey mandated by our heritage–an insistence upon erasing artificial boundaries and binding us all–Germans every one–into a single Reich! A single nation! A single *Volk*! Now is that time," he said, his voice rising for the first time, injecting a sense of urgency. "Now is the time for us to be united with the Fatherland. Now is the time for Austria to become Germany."

Drawing himself up and issuing the stiff right arm salute, he exclaimed loudly, for all to hear, *"Heil Hitler!"*

The crowd responded and broke into the *Horst Vessel* song, the anthem of the Nazi Party.

Muller, standing with Hamilton, just a few yards from the reviewing stand, marveled at the passion and intensity of the response, as the crowd surged and seemed to take on a life of its own, losing itself in a jubilant collective embrace.

Hamilton tugged at Muller's elbow and they edged back into the station so they would not be noticed as only observing what was transpiring. In a corner sat a small knot of men in workers clothing, drinking their beers, unmoved by the excitement outside.

Muller spotted the laborer who had spoken to Hamilton.

The man stood and pointed Hamilton and Muller toward the bar. "Have a drink, boys," he said loudly to the cheers of his comrades. "They'll be coming after all of us soon enough. You'd better make the best of the time you've got left."

Hamilton tipped his mug back at them and told the bartender to buy them a round.

As they stepped out on the platform to await the 10:50 Express train that would return them to Vienna, Hamilton gazed back at the station bar.

"You never see workers at these bloody Nazi rallies," he said. "The guy was right; they'll come after his crowd. It's a bad time to be a trade unionist or a Social Democrat."

Muller uncorked a pint of whiskey that he extracted from his valise and passed it to Hamilton as they boarded the train.

"I'll save some for the traitor," Hamilton said quietly, pointing as Seyss-Inquart and his delegation walked past to the next compartment.

"Your contact was certainly on the money," said Muller. "No nuance; just a total embrace of Hitler. So how does this play out? The end must be near."

"This is Austria, Muller," Hamilton replied, handing back the flask, "home to great opera. I think there's probably another act or two left in this drama."

# CHAPTER 32

Thursday evening Viktor Keinböck was waiting as planned on the bench overlooking the Danube.

"You have the passport photos?" Muller asked. Keinböck nodded. "Three of them, each one a little different."

"Good; we're off then," Muller said.

They took the lengthy circuitous route to the Heinrichshof Café and found seats in a small booth along the wall, each ordering a beer while awaiting the appearance of Franz.

Keinböck unwrapped a pack of Pall Mall cigarettes and offered one to Muller who accepted and flicked his lighter for both of them.

"I found a last pack in my desk drawer this afternoon," he said. "I thought they might bring us luck; hopefully good luck," he added.

"Have you noticed the streets, how much more brazen the Nazis have become about displaying their affiliation in the last few days? It's like someone has given them instructions to step up the pressure, but only so far," he said.

Muller blew a smoke ring. "I've taken to walking the Karnerstrasse in the early evening just to watch the show," he said. "And you're right. It seems tightly controlled; as if they're playing a game. Flash a Party lapel button here, a Party hat pin or a Party badge there, but not the whole show. The police seem to be playing along as well. There seems to be a cat and mouse game going on."

Franz appeared at the doorway and beckoned them. They quickly paid their bill and followed him around to the back of the building where a small battered Daimler truck was parked. It had a faded sign painted on the door advertising 'Alpine Iron Castings'. Franz motioned them into the back under a canvas cover; two benches provided places to sit.

"This will take a while," he said. "Be patient and stay out of sight."

After thirty minutes of rattling slowly along the cobblestone streets, the truck braked to a stop and Franz lowered the gate for them to dismount. There was a dim street light at the corner but Franz skirted it and ducked into a dark alley where Muller reached out to steady himself against the wall as they slowly walked in single file. Franz stopped at a set of narrow stairs that led down to a doorway, scarcely visible in the gloom. He knocked three times. They waited. Then the door opened and they stepped across a threshold into a room lit by a single light bulb hanging above a table piled high with paper. The man who had opened the door motioned them to chairs around the table, then sat in one of the chairs himself, moving two piles of paper to the floor.

He was fat, with greasy hair slicked across his balding pate. Suspenders held up trousers below a dirty shirt and a stained necktie with a floral design. He looked at Franz and said something in a tongue that Muller didn't recognize.

"Please give him the pictures and the blank passports," said Franz.

Muller unwrapped an oil cloth purse and laid two Swiss passports on the table. Keinböck handed over his photos, which the man studied, glancing at Keinböck several times. Then he picked up the passports and flicked through them saying something to Franz.

"He says these are okay," Franz translated.

Muller was about to say that they damned well should be okay since they came from the Swiss Passport Office. But he decided to hold his tongue.

The man turned his chair to face behind him and switched on a bright light above a desk that held a large blotter and at least a dozen small inkwells. The man selected one of Keinböck's photos and spit on it, rubbing it with his right thumb.

"I have to age it," he said in heavily accented German. Reaching into his desk he brought out a bottle of clear glue that he applied to the back of the photo with a small brush. He then flattened one of the passports and carefully affixed the photo in the allotted space. Removing his thumb, he pressed down on the photo with a blotter, then closed the passport and placed a heavy book on it.

"We give it a few minutes to stick," he said. Then he asked Franz for Muller's passport. Muller looked at Franz, but Franz nodded and Muller handed it to the man.

He opened it and carefully studied the line where Muller's name had been written and the raised letters of the stamp that been applied.

Returning it to Muller, he removed the book from atop the new passport and opened it. Then he selected one of the inkwells and a nearby pen.

"What name?" he asked.

Muller and Keinböck looked at one another. How could they have forgotten that?

Shit!

Thinking quickly, Muller pulled Keinböck to his side. "An Appenzell first name," he said. "Rudi; very common. Agreed?" Last name? he wondered. Then it came to him. The driver for Büro Ha. Dunkel. Certainly a false name.

"Rudi Dunkel," he said. "That'll do it." He smiled thinly at Keinböck.

The man dipped his pen carefully and wrote the name confidently. "Special government ink," he said with a note of pride.

Then he blotted the name and reached into another drawer to bring up a small device that he placed on the desk and, lifting a lever, opened it. He fit the page of the passport into the machine flush to one of the edges then pushed the lever down to squeeze it.

When he released the lever and removed the passport, they could see the raised franking stamp that seemed identical to the one used on Muller's passport.

"Will be good," he said with a smile that revealed a missing tooth, and handed the passport to Keinböck.

Franz handed the man a thick envelope and they returned to the truck for the trip back to the Heinrichshof.

# CHAPTER 33

Muller had been able to obtain two tickets for Steffi and him to attend a Vienna Philharmonic Symphony performance at the Konzerthaus that Saturday evening. It was an all-Mozart program, the 'Prague' symphony, number 38, and his last two, symphony number 40 and the great 'Jupiter' symphony, number 41. They were among Muller's favorite works and the prospect of hearing them performed all together was exciting.

They decided to dress for the concert, Muller in white tie and Steffi in a light blue gown that she had bought for an earlier formal event, but that had become a favorite. She had added a pearl choker necklace and matching bracelet. Muller thought she looked lovely and very sophisticated. She responded with a smile and a curtsey.

They arrived early and sipped champagne, mingling with the well-dressed crowd in the large, ornate Konzerthaus foyer, its high ceiling and cream-colored walls decorated with gold leaf design, beneath a vast overhanging chandelier. The mood was light and a hum of laughter and smiling conversation pervaded the room.

Then, as the lights flickered and subtle tones rang to signal it was time, they entered the concert hall itself.

It was even more ornate than Muller expected, with a high, scallop-shaped vault behind the stage dominated by six vertical marble columns, each topped with gold Doric orders, and the walls to each side displayed intricate gold and inlay patterns. Deep crimson velvet curtains added rich contrast to the shiny gold leaf.

Muller had been able to secure orchestra seats about halfway back, just off the left-hand aisle; they were good seats, and he was pleased.

The members of the orchestra were seated and in a moment the concertmaster strode onto the stage with his violin in hand. They all dutifully tuned their instruments and the concertmaster took his seat. Then the conductor, Bruno Walter, a young man but already a Vienna favorite, entered from the left and took the podium, bowing to the audience, which responded with warm applause.

The audience grew quiet and Walter turned to the orchestra, ready to begin. But then there was a stir in the rear, where the boxes were located, and ripples of applause began, causing Walter to lower his hands, turn and look back. The audience suddenly recognized that the Chancellor, Kurt von Schuschnigg, had entered one of the boxes, and everyone rose to greet him with cheers and applause, some even chanting '*Kurt von Schuschnigg, Kurt von Schuschnigg.*" Bruno Walter on the podium began to applaud and members of the orchestra stood too, clapping enthusiastically.

In the box, Schuschnigg, was clearly embarrassed and sought to quiet the display, motioning for the audience to be seated, then, when it was clear they had no intention of doing so, attempting to direct the applause toward the orchestra.

A spontaneous display of enthusiasm and support, Muller thought, nudging Steffi's shoulder and whispering to her. She nodded, watching intently. Finally, after nearly ten minutes, Schuschnigg took his seat, smiling, and invited the audience to do so too, which they finally did, quieting the hall. Walter turned back to the orchestra and, raising his hands, gave the downbeat.

The Prague Symphony was warmly applauded by the audience when it drew to its melodic close and Bruno Walter exited stage left for the traditional pause before returning to begin the second work of the evening.

Suddenly, an usher appeared in the aisle at their row and, using a penlight, pointed at Steffi, handing her a note. She took it and whispered to Muller.

"It's the hospital; emergency. I have to leave." She stood and gathered her coat from the floor beneath her chair. Muller did the same and they both walked up the aisle to curious stares from other audience members.

Steffi stopped.

"No, you should stay," she said. But Muller shook his head and firmly took her elbow to guide her toward the exit.

As they made their way into the deserted foyer, Steffi again said to him "Paul, you should stay. I hate to ruin your evening too."

"No, it's all right," he said. "What's happened?"

Steffi put on her coat as they walked toward the exit.

"It's a problem with a patient who just delivered a baby. The whole thing was botched. She was in labor for over 24 hours and the nuns wouldn't give her any painkillers. You know how self-righteous nuns are about childbirth."

Steffi paused as they descended the steps and found a taxi.

"Anyway, she was at the end of her rope when one of the doctors decided to intervene with a cesarean operation," she continued, settling in the back seat. "But then during the actual operation, we had one of these anti-Jew attacks when gangs stormed the corridors of the hospital looking for Jews–doctors, nurses, patients, anyone, actually–to beat up. It was pretty horrible, actually," she went on. "I don't have any love for the Jews–they don't belong here as far as I'm concerned; I'm glad to have them out of the way. But you don't just unleash a mob to chase them down in a hospital, for goodness sake.

"Well, the doctor performing the operation is a Jew and he literally ran for his life, leaving the incision open and the surgery incomplete. They called me in to finish it, but it was a chaotic situation. The child was born and is apparently doing fine, but something's happened to the mother, so they called me. Sorry." Steffi patted his hand.

"Actually, you may know the family," she added. "The father's an American radio reporter; isn't he one of the journalists you spend time with?"

"William Shirer?" said Muller.

"Yes, that's it," Steffi responded. "The wife is Tess Shirer."

"I don't know her, but Bill Shirer's become a friend," said Muller. "She's in bad shape?"

Steffi nodded. "That's why they called me. Maybe her husband is here. You could help take care of him while I try to sort out what's wrong with Tess."

"Right," said Muller as the taxi pulled up to the hospital. He paid the fare and they alighted, hurrying up the steps.

"We're certainly dressed for it," he said with a smile.

Muller waited as Steffi ducked into a supply room and emerged a moment later wearing a surgical gown over her dress and a stethoscope hanging around her neck over her pearl necklace.

She checked with an attendant at the desk, then led the way down a corridor and pushed open the door to a room where a woman lay still on a bed with an oxygen mask over her nose and mouth. Peering over Steffi's shoulder, Muller saw Bill Shirer seated next to the bed holding his wife's hand.

"Muller," said Shirer in surprise, looking up at him. "What are you doing here?"

"Surgeon Farber is my...er, my friend; we had a date tonight when she was called here to see your wife," Muller replied. "So sorry there's a problem. I'm here to help too."

"Mr. Shirer; Paul," Steffi said, "the first thing I need you both to do is leave the room so I can conduct an examination. There's a waiting room at the end of that corridor," she pointed. "I'll come find you as soon as I have news. Now go."

They found chairs in the waiting room and Shirer slumped down in exhaustion.

"I can't tell you how bad it's been, Muller," he said. "I was off on assignment when Tess went into labor. CBS had me covering another one of those damned children's choirs–this one in Split on the Adriatic; hard to get to. Ed Murrow was here and managed to deliver Tess to the hospital, but then he had to leave, so there she was, all alone. She had a terrible time in labor but the nuns wouldn't do anything for her. What hypocrites!" He shook his head.

"Dr. Stein finally found out what was happening and took her off to surgery to do a cesarean. Then–while he was performing the operation–a mob stormed the hospital looking for Jews. They literally raced through the corridors grabbing people and using clubs to beat them bloody. Can you imagine it?" Shirer looked at Muller with an expression of disbelief.

"Well, Stein's a Jew. He realized what was happening and just barely escaped down a back staircase. But there was Tess, still on the operating table. Someone ran to find Surgeon Farber and she came in to finish the job the best she could. Somehow our baby girl was born and is doing fine–the nuns at least found a wet nurse for her–but Tess is in terrible pain. She can't move without agony in the wound. I got off the train to come directly here and insisted the hospital get Farber back here to find out what's wrong.

"Where were you when you got the message?" Shirer asked.

"At the Philharmonic performance," Muller replied. "They passed Steffi a note and we left to come right over."

"Well thank you for that," Shirer replied, tapping tobacco into his pipe. "No wonder you're dressed to the nines."

"The most amazing thing happened, Shirer," Muller continued. "Just as the program was about to begin, Schuschnigg ducked into a box in back to attend the concert. He was obviously trying to avoid calling attention to himself by arriving at the very last moment. But people sitting nearby saw him and they began what turned into an absolutely thunderous ovation that went on and on. It was wholly spontaneous and very enthusiastic. Somehow he's struck a patriotic nerve and people are responding to it."

Muller lit a Gitane and pocketed his lighter.

"I wonder if he has the nerve to use this new-found popularity to confront Hitler, somehow," Muller mused. "He hasn't been very imaginative so far; I wonder if he's got something different up his sleeve now?"

At that moment, Steffi Farber appeared in the doorway and sat down next to Shirer. Her surgeon's gown–and her dress beneath, Muller noted–were both streaked with blood.

"Good news, Mr. Shirer. I reopened the incision and immediately discovered that someone–I don't know if it was Dr. Stein or me–had left a small instrument in the wound which was the source of Tess's intense pain. I don't know how it happened; inexcusable, but in the chaotic confusion...." Steffi shook her head.

"I'm deeply embarrassed at the error and the terrible consequences for Tess," she said. "The combination of Jew-haters chasing Jews is no excuse."

"Anyway, I removed it and sewed Tess back up. I've given her sedatives to knock her out for the night; she'll feel better in the morning I'm sure." Steffi stood, turning to Muller.

"Paul, I have to stay. There's practically a war in the emergency room with competing gangs bringing in their wounded and fighting over who's to be treated first. I won't be finished until early morning."

She leaned toward him and planted a kiss on his cheek. "Take Mr. Shirer out for a drink to celebrate his new daughter and a wife who's now out of danger."

# CHAPTER 34

The following Monday, Muller left the hotel early. Ordinarily he didn't arrive at his office with a smile on his face. But this morning was different.

"Frau Metzinger," he said, "walking along the Ringstrasse, I saw a flyer on one of the newsstand kiosk advertising a new Hollywood movie called *Algiers.* It's one I want to see. Can you find out for me where it's playing and the show times?"

"Certainly, Commissioner," she replied and a few minutes later entered his office handing him a note with the theatre address. "Show times are 2PM, 4PM, 6PM and 8PM," she said, adding, "I can't imagine why there would be so many performances of a film about Africa."

Frau Metzinger was unfailingly efficient in matters related to the office, but she certainly was not a movie aficionado, Muller thought as he took the note and thanked her. He was confident that Austrians would flock to the theatre to see this new Hollywood blockbuster about the famed jewel thief Pepe Le Moko holed up in the Casbah. Austrian women would swoon over the suave Charles

Boyer and Austrian men would ogle Hedy Lamarr, the dark-haired beauty making her widely-anticipated American film debut.

"And the theatre is in a rough part of town too," Frau Metzinger sniffed on her way out of the office. "Close to Floridsdorf, where those Socialists still live." She shut the office door firmly with obvious disapproval.

Muller ignored her disdain. He wasn't about to let her pour cold water on the warm memories he had of his time in Hollywood last year and of the friendship he'd kindled with Charles Boyer. He sat back in his office chair and let his mind wander.

Sam and Elise had invited him to a reception at the Brown Derby, the iconic restaurant built to resemble a man's derby hat that was a favorite of the Hollywood glamour set. It was situated on Wilshire Boulevard just up the street from the Ambassador Hotel and its lavish Cocoanut Grove Club.

"The Derby's owned by Jack Warner," Elise informed him," so it's the best. The Grove is where the MGM people hang out; not our kind of place."

Muller smiled, bemused; Hollywood competition even extended to watering holes. He supposed it made sense if you were part of what he'd come to view as a seemingly unending race for one-upsmanship.

His light-hearted mood had continued as Elise and Sam introduced him to guests at the party. He helped himself to champagne flutes being passed and people-watched, moving easily among the formally attired men and women in dazzling gowns. He didn't know anyone, of course; but it amused him to move around in the crowd, listening to snippets of conversation and admiring–he readily admitted–the striking beauty of so many of the women.

At some point, he'd found himself encircled by a clutch of guests. He heard a man over his shoulder speaking English with a decidedly French accent and turned to find himself standing directly before a slender man about his age with dark hair and striking good looks. The man extended his hand.

"Hello," he said, "I'm Charles Boyer," pronouncing his name as a Frenchman would.

Mischievously–maybe it was the champagne, he supposed later–Muller responded in French. "Bonsoir, monsieur. enchanté. Je m'appelle Paul Muller."

Boyer's face lit up in a broad grin. "Encore un Français!" he exclaimed. "Merveilleux! Quelle surprise."

"En effect Suisse," Muller replied, "mais..." and he mimed his best Gallic shrug.

"Ha." Boyer guffawed. He shook Muller's right hand again and draped his left arm over Muller's shoulder, continuing to address him in French. "How splendid to hear our glorious language, even from a Swiss. Hardly anyone here speaks a word, and those that do have a terrible accent."

"Come," he said, taking Muller's elbow and steering them both out of the crowd toward a small cocktail table with two chairs along the wall. "Take a seat and let's chat a moment."

When they were seated, Boyer pulled out a cigarette case and offered one to Muller.

"My God," exclaimed Muller, "are those Gitanes? My very favorite," he said quickly taking one from the case and examining it as Boyer flourished his lighter. "I haven't been able to find them anywhere here in the States," Muller went on. "I ran out months ago, so I've been reduced to Luckies and Camels; I can't decide which is worse."

Boyer laughed. "I have a very secret source that I won't divulge," he said, his eyes sparkling in mirth. "But I can see to it that you receive a couple of cartons right away."

They both sat back, inhaling.

"So, it's Mr. Muller, you said?" Boyer inquired, continuing to converse in French. "I don't believe we've met before. Do you live here or just passing through?"

Muller explained that he was visiting his cousin and her husband, pointing out Elise in her dark purple gown across the way. Boyer inquired further and Muller had finally admitted that he'd spent time in Danzig as a diplomat, but that he he'd resigned and decided to leave the travails of Europe behind and travel in the United States.

Boyer's face turned serious.

Muller immediately regretted raising the subject, but Boyer raised his palm.

"Mr. Muller, I'm very apprehensive about what is happening now in Europe. There seems to be nobody in this town who knows much of anything about it–or cares, for that matter–and it's damnably difficult to get any European news here. It's intensely frustrating, so I'm delighted to meet a fellow European who actually seems to know something about the subject–and can even converse about it in French. So don't apologize even for an instant; you've made my evening."

Boyer stood and motioned for a waiter with a tray of champagne flutes, exchanged their empty ones, then sat down, lifting his glass to clink Muller's.

"Santé," he said with a smile.

"Tell me about your involvement with Danzig, that symbolic little city situated between the Nazis and the Poles."

Muller had just begun to describe his League of Nations assignment when a white-tied formally-attired head waiter began striking a triangle and requesting guests to move to the dining room where dinner was about to be served. At that moment, an attractive brunette in a striking red gown approached their table.

"Darling, it's time to go in," she said to Boyer, speaking with a very evident British accent.

Muller and Boyer immediately stood.

Switching back to English, Boyer greeted her and gestured toward Muller.

"I've discovered another French speaker, cherie," he said, taking her hand. "Mr. Muller, this is my wife Pat; Pat, meet Mr. Muller my new Swiss friend."

Muller bowed and raised Pat's gloved hand to his lips in a very continental fashion. "Enchantė," he said, adding "It's very nice to meet you," in English.

Boyer laughed. "See what I mean, cherie? He even has proper manners in addition to his language skills."

Pat Boyer put her arm through her husband's.

"Charles does enjoy discovering Europeans," she said smiling at Muller. "I'm British and, along with our American hosts, we are dismissed as 'Anglo Saxons' by the haughty French. But I'm afraid we second-class citizens must summon you both to dinner."

"Yes, yes," Boyer responded, "but Mr. Muller, we must fix a date to meet. Will you join me–us," he added, glancing at his wife, "for dinner Monday night at the Beverly Hills Tennis Club? They have a marvelous terrace."

Something in Muller's demeanor must have given him away.

"Wait, you play, don't you?" Boyer asked.

Muller grinned and nodded. "Not as often as I'd like, but yes."

"Splendid," Boyer replied with a broad smile. "Come at 5 with your kit and we'll play a set before cocktails."

Muller agreed and they shook hands. Boyer and his wife headed for their table in the dining room, while Muller searched for Elise and Sam and their hosts, whom he found at the bar.

"Paul," said Elise as they strode toward the dining room, "do you realize whom you were just speaking with?

Muller replied, "Well, yes; he's a Frenchman named Charles Boyer.

"That's not just Charles Boyer," she said; "that's *Charles Boyer*! He's one of the biggest movie stars in the *world*!" She covered her mouth with her hand, giggling. "Every woman in the room was watching," she said speaking in an undertone. "He's a matinee idol and such a Hollywood *heartthrob*." She burst out laughing again.

When they were seated, Muller could see Boyer several tables away. He'd never met a movie star before, but looking at him now, Muller could see that the man really did have a striking appearance. He had an oval face with perfectly-centered eyebrows arched above wide set dark eyes and a long, very straight aquiline nose. His sleek dark hair was parted just so, above his left eyebrow. His new movie star friend looked very handsome indeed, Muller decided, and smiled to himself.

Toward the end of the evening, on his way out, Boyer came up to their table and nodded to the guests before placing two Gitane cigarettes next to Muller's plate.

"These are all that remain, I'm afraid," he said. "But I'll have a supply for you when we see each other on Monday." He tapped Muller's shoulder in a friendly gesture and waved as he walked away.

"Bonsoir, tout le monde."

Elise burst out laughing and poked Muller in the ribs.

The following Monday, Muller drove his rented Chevrolet to the Beverly Hills Tennis Club, an extravagant structure with incongruous Federal style columns facing a circular drive that was lined with towering palm trees. He handed the keys to a valet and was ushered into a wide entryway with a view of red clay courts and the San Bernardino Mountains rising beyond.

He was shown to the men's locker room where an attendant led him to a locker that had been set aside for him. Mr. Boyer had not yet arrived, he was told, but was expected at any moment.

Ready to play his part, Muller changed into his white tennis trousers and short-sleeved shirt; he pulled on his white tennis sneakers, picked up his racket and strode out toward the courts. A bronzed, athletic-appearing man came up to him and introduced himself as the head professional.

"Ned Roundtree, sir," he said. "Mr. Boyer's staff just called to say he was delayed on the set but was on his way and suggested that we rally for a few minutes until he arrives."

Ten minutes later Charles Boyer jogged over to their court.

"Thanks, Ned for taking care of my guest," he said to the pro, then walked to Muller's side of the court smiling and shook hands warmly, shifting into French.

"Sorry to be late," he said. "Hedy Lamarr is just impossible. Beautiful woman, but no actress at all; every scene takes forever. She can't even get her lines right." Boyer shook his head. "But finally we finished for the day and here I am, ready to conquer. Let's start. You serve."

They played a spirited set. Muller was the better player and won the set 6-3, but Boyer had a clever serve with spin that was hard to handle and the occasional effective cross-court backhand. It was getting dark though, so they decided one set was enough.

Back inside the clubhouse, Boyer reached into his locker, a few spaces down from Muller's and handed him two cartons of Gitanes.

"Enjoy them," he said, ignoring Muller's protestations. "I can get plenty more."

After they showered and changed, Boyer led the way to the terrace bar. They ordered drinks and took seats at a table where they could watch the setting sun reflect on the distant mountains.

"I am really sorry for being late," Boyer said accepting one of Muller's Gitanes and his light. "I'm doing a film called *Algiers*, he said, "You probably know the French film *Pepė Le Moko* from last year?

Muller nodded. "Jean Gabin played Pepé, I think."

"Right," said Boyer. "Well, Hollywood has decided that America is ready to be introduced to that clever jewel thief and to the souks of the Casbah. This time, I'm Pepė." He added smiling, "much better looking than Jean Gabin.

Quickly he became serious. "But it's become a nightmare to film. Along with the problems with Hedy, the cinematographer, Jimmy Wong, keeps fiddling with the lighting, trying to get the shadows so they correspond with some real takes of Algiers that were shot on site."

He sighed, "So it's slow going, but in the end, I think it'll be good."

Then with a sly expression, he switched back to English

"Come wiz me to zee Casbah," he said, his French accent on full display. "That's how it'll be known." He winked; then burst out laughing.

"Showbiz," he said, again in English with a grin. Then, switching back to French, "But let's speak of more serious matters. Tell me what you were doing in Danzig."

Muller related the tale of his appointment by the League of Nations as Secretary to the League's High Commissioner and the struggle that ensued to keep the Free City from falling into the hands of the Nazis. Boyer knew only fragments of the story and kept interrupting, wanting more details, obviously intrigued with the politics of the conflict as it had unfolded.

Several cocktails later, still deep in conversation, they didn't notice Pat Boyer who'd approached the table. Finally, she reached out and put her hand on her husband's shoulder. Boyer was startled, then both he and Muller leapt to their feet in embarrassment.

She motioned them to resume their places and seated herself on the chair nearest Muller.

"I'm only here for a moment," she said. "I don't want to interrupt you and I'll only stay for one drink, but I didn't want to leave without saying hello."

Muller was again struck by her heavy British accent.

"Welcome cherie'" said Boyer. "Mr. Muller was just explaining to me his role in Danzig and his dealings with your friend Anthony Eden."

Pat Boyer took the olive from the martini that had been delivered and popped it into her mouth. "I wish he *were* a friend," she said with a smile. "He's very handsome with that sandy red hair and matching mustache. And I do admire his leadership in advancing Britain's appeasement policy." She turned to Muller, "You must be an admirer too if you dealt with him on that issue."

Muller hesitated, and Boyer broke in.

"Actually, cherie, he's not a supporter of appeasement at all," he said, smiling at her, but being deliberately provocative.

"So are you a warmonger, then?" Pat asked Muller, in an equally provocative way.

Before Muller could respond, Boyer interrupted again.

"No, cherie, Mr. Muller's not the warmonger; *Hitler* is." He grinned triumphantly at his wife before turning back to Muller.

"Mr. Muller, my wife and I have this kind of friendly but quite profound disagreement about British policy toward Hitler nearly every day. I'm so glad you could be here to witness today's version and I'm hoping you'll also be brave enough to inform the intrepid Mrs. Boyer why her support for Mr. Eden and his policy is so much poppycock."

Muller found himself amused by this exchange, but also a little nonplussed about how to respond.

He bought a little time to think by offering up his Gitanes and a light, but they were obviously waiting for him to proceed.

"I have no reason to doubt for a moment the seriousness with which Minister Eden approaches his dealings with Chancellor Hitler," he said a little stiffly. Feeling awkward, but having begun, Muller decided to plunge on, "but I'm afraid I fail to see that appeasement has delivered any results. Britain–and France for that matter too, though to a lesser extent–has made one concession after another to Germany, seeking to entice Hitler into some kind of new European peace agreement. But my impression is that Hitler has simply pocketed their concessions, then upped the ante by making more–and more unacceptable–demands, all the while refusing to entertain the broader arrangement that Eden's trying to negotiate. So I think it's been a bust, frankly."

"I don't mean to sound impolite," he added, smiling at Pat and spreading his hands in a friendly fashion. "There are many statesmen wiser than I who would strongly disagree, and who continue to applaud appeasement as being absolutely the correct approach. But for whatever its worth, that's my opinion."

Pat Boyer took a long drag on her cigarette, fixing Muller with a level gaze.

"Mr. Muller, I very much hope that you're mistaken," she said. Then smiling at both men she added, "but I certainly understand why my husband was looking forward to speaking with you this evening."

Finishing her drink and stubbing out her cigarette, she stood to leave. "Don't be too late," she said to Boyer.

"Come wiz me to zee Casbah," he said to her in a stage whisper, then grinned and kissed her lightly on the cheek.

They had continued to converse over dinner and into the evening, Muller remembered. Boyer was a sophisticated observer of European politics and they had a spirited discussion. It had been thoroughly enjoyable and they had met twice more before Muller departed for New York a month later. At these subsequent dinners, in addition to their political discussions, Boyer had shared gossip and funny stories about filming *Algiers.* By the time he left California, Muller had felt a little like one of the stagehands on the set.

So he was not about to miss the chance now to finally see the finished product. As Muller exited his office in mid-afternoon to catch the 4 PM show, he walked past the desk where Frau Metzinger was typing, studiously ignoring his departure.

He was able to restrain himself from whispering 'Come wiz me to zee Casbah'.

# CHAPTER 35

Muller thoroughly enjoyed the movie. While the plot was thin and the dialogue stilted, the lighting and the face shots were hugely entertaining. It quickly became apparent that James Wong, the cinematographer, had succeeded brilliantly in creating an atmosphere of mystery and intrigue with his almost magical black and white imagery of the souks. And by God, Hedy Lamarr looked gorgeous as the camera lingered over her perfect face and hair. But it was Charles Boyer's performance in bringing Pepé Le Moko to life that Muller enjoyed most–especially the funny scenes where he wore a fez. Boyer had told him that the fez was made of wool and was so uncomfortable that he made them sew in a silk liner. Well, it certainly looked good on screen to Muller. At the end, when Pepé–hopelessly smitten with Gaby, Lamarr's character–leaves the protection of the Casbah, Muller was rooting for him to get aboard the waiting steamship and escape. But of course, he was shot and killed by the detective, with Gaby–unaware of the drama–departing on the vessel.

The lights in the theatre came up and Muller's mind was still on the film as he put on his hat and coat and exited through the glass doors. He was smiling at the image of Boyer leading the police on merry chases through the souks, always able to lose them and laughing as they plunged past his hiding places.

Muller had just stepped outside when, suddenly, a projectile struck the wall above him, showering him with plaster and glass, and he was shoved back against the theatre doors by a surge of bodies pushing one another. Muller tried to refocus his attention. What was happening? The overhead lights of the theatre canopy made it difficult to see into the street where darkness had fallen. Suddenly alert, he could hear loud shouts but couldn't identify them. The crowd of moviegoers exiting the theatre seemed to be getting pinned back against the theater doors by another crowd in the street. Then he caught sight of clubs being swung and heard the unmistakable sound of fighting.

Christ! They'd walked out of the theatre directly into a street brawl.

The crowd suddenly was shoved to its right and several club-wielding men began shouting and pushing around the edge. Another projectile struck the wall to Muller's left and glass splinters fell causing some in the crowd to scream and creating a sense of panic. The theatre doors behind them were locked and people began flailing at one another trying to find a way to escape. One of the brawlers, a big man with a beard and a bloody wound on his head was driven into the crowd, knocking people to the ground. Muller saw a red bandana on the man's sleeve and realized he was a Nazi fighter. That was not an encouraging sign.

Two other fighters crashed into the theatre-goers as they wrestled with one another. People were shoved to the ground and more fighters seemed to wade into the crowd, which was now in a full panic. Muller was nearly bowled over by a fighter who was knocked down by two attackers. He elbowed his way over the prone body, gaining a few feet of room before another crowd surge drove him to his knees. Using his elbows for leverage, he was able to regain his footing and as he finally straightened up he found himself pressed against a woman whose back was against the theatre doors. He realized with a start that he was looking directly into the face of Marte von Papen, the wife of the German Ambassador. Her eyes were wide with terror and her mouth hung slack. Acting on instinct, Muller circled her waist with his right arm and used his left shoulder and arm to try and gain traction and move toward the corner of the theatre entryway.

"Frau von Papen," Muller shouted in her ear, "we need to get out of here. Please hang onto my arm."

Marte's eyes blinked as she tried to focus on Muller, but she nodded and began to slide along the locked doors in the direction he was trying to lead.

By this time, more brawlers had crashed into the theatre crowd and bodies were hopelessly entangled as people were shoved and pushed against one another in the struggle. Muller kept pressing on to his right, using his elbow and shoulder and occasionally kicking or using his knee to push his way along. Finally, he spied the edge of the entryway and with one final shove was able to propel both himself and Marte around a corner. But they stumbled into another maelstrom of bodies struggling with one another. Suddenly a series of projectiles–paving stones, Muller reckoned–struck several of the men, knocking them to the ground. Grabbing Marte hard by her waist and forcing them both to duck their heads, Muller found a way for them to step over the prone bodies and gain some room to run several steps past the corner.

Glancing up and looking for more space to move away, he could dimly see men running in their direction, waving clubs and screaming loudly, clearly headed for the brawl. Muller threw Marte to the ground against the wall and fell atop her trying to protect them both against attack, but the reinforcements ran past them toward the main brawl at the corner. Once they were past, Muller rose, with his arm tightly around Marte's waist, and they began to trot along the street away from the fighting.

By now, Muller's eyes had adjusted to the dark and streetlights offered enough illumination to allow him to get better oriented. In a few steps they were at another corner and he led them into a street that was a bit wider and better lit and didn't seem to harbor more fighters.

Stopping a moment to look around, Muller turned to Marte.

"Can you run another block or so? I think we can get out of here."

"Yes," she replied, and they scuttled along, bent over and keeping to the shadows, moving as fast as they could. Finally a still wider street appeared to their left. Muller couldn't read the street name but he led them around the corner. Suddenly everything appeared normal; they could see shoppers strolling on the sidewalks and automobiles on the street; everyone seemed to be going about their ordinary business.

A coffeehouse was near the corner. Muller motioned toward it and Marte nodded.

The proprietor looked at them in surprise as they entered, shoving open the door hard and panting, looking over their shoulders.

"What's going on?" he asked, "Are you all right?" He took the towel off his shoulder and began wiping pieces of plaster and glass shards off their coats.

"We walked out of the movie theatre and got caught in a street brawl," said Muller. They were both breathing hard and they stood, looking at the room half-filled with patrons quietly seated at tables.

"We're lucky to be alive."

The proprietor led them to a booth and took their coats, hanging them on a peg and wiping off more debris.

"What terrible times we're living in," he said shaking his head. "But it's safe here."

"Can you bring us two double whiskies?" asked Muller.

"Right away, sir," said the proprietor.

Marte slid into the booth and seemed to melt into the back corner, her head against the wall and her eyes closed. She trembled and Muller could see her clenching and unclenching her fists.

"Fucking...Nazi...Swine...," she said slowly, hissing the individual words, her eyes still closed.

Then she sat up eyes wide open and pounded a fist on the table.

"God, how I detest them."

She grabbed the drink that had been placed in front of her and took a long gulp, choking and coughing slightly at the whiskey's bite. She placed the drink back on the table and looked directly at Muller, who had taken the seat across from her in the booth.

"I don't know who you are, but thank you for rescuing me from those Nazi brutes," she said angrily, shaking her head. "They are such bastards, and they just don't care. I'd probably be lying dead in the gutter if you hadn't gotten me out of there. So thank you."

She took another long swallow of whiskey.

"Frau von Papen, my name is Paul Muller, I'm the League of Nations Commissioner General for Austria and we met–well, not met, but we spoke to one another–at the reception in the Chancellery a few nights ago. I recognized you," Muller said.

"You were at the movie tonight too?" Marte asked.

Muller nodded. "I had no idea that we were walking out of the theatre into a street riot. We were lucky to escape."

Marte finished her drink and Muller signaled for two more.

"I don't know that I've ever met a Commissioner General," she said, a slight smile softening her features. "That's a formidable title. You say that we spoke to one another at that reception? I would have thought I'd remember."

"It was very quick and unimportant," Muller replied. "Your husband was making his way toward other more important guests and brushed past me without a word. You followed a couple of steps behind and apologized, saying that your husband was sometimes a bit rude when he was headed through a crowd toward someone he needed to speak to. That was it; but I was flattered that you had spoken to me and, well–I remembered your face tonight when we were shoved into one another."

Marte smiled at him. "I'm afraid I still don't recall," she said. "But I'm sure it happened that way. I'd like to have a pfennig for every time I've had to apologize for Franz' boorish behavior. For once a good deed goes unpunished."

Marte picked up her new drink and clinked the glass against Muller's glass.

"So, Mr. Muller, what is it that the Commissioner General of the League of Nations for Austria does here in Vienna?"

When Muller thought back about it later, he couldn't explain what prompted his response–relief at escaping the mob, a hangover of bravado from the movie, a sense of attraction to Marte?

But he'd proceeded to reply, "Well, among other things I'm trying to stop Hitler's plan to take over Austria that your husband is busy promoting."

Marte's face registered surprise and she drew back her head as if to absorb what Muller had just said. Then she slapped the table with her hand and broke into peals of laughter.

"Oh my," she said continuing to laugh, wiping her eyes that were beginning to tear up in mirth. "That is *so rich*; I love it," and she burst into a new round of laughter, again slapping the table, this time more softly.

"Ahh," she said finally, blowing her nose and shaking her head. "I can just see the headline, 'League Diplomat Rescues German Ambassador's Wife in Plot to Thwart Hitler'

"Ha!" she said, pausing to blow her nose again. "This is simply *too wonderful*."

Muller felt embarrassed.

"I shouldn't have said that," he said, looking around him for eavesdroppers. "I just blurted it out. Sorry."

"Don't be sorry," Marte said. "I'll help you. I don't want that vulgar little Austrian housepainter to succeed; I want him taken down a few pegs–the way it was meant to be at the start when we were supposed to control him, not the other way around."

She accepted Muller's offer of a Gitane and his light, taking another large swallow from her drink.

"So is taking in a movie matinee part of your plan to derail Hitler's takeover plot?" she asked, with a playful smile. "If so, you can certainly count me in for that part."

"I'm afraid that was a bit of indulgence," Muller replied, still feeling embarrassed. "You see, I was in California last year–in

Hollywood, actually, visiting a cousin–and through a series of coincidences I became acquainted with Charles Boyer. We played tennis and had drinks and dinner a few times; he shared stories with me about filming *Algiers* and when I saw it was playing, I had to come see it.

Muller spread his hands. "No secret plan; just a case of playing hooky, I'm afraid."

Marte fixed Muller with a gaze of such intensity that he was startled and sat back against the wall of the booth.

"What's the matter?" he asked.

Marte wagged her head slowly, still gazing intently at him. Finally she spoke.

"Charles Boyer too?" She took a deep breath.

"This is about the most remarkable afternoon I've ever experienced," she said, finishing her drink and nodding when he motioned for another round.

"I snuck out of the residence to go see *Algiers* because I'm hopelessly smitten with Charles Boyer–who's the handsomest man in the entire world; I fantasize about him nearly every night. So I had to come and see the movie. I was enchanted by it and then, when it was over, I walk outside and find myself attacked in a street brawl where I thought I would be killed; I'm rescued by man who turns out to be a diplomat, in fact a 'Commissioner General'– which is itself, by the way, a highly attractive title–who's trying to defeat Hitler's–and my husband's–plan to take over Austria. This is itself a very full plate for a single afternoon.

"Then it turns out that this gallant Commissioner General is also best friends with my heartthrob Charles Boyer."

Marte then put her hand over Muller's on the table top and gave him a big smile.

"As I see it, the only proper way to finish off a day like this is for you to take me back to your room and play Charles Boyer while I fuck you as hard as I can."

"What do you say, Mr. Commissioner General?"

# CHAPTER 36

Muller lay in the tangled bedsheets, half sitting with a pillow behind him as he smoked his Gitane. Marte had unwound herself from his body and gone into the bathroom to draw a warm bath. He stretched and flexed his muscles; it had been a very vigorous session of passionate lovemaking. Muller realized that he had never been with an older woman before–he thought Marte was surely over forty–but that certainly had been no deterrent. When they got to his suite at the hotel, they'd torn off their clothes, flung the bedcovers aside and Marte had mounted him with such urgency that they'd both climaxed almost immediately. She then rolled under him, locked her legs behind his neck and they began again. And again.

Muller reached over to the phone on the nearby bed table and called room service to order a plate of cold meats and a nice bottle of Gevrey-Chambertin burgundy. He threw on a pair of trousers and a sweater, and lit two candles on the small table close to the window. When the waiter came, Muller had him set the plates and wine properly before departing discreetly.

Marte came out of the bathroom clad in his large white bathrobe, her hair rolled up in a towel. She paused at the doorway, looking at him, curtsied, and blew him a kiss as she entered the sitting room.

"You look very nice, Frau von Papen," Muller said.

"Oh please," she replied smiling, "I think we know each other well enough now for you to address me as Marte." She walked up to where he was seated and ruffled his hair before taking the other chair.

"But of course, you shall remain my 'gallant Commissioner General', not just Paul Muller aka Charles Boyer."

She toasted him with the glass of wine, "Santé," and began nibbling at the assorted meats.

"I've been thinking about ways I can sabotage my husband's plans to help Hitler take over Austria," she said matter-of-factly. "I'm afraid I haven't come up with a solution yet. But be confident that your secret is safe with me. I'll do nothing to help that nasty little Austrian housepainter succeed."

Marte accepted Muller's Gitane and light.

"There are some things you need to know," she said.

"First, while my husband and I remain married, we've not lived together as husband and wife for a long time. That's one of the reasons I am here with you tonight," she said. "A woman needs to have a little fun now and then," she added, smiling. "But the more important point is that while I have continued to perform my public responsibilities as the wife of a high-ranking official in the

German government, I despise that government and I especially despise Herr Hitler, whom I consider to be both vulgar and a menace.

"Franz doesn't disagree with these sentiments," she continued; "he considers the whole Nazi apparatus to be beneath him and he constantly looks down on them. I remember him telling me years ago, when he first met Hitler, how absurd he found his appearance–the silly little mustache and those garish uniforms–and how contemptuous he was of Hitler's lower class accent. So we share a common disdain for the man.

"But Franz is an inveterate schemer. He's always chased power, and having tasted it–you'll remember he was briefly the Chancellor in 1932–he's obsessed with getting it back, and he's always looking for ways to pull strings and exercise influence. So he continues to engage with Hitler, doing whatever he needs to do to remain in the game.

"And I," said Marte as she stubbed out her butt, "grit my teeth and, always smiling, dutifully follow along in his wake."

"You find that distasteful," said Muller refilling their wine glasses.

"Very," she replied. Then she paused, swirling her wine in the glass.

"I suppose we're both really waiting in the wings in the hope that Hitler will stumble and be pushed out of power," she added. "He's taken huge risks and he's made a lot of enemies; he may well be vulnerable. If that should happen, Franz will try to take advantage of the fallout that would ensue. So I'm sticking around, at least for now."

"I just wish I had more confidence in Franz' skills at political intrigue," she added. "He doesn't have a very good track record of success."

"He's prone to making mistakes?" Muller asked.

Unfortunately, that's been a pattern," Marte replied.

"Actually, some of the schemes are amusing," she went on. "For example, he began his career as a German diplomat in Mexico when the Mexican Revolution broke out. He got right in the middle of things and began running guns to the Mexican General who'd mounted the coup. But he was backing the wrong horse; the Americans supported a different General who proceeded to take power and Franz had to flee for his life. Not an auspicious start to a career," she added.

"But then he was sent to Washington as a military attaché at the outbreak of the Great War. Well, Franz proceeded to stir up all the trouble he could there. He sabotaged companies in the U.S. that were allied with the British and French and set up an operation to forge U.S. passports for Germans in the Western hemisphere to use in returning to Germany. His most bizarre plan was to organize German-Americans to invade Canada and knock it out of the war."

"Is that true?" Muller asked.

"Absolutely," Marte replied. "His plan was to blow up bridges and railroads in Canada on a scale that would force them to abandon plans to send soldiers to Europe to fight the Germans. He organized a scheme to destroy the Welland Canal in the Great Lakes and he hired someone who actually blew up a railroad bridge somewhere in Maine that was owned by the Canadian Pacific Railroad. But the guy got caught and the subsequent investigation led right to Franz. His diplomatic immunity protected him from arrest, but ultimately the U.S. declared him *persona non grata* and deported him back to Germany."

"In fact," Marte added, "Franz was indicted in the U.S. for his Welland Canal plot and that indictment remained on the books until 1932 when he became Chancellor and he managed to get it dropped." Marte shook her head ruefully. "So we couldn't visit the U.S. during all that time, because he'd be arrested and put on trial."

Muller smiled. "I see what you're getting at.

"But earlier tonight, at the coffee shop, you said that you wanted to take Hitler down a few pegs so you–I assume that means Ambassador von Papen–would control him and not the other way around. Then you went on to say, 'that's the way it was meant to be at the start'.

"What did you mean by that, if I may ask?"

Marte sighed. "Well, that's his biggest failure of all. You see, Franz was the man most responsible for Hitler being named Chancellor in 1933. He was confident that he and other German political leaders in the cabinet could control Hitler like a harmless puppet while they really ran everything.

"Ha." she added bitterly, reaching for another Gitane. "As we all know, that plan didn't work out so well. Hitler completely outmaneuvered them all in a matter of weeks and assumed total control."

"What actually happened?" asked Muller. "How did your husband become the key to Hitler's appointment?"

"It's so depressing to recall," Marte replied, shrugging further into the bathrobe and pulling her legs up beneath herself. "It's a big part of why we became estranged." She took a sip of wine and paused, as if lost in thought, before continuing.

"My Franz–when he chooses to be–can be utterly charming, and for years, he lavished his attentions on Paul von Hindenburg, who was President of the Weimar Republic–which was the German government at the time, as you will remember. Hindenburg by then was in his mid-80s and increasingly he leaned on Franz, who flattered him, beguiled him with funny stories and became practically a member of his household. Franz was a prominent Catholic Conservative but he had no independent powerbase and his sudden appointment as Chancellor in June 1932 was attributable solely to Hindenburg's affection for him. But that autumn, Franz was forced to resign and new elections took place. Hitler's Nazi Party won about a third of the votes and he demanded that Hindenburg appoint him Chancellor. Hindenburg was disdainful of Hitler and refused, so there was a deadlock.

"This was a bad time in Germany, Paul," Marte went on, spearing a few slices of meat with her fork and taking another sip of wine. "It was the depths of the Depression, with millions out of work; rival gangs of Communists, trade unionists and Nazis were roaming the streets–and not just in Berlin, but across Germany.

"Something had to be done to break the impasse, and my Franz came up with the solution: name Hitler Chancellor, but name him–Franz–Vice-Chancellor and let him oversee appointment of a cabinet in which politicians opposed to Hitler would make up a majority. All Cabinet decisions required a majority vote to become law, so since Franz would run the Cabinet, he would hold all the cards and Hitler would be effectively under his thumb.

"And that's essentially what happened. Hindenburg appointed Hitler, believing he could rely upon Franz to run things and keep Hitler in check."

"Except he couldn't," said Muller.

Marte nodded. "Hitler may be vulgar and a menace, as I said a moment ago. But he's also very clever–and he's absolutely ruthless. He never hesitated a moment.

"Only three days after being appointed to office, Hitler disbanded the Parliament demanding a new vote. Then, three weeks later, the Nazis staged the Reichstag fire which burned the parliament building to the ground. That incident was a terrible shock to the entire country. Hitler blamed the Communists for the fire and Hindenburg granted him emergency powers to suspend civil liberties and restore order. In the ensuing uproar, Hitler replaced the Weimar Constitution with a measure called the Enabling Act, which empowered the Chancellor to rule the nation by decree.

"So, within sixty days of assuming office as Franz' puppet Chancellor, Hitler had completely changed the system. No more Weimar, no more cabinet, and no more Parliament. The only office left standing was that of the Chancellor–occupied of course by Adolf Hitler–who was now the dictator of Germany."

"It all happened so quickly," Marte said quietly; "in the blink of an eye."

"So did Hitler remove your husband from office?" asked Muller, pouring the last of the wine.

"No," replied Marte. "That was the strange part," she went on, unwinding, then rewinding her hair in the towel. "Nothing seemed to have changed. Franz remained in office and went about his business as usual, even continuing to nurture his relationship with Hindenburg, the two of them plotting ways to restore Franz' plan of cabinet government that would oversee Hitler and keep him under control.

"And it wasn't just Franz," said Marte. "No one at the time seemed to grasp the fact that they had just become powerless.

"Well, that illusion was abruptly shattered by all the murders–the Night of the Long Knives." Marte paused, swirling her wine. "The spectacle of the German Chancellor murdering his political adversaries–how many, a hundred or more; who really knows?–was a complete shock. It was horrible. People don't behave that way–or so we thought–until confronted with the reality that Hitler *did* act that way. He even went on the radio to brag about the murders and to warn any future opponents that he would kill them too."

"It must have been terrifying for you and your husband," said Muller. "Were you targets?"

"Franz certainly was," Marte replied. "The SS raided his office in the Chancellery and shot two of his staff members."

"He escaped?"

Marte shook her head. "We were placed under house arrest at our villa in Berlin. Soldiers surrounded the whole place and cut our telephone lines. We knew something was going on, but neither of us was expecting Hitler to unleash the SS and commit wholesale murder.

"Bang, bang!" she said, flicking her hand like a pistol; "Just like that.

"It was unforgiveable." Marte used the back of her hand to wipe her eyes that had teared up.

She sighed. "When they finally released us, Franz went to the Chancellery. His office had been ransacked and there was blood everywhere. Hitler was meeting in a nearby conference room with the Nazi leadership–the ones that had survived the purge, at least–and there was no seat for Franz at the table. So he resigned. Hitler accepted and no successor was appointed.

"But that wasn't the end of it," Marte continued, using a napkin to blow her nose. "A little while later Hitler summoned Franz to his office and–as if nothing had happened–assured him that he remained in Hitler's good graces. He told Franz that he thought it would be smart for him to absent himself from Berlin for a while, so he was appointing him Ambassador to Austria. 'I have important business to accomplish there,' he told Franz, and 'I'm going to depend on you to help me succeed'.

"Franz, ever alert to the opportunity to regain influence, accepted immediately, assuring Hitler that he would do whatever was required to achieve Hitler's goals in Austria.

"Which we now know, gallant Commissioner General, means helping Hitler gobble up Austria–a goal which you've told me that you oppose."

Marte looked levelly at Muller.

"Unfortunately, it's not Franz' plans that you're opposing; those have a way of failing, as I've described.

"No," she said; "you're opposing Hitler's plans, and *his* plans always seem to succeed."

Marte stood.

It's time for me to get dressed and leave," she said smiling at him, bending to plant a kiss on his cheek as she walked to the bathroom.

"I was going to invite you to ravish me one more time, but I'm afraid I'm not in the mood anymore."

## CHAPTER 37

Otto Schultz met Muller for lunch the next day, choosing Wolfe's, as usual. He appeared haggard and Muller noticed that his shirt was wrinkled and spotted.

"It's a very difficult time," Schultz said, as if reading Muller's mind. "You can't imagine the pressure Schuschnigg's under. He's been betrayed and he's angry about it. He and Seyss-Inquart are practically at sword's points; they quarrel in cabinet and Seyss-Inquart has done us real damage in the countryside. But Schuschnigg is courageous and, as I've described him to you before, he's very stubborn. He refuses to capitulate to Hitler and he's taken new steps to change the lineup of forces in his favor."

Schultz waved away the sausage and sauerkraut that Wolfe brought to the table. "I'm too tired to eat," he said, thanking Wolfe.

Turning back to Muller, he said, "Schuschnigg has laid the foundation for empowering the Left and deploying them against his Nazi adversaries. It's a bold move that could mobilize a big chunk of society that's been essentially marginalized and bring it into the fight on his side. Together, the Fatherland Front and the

Left could generate enough strength to overwhelm the local Nazis. He thinks Hitler's threat of invasion is a bluff and that he'll be forced to back down when he sees the Austrian Nazis losing power to this new alliance. He concluded that it's a way to win and preserve Austria–which he's determined to do, even if it means resurrecting old enemies.

"But it would be a big change," Schultz went on, "make no mistake about that. The Fatherland Front has effectively been at war with the Left for 20 years or more, so there's fierce resistance to this policy change within the party. For some, it's an unthinkable maneuver. But it's the only hope we've got to avoid being swallowed up by the Nazis, and I've been encouraging it."

"How did this come about?" Muller asked, offering Schultz a Gitane and a light which he accepted, coughing as he inhaled, then wiping his mouth with the back of his hand before continuing.

"The key leadership of the Left–the men who've been exiled but remain in charge and continue to call the shots–concluded that they need to join forces with the Fatherland Front to oppose Hitler. It's that simple. They and their members hate the Front. But they look at what the Nazis have done to labor and the Social Democrats in Germany and they're terrified that the same thing will be repeated here if Hitler takes over. So, they prepared a plan to back Schuschnigg and resist the Nazis if he agrees to restore their basic rights. They presented the plan to me and I gave it to Schuschnigg. The timing was right, because Schuschnigg had concluded that finding allies on the Left was his only available option. So, he agreed to meet with them and the process has started."

Schultz paused and asked Wolfe to bring him some toasted bread with butter and a cup of tea.

"Have you noticed that in the streets you now see men wearing the socialist Three Arrow badge?" he asked. "It was banned, of course; jail time if you were caught wearing it. But now, it's competing with the Swastikas that are being more openly flaunted too."

"Well, no," Muller replied. "I wouldn't have known to look for it. But I certainly have seen the swastika appearing nearly everywhere. The last several nights have been filled with demonstrations and marches. No uniforms, but everything else. They seem to be trying to take over the city. It looks like just a matter of time until they mount some kind of coup to get rid of Schuschnigg."

"It looks that way to him too," said Schultz, spilling crumbs of toast as he spoke. "That's why he's going to drop a bombshell in a speech tomorrow night that will change the whole equation. The new alliance with the Left is a key part of the plan and it will set everyone back on their heels."

"I suppose you won't tell me the plan," Muller said teasingly.

"Listen to the speech and decide for yourself," Schultz replied, rising to leave. "It had better work or Austria is doomed."

He waved at Muller and disappeared through the doorway.

# CHAPTER 38

When Muller arrived back at his hotel, the concierge handed him an envelope.

"A message came in for you on the telex, Mr. Muller," he said. "I took the liberty of treating it confidentially."

Muller thanked him and took the envelope into the bar to open. He extracted the telex flimsy.

"AE resigned last evening. Spoke to House today. Backed away from challenge to NC. Off to Cap Ferrat with tennis racquet. Pity." RCS Stevenson.

Muller ordered a nightcap and reflected on the news. At least he'd tried; he'd gotten to meet with Eden and made his case. He couldn't very well put himself in Eden's shoes, but he found it strange that a man with Eden's unquestioned gifts of political and leadership skills would, when the chance presented itself, shrink from reaching for the gold ring.

Muller sighed and finished the last of his brandy. There would be no help for Austria from the British Government; its isolation was now confirmed.

# CHAPTER 39

The next day, Vienna was shut down for business as political demonstrations surged through downtown and nearby neighborhoods. Police didn't attempt to break up the marches but for the most part were able to steer marchers away from challenging one another. There were a few melees and ambulances could be heard delivering bloodied brawlers to local hospitals. But much of the day passed without major violence as organizers seemed content to avoid direct confrontations. Word had spread about the Chancellor's evening speech and there was a sense of anticipation that something important was about to happen.

That afternoon, the Fatherland Front organized a rally at the West Banhof as a sendoff for Schuschnigg, who had decided to deliver his speech in Innsbruck–his birthplace and the city that had been his political base since entering political life. He still spoke with a Tyrol accent and over the years he had regularly invoked the nearby Alpine mountains as a source of personal and political strength.

He was probably going to need all the strength he could muster, Muller thought as he tried to navigate the city and avoid the competing demonstrations.

Back in his hotel room, Muller decided to it was time to take precautions and prepare for what might need to be a hasty exit. He hauled his trunk out from the back of a closet where he had stowed it upon his arrival in Vienna two months earlier. Had it really been only two months, he thought to himself; it certainly seemed a lot longer. He pushed the trunk over toward his bed where the lamp offered more light. He unlocked it then, using a pen knife, he carefully opened the false bottom and removed a pistol and three ammunition clips along with a forged Swiss passport that had been prepared for him. He placed them in his valise. He pushed the trunk back in his closet then picked up his valise and walked quickly to his office, which, it being after hours, was deserted, as he had expected.

Turning on the desk lamp, he took the forged passport from his valise and began to page through it. The document had been issued in the name of Rolf Munger, a resident of Dielsdorf, a suburb of Zurich located just north of the city where, according to his cover story, he was employed as a scrap paper salesman. The photograph was a good likeness of Muller, but the lighting and shadows had been altered enough so it didn't entirely resemble the photo in his League of Nations diplomatic passport. The forgery was a little dog-eared and contained entry and exit stamps from Switzerland, Austria and the Netherlands. He had been assured by

Rudi Dunkel that Büro Ha forgeries were actually prepared in the passport section of the Swiss Customs Office to avoid any errors and that all the backup documentation was on file to permit prompt reply to any inquiries made by border authorities. It was as close to the real thing as a forgery could be, he'd been told.

He compared the two documents, passing them from one hand to the next. The League of Nations passport was certainly compromised; he was confident that German authorities had photographed it and entered all the information in whatever file they'd opened on him when he had been detained in Berlin. He had to hope the forgery was as good as advertised.

He stood and went to the office safe where he changed the combination so he was sure no one else had it and he locked away the forged passport and the valise containing the pistol and ammunition. Returning to his desk, Muller sat and took stock, pouring himself a whiskey from the bottle he kept stored in a desk drawer and lighting a Gitane.

This is all going to come to a conclusion soon, he thought to himself. One way or another; the pressure was too high to last much longer. Franz, his handler, had given him reassurance that he had made arrangements to smuggle him out of Vienna to Czechoslovakia when the time came. He didn't provide any details and Muller didn't press him; better not to know. But they'd introduced a new system for communicating more quickly with one another, using chalk to write a number on the back of the bench that Muller and Keinböck frequented on the bank of the

Danube. The number denoted a time to meet later the same day at Heinrichshof Café. Hopefully, it would enable them to act fast when the time came. It would have to do, Muller decided.

Finishing the last of his whiskey and stubbing out his butt, he rose and locked the office door on this way out.

Muller strolled along Karntner Strasse to observe the atmosphere and see the competing political badges on display. To his surprise, he began to notice the Three Arrow medal that Schultz had described. Generally, it was worn by men in working garb, whom Muller assumed were trade unionists. But he also saw it on the lapels of well-dressed men who appeared to be part of the gentry. It was far outnumbered by Nazi gear–medals, buttons, badges, even hatpins worn by ladies–that were now even more ostentatiously on display. The police were, once again, content to stand by without interfering and the strollers seemed consciously to avoid criticizing one another's displays of allegiance. There were occasional scuffles–especially involving young Nazi sympathizers who seemed determined to stir up trouble. But by and large, it was a relaxed and peaceful gathering, the atmosphere perhaps enhanced by fine weather that offered the promise of an early spring.

Muller had decided he would listen to Schuschnigg's speech at the Café Louvre with his journalist friends. When he arrived, he found them clustered, as usual, around the booth toward the back even though the place was nearly empty. Shirer was among them and he greeted Muller warmly, thanking him for his help–and

Steffi's–a few nights earlier at the hospital, telling him that Tess's condition was much improved. He had evidently shared the information with the others, because they all joined in offering Muller appreciation–Hamilton going so far as to say they wouldn't let Muller buy a round that night–well, at least not for a while.

Muller thanked them, then sought to change the subject, asking what the rumor mill currently thought Schuschnigg would say that evening in his speech. He decided not to share what Schultz had told him about Schuschnigg's pending invitation to the political Left to join with the Fatherland Front in opposing a Nazi takeover.

His question brought a chorus of conflicting observations, leading Shirer–whom Muller had come to observe as the most grounded of the group–to intervene.

"The correct answer to your question is that none of us knows," he said genially, puffing on his pipe." Looking at his watch, he added, "We're going to find out in about fifteen minutes, so let's get to the bar where the radio is and make sure Kreutzer to tunes in to the right frequency so we can listen to what the Chancellor is going to say."

As they gathered at the bar, in front of the Volksempfänger radio, the bartender stood them a round of drinks on the house and fiddled with the dial to catch the proper frequency. Reception was scratchy with some static, but clear enough and they could hear the crowd assembled for the speech, chanting and cheering.

Schuschnigg was announced to an outburst of applause and cheering. Finally, the crowd grew quiet and he began to speak. His voice sounded thin and reedy to Muller. Maybe it's just the reception, he thought, but it had to be nerves too. This was another defining moment for the Chancellor in what had become a seemingly endless series of crises.

He began by extolling the strength of the Austrian economy, the plentiful availability of food, clothing and other consumer goods, "especially by contrast with some of our neighbors," he observed. Another obvious dig at Germany, thought Muller.

"Do we want to return to those days of hardship?" he asked, "to the days of standing in line and doing without?"

"No," roared the crowd. "No!"

"There are those among us who want us to go beyond being a neighbor to the German Reich," Schuschnigg said. "They want us to give up Austria, to forfeit our Austrian heritage and to become part of Germany. I oppose such an outcome. But I must know, where do Austrians stand on this question?

"So, my friends," he continued, his voice sounding ever more confident, "I am ordering a plebiscite–a nationwide vote–next Sunday, four days from now, in which Austrians will be asked to decide the answer to a simple question: shall Austria remain an independent nation; yes or no."

The crowd now began chanting in the background "Yes, Yes, Yes."

Schuschnigg continued. "I want all eligible Austrian voters aged 26 and above to participate in this vote so it is truly representative of the nation. To that end, I am declaring members of the outlawed Social Democratic Party eligible to participate in this plebiscite. We in the Fatherland Front continue to oppose Socialism and Communism," he went on, "but the question of national sovereignty transcends our doctrinal differences. All Austrians must vote on Sunday to answer the question: a free, Christian, Germanic, independent Austria: Yes or No?"

And the speech came to an end, the crowd chanting *"ja, ja, ja, Oesterreich, Oesterreich."*

Music resumed on the radio frequency and Kreutzer switched it off as the journalists and Muller traipsed back to their favorite booth, drinks in hand.

They took their seats without speaking, looking at one another with disbelief, not knowing quite what to say.

Finally, Hamilton, in an uncharacteristically low voice, broke the silence. "That's the Goddamned-ist speech I've ever heard. Whooo!" He exhaled loudly.

"A national vote–and he invited the Left to participate," said Henry Fodor. "As I recall, Hamilton," he said chidingly, "you said ten days or so ago, 'Never in our lifetime'."

Hamilton nodded. "I did indeed," he said, "and I'm in shock at what I just heard."

Hamilton downed the rest of a very large whiskey and ordered another, shaking his head as if to clear his brain. "Let's think this through," he said concentrating on the water rings his glass was making on the table as he swirled it around. "It's now late Wednesday night; that gives them three days to organize the national vote. Hard to do," he said. "But the government will control all the levers. They're the ones that'll print the ballots, get them distributed, man the polling stations and run the counting process. They ought to be able to dictate the outcome pretty easily, it seems to me."

Shirer nodded. "Calling it a plebiscite won't make it a free election. They'll simply lock out the Nazis one way or another. They've been fixing elections here for years and they're pretty good at it; so, I think we can safely assume the government will win this thing easily as Hamilton just said."

"Invoking the 26-year-old voter eligibility standard was clever too," said Boothby. "All those young Nazis strutting around, especially out in the countryside, are taken off the board."

"And he's invited the Left into the tent," added Fodor. "That's a lot of votes."

"I wonder if there's more to that move," said Shirer. "He doesn't really need their votes to win this thing; the Fatherland Front's been holding sham elections and winning them for years without any participation by the Socialists. Perhaps what he's really doing is recruiting them as fighters if it comes to that."

There were murmurs of agreement around the table.

"Maybe we can find someone who can tell us if he's opening the armory and handing out guns to them," said Boothby, scribbling himself a note.

"This announcement will play well with the public in France and Great Britain, probably in America too," Muller observed.

"Yeah, but a fat lot of good it will do them," Hamilton snorted. "Eden's resigned and Chamberlain won't lift a finger to help. And Paris is absolutely paralyzed. Leon Blum is to be sworn in as Prime Minister on Sunday, bringing the Popular Front to power for the second time with all its Socialist and Communist baggage; I can't imagine the French government galvanizing itself to oppose Hitler if he calls Schuschnigg's bluff."

"And will he do that?" Muller asked.

"That's the question, isn't it?" Hamilton replied, shrugging. "Someone's bluff is going to be called and I wouldn't bet against Herr Hitler."

As Muller strolled Back to the hotel, he was reminded of what Marte von Papen had said to him when she was leaving his room the other night: It was Hitler's plan he was opposing, she'd said, and Hitler always seemed to win.

Well, he thought, we'll soon find out; events were hurtling toward some kind of conclusion.

# CHAPTER 40

The next day Muller decided to inquire if Edgar Raditz was still at the German Embassy. If the likelihood of a sweeping Schuschnigg victory were so apparent to his journalist friends, then it must be equally obvious to Hitler and the pressing question was what Hitler intended to do about it. Raditz, if he hadn't been sent back to Berlin, would be his best source of information.

Muller used a call box at a small café near a tram stop on Kaiserplatz. To his surprise, the Ministry switchboard operator informed him that Mr. Raditz was expected in the office shortly after noontime. "Please leave him a message that Karl called," said Muller and hung up.

When he returned to the Palace, he was obliged to enter by a side door. The massive front entryway was being secured by soldiers laying out sandbags to create guard posts, two of them already set up with machine gun emplacements, Muller noticed. Barbed wire was being strung around the edges of the security perimeter for added protection. Officials at the side entrance, armed with clipboards, were checking people in. Muller identified himself and the official checked his name off the list on his clipboard. Then he handed Muller a stiff blue card bearing an official seal.

"Please use this temporary pass for entering and exiting the building, sir," he said. "We will be issuing official passes in the next few days with your name and a photo. There have been threats to the building and to some officials, so we're imposing new security arrangements."

"So, I'll need to show this card?" Muller wanted to understand how the new system might restrict his movements.

"Yes sir," The man said. "Once the guard stations are set up you can continue to use the front entrance. You won't have any difficulty once you show them this card. It's outside visitors and potential demonstrators we're concerned about; they'll be the focus of attention."

"Will this side door remain available?" Muller asked.

"Only from the inside, sir," he replied. "It can still be used as an exit, but you'll have to enter the building through the guard stations in front."

That should not pose any new problems, Muller thought to himself. In fact, if violence broke out, having the army guarding the Palace would probably be an advantage.

Getting to his 7 PM meeting with Raditz at Café Clover was going to be a challenge, Muller realized, as he set out from his office at the Palace. The city had once again been shut down most of the day by demonstrations and the government had set up checkpoints at key road intersections; Muller noticed both police and army units were now deployed and were using more aggressive tactics. New barricades had been erected to separate the adversaries, but scuffles were constantly breaking out, especially as the crowds seemed to have been fueled by afternoon and early evening drinking.

Muller found he was forced to make detours around the obstacles and he had to dodge several altercations as young men, some obviously drunk, taunted one another and began throwing punches and hurling rocks. Muller fingered the brass knuckles in his pocket, hoping he wouldn't need to use them–but glad he had them. He pulled down the brim of his hat while working his way around the edges of the crowds and tried to avoid calling attention to himself.

When Muller finally reached the café, he found Raditz in his accustomed alcove near the bar, a drink on the table in front of him. He was reading a broadsheet which Muller could see bore a large headline reading simply *"Ja".* Raditz looked up and greeted Muller as he hung up his coat and hat and slipped in to the other seat at the table.

"Seen this?" Raditz asked, showing him the broadsheet.

"No," Muller shook his head.

"It's an election handout being distributed by the Left," Raditz said. "Some group calling itself," he picked up the sheet and checked the name, "*the Committee of Revolutionary Socialists*." Fascinating; it's a long manifesto regurgitating all their complaints against both Schuschnigg and the Fatherland Front's Fascist agenda before finally urging a 'yes' vote."

"Listen to this," Raditz said reading from the sheet.

"*Sunday is not the day to repay Austrian Fascism for the crimes it has committed against workers since February 1934. Sunday is the day for showing our bitter hostility to Hitler and Nazism. On that day, the whole worker class must vote YES.*"

Raditz put the sheet down and smiled.

"They have to nurse their grudges before they can bring themselves to vote with the Front," he said. "It's hardly a full embrace or a vote of confidence; more like 'hold your nose but vote yes'." He tapped Muller's glass with his and they drank.

"It was difficult just getting here," Muller said. "This kind of upheaval can't go on much longer; the city's virtually impassable and the atmosphere is explosive."

"Well, it's about to come to an end," Raditz said. "I'm glad you called for the meeting because I was about to call you."

Raditz glanced around for eavesdroppers then bent his head toward Muller.

"Hitler's issued the order to invade," he said quietly. "The *Wehrmacht* is mobilizing on the border tonight and the invasion will begin sometime tomorrow or Saturday at the latest.

"You better find a way to get out quickly, Mr. Muller," he said in the same low voice. "I know you have diplomatic status, but Germany's not a member of the League and they don't view it sympathetically–as you well know. So, I'd look for a quick way to exit."

"You're not being recalled?" Muller asked.

Raditz smiled and began chuckling. "No," he said, "Instead I'm going to be one of the ringmasters for the elaborate show Hitler's planning to mark his triumphant return to Austria. He hasn't replaced von Papen as the German ambassador here–Hell, why do that when there won't even be an Austria in a day or two?–so those of us who are still here are charged with organizing his grand entrance.

"In fact," he said, "the plan is to have Hitler deliver his triumphal speech from the balcony of your very own historic Palace, Mr. Muller. We're to fill the plaza with enthusiastic Austrians–who will not be difficult to find once the invasion takes place–and our *Führer* will make his appearance on that famous balcony to greet them as their new emperor, just like the Hapsburgs did in the good old days."

Raditz clinked his glass against Muller's again in mock tribute.

"Well, right now that plaza is surrounded by barbed wire and protected by sandbags and machine guns," Muller said.

Raditz waved his comment away. "They'll be long gone," he said confidently.

He looked at his watch. "Hitler's ultimatum to Schuschnigg is being delivered as we speak," Raditz said. "He is being told to resign and surrender the Austrian Army or face the consequences of triggering a war instead of a peaceful takeover. Every ounce of German pressure is being mounted to force his hand."

"When will this be made public?" asked Muller.

"The plan is to make an announcement right after Schuschnigg resigns–which I assume will be no later than tomorrow," Raditz replied. "Seyss-Inquart will replace him and invite the Germans in. No fighting, no bombing or cannons, just 100,000 nice German soldiers driving their tanks and lorries to Vienna."

Raditz leaned in again, adding quietly, "Of course, they'll be preceded by Gestapo and SS units to help prepare the way. As you know, Mr. Muller, they're often not so nice. So, I repeat my message that you should get out. No later than tomorrow."

Raditz stood up and retrieved his hat and coat. "I have to get to work on preparing Hitler's celebration."

They shook hands and Raditz strode toward the door.

Muller lit a Gitane and sat, nursing his drink.

Tomorrow, he said to himself; and he began thinking of what to do.

# CHAPTER 41

The next day, Friday March 11, dawned clear and unseasonably warm, a sure sign that spring was on the way. Muller left the hotel carrying a small canvas bag that he had packed the previous night containing a change of clothes–a cheap suit that was a bit baggy, a brown coat that looked very different from his customary tailored tweed overcoat and a battered fedora. Everything else he'd need if he had to flee was in the office safe.

Stopping at the corner kiosk, Muller glanced at the newspaper headlines. Nothing about an imminent invasion; all the headlines were about Sunday's vote. Hearing a low-flying airplane, Muller looked up and saw an old two-seat bi-plane circling overhead towing a banner reading *Ja Oesterreich Ja.* He could make out a figure in the rear seat tossing out leaflets that floated down to the streets. He turned onto the Ringstrasse and bent to pick one up. It bore the symbol of the Fatherland Front Party and urged voters to cast their ballots. *Oesterreich, Ja.*

Well, they were certainly getting out the message, he thought to himself, turning back to find a trash can. As he did so, he caught sight of sanitary department workers pasting notices on the walls of nearby buildings. One carried a pail of what was evidently glue and as the other put the notice on a wall, the first applied the glue with a large brush. They worked quickly, evidently in a rush.

Muller walked toward the closest notice. His stomach tightened as he got close enough to read it:

**ATTENTION!**
**MOBILIZATION ORDER**

**ALL RESERVISTS**
**REPORT FOR DUTY IMMEDIATELY**

What? Was this a directive to resist the coming invasion? A way to forestall some kind of Nazi coup d'etat?

Muller began walking rapidly to the Palace. He needed to find out what was going on and meet with Keinböck.

There was a queue at the entry to the security perimeter that had been set up in the plaza in front of the Palace entrance. As he stood impatiently in line, Muller instinctively lifted his gaze to the elaborate baroque balcony above the ornate entryway. Would Hitler really be speaking from that balcony in a day or two?

When it was his turn, the guard glanced at his identity card and quickly waved him through the gate. Striding briskly up the staircase, Muller saw knots of people congregating in the corridors and the vast hallway below, talking and gesticulating; there was a sense of agitation.

Walking into his office suite, he found Frau Metzinger and Fraulein Heinz seated on the entryway couch holding hands and wiping tears from their faces. They stood but looked stricken as he entered the office.

"Commissioner," said Frau Metzinger, "My Jens is called to mobilization; my dearest husband. I must go to him.

"And my brother, too," said Fraulein Heinz. "Why is this happening? Why do they need to take Willi away? He's only a boy!" she began sobbing.

Muller saw they had turned on the radio and had just heard the news of the mobilization order. At that moment, the announcer broke into the music to repeat the call for reservists to report to their units at once.

Muller put down his bag and laid a hand on the shoulder of each of the quivering women.

"You must go home at once and see to your men," he said. "I don't know the reason this is happening, but it must be serious, so–yes–by all means; leave at once. I'll see to the office and lock up when I leave.

"Let's all hope for the best," he said to them as they quickly put on their hats and shrugged into their coats on their way out the door.

Muller entered his large office, shutting the door behind him, and placed the canvas bag under his desk so it couldn't be seen. Then he walked to the safe and opened it. He removed the Luger pistol and put it in his top desk drawer along with the three ammunition clips. He checked to make certain his false passport was in its pouch and put it in the drawer too, next to the pistol. Then, reaching into the back of the safe, he took out the document that he was looking for. He carefully folded it and placed it in an official envelope, marked with the Commissioner General's embossed title, tucking it into the pocket of his suit jacket and patting it to make sure it was secure. Then he closed the safe and spun the dial. Walking out of his suite, he carefully locked the door behind him.

Descending the grand staircase, he saw the National Bank offices on the first floor, ordinarily a calm island of quiet order, were a beehive of activity, clerks scurrying about, telephones ringing and an undercurrent of urgent conversation.

Keinböck's office door was open and he motioned for Muller to come in.

"What a mess," he said. "The banks here in Vienna have been in turmoil all week with closures caused by the demonstrations. Terrible problems in the regions with Nazis trying to seize control in various places and now the banks on the German border are sending in teletype messages telling us they're closing because the German Army is set to invade–maybe as early as today. Plus, I've got to let a big part of my staff leave for the Mobilization."

Keinböck ran his hands through his thinning short grey hair.

"Things seem to be coming apart," he said, "even though the government should easily win the Sunday vote. The question is whether we can get there."

Muller offered him a Gitane and put his fingers to his lips, rolling his eyes at the ceiling.

"Fresh air and a cigarette, Muller," Keinböck said loudly, nodding, "That's what I need. Step outside with me."

"Certainly." said Muller.

They stepped into the corridor. "Let's find a vacant office where we can talk quietly without going outside and having to deal with all those new guards and checkpoints they've set up," Keinböck said.

"Freida," he called over his shoulder to one of the secretaries, "has Wagner gone off to the mobilization?"

"Yes, sir," she replied.

Keinböck took Muller by the elbow. "We can use that office, then," he said, striding down the corridor, opening the door to a small office with papers neatly stacked on the desk, and motioned Muller to enter, shutting the door behind them.

"You're getting messages from your banks at the border that an invasion is imminent?" Muller asked.

"That's what they're saying," Keinböck replied, nodding. "They're telling me they can see army units lining up their tanks and getting soldiers into the backs of lorries ready to go. I'm also told that Hitler sent messages to Schuschnigg last night and again this morning demanding that he resign and surrender immediately."

Keinböck ran his hands through his thinning hair again. "I got a telephone call this morning ordering me to a meeting at the

Chancellery at 11AM. But then they called back and said the meeting was postponed; no new time."

Muller found an ash tray to stub out his Gitane. "I don't think you should go to any Chancellery meeting. They might sack you or demand your resignation; that would spoil our plan."

Keinböck nodded again. "I thought about that too. Look, this is proving a lot more difficult than I'd ever imagined. We're facing invasion by the Germans–maybe as soon as today or tomorrow. If we resist, we'll need all the money we can find to pay for our defense, and if somehow, we get to Sunday, the Chancellor's likely to win the vote and the resistance will go on. I can't even consider pulling the plug and draining the Treasury under these circumstances. It's out of the question."

"Are you telling me that you're abandoning the plan?" Muller asked.

"No," said Keinböck firmly. "But I'm very concerned about how I'm going to know when to go into action. And there's still a vital piece missing, Muller. I don't have a formal notice of default and demand for payment. I need that before I can activate a transfer of funds and I don't see how I'm going to be able to get that in this chaotic situation."

There was a rap at the door and Freida stuck her head in. "A call from the Chancellery, sir," she said.

Keinböck rose. "I'll take it in my office. Muller, you wait here."

Muller plopped down on a chair and let his shoulders sag. He understood Keinböck's frustration. It was damnably difficult to know what was actually happening and where this crisis was headed; it just wasn't clear. He was reminded of the runway fog that had delayed his flight to Vienna back in January. There were many possible outcomes that lay just ahead, but they were all shrouded in impenetrable clouds of uncertainty.

He hadn't told Keinböck that he had the formal demand to repay the loan that he was looking for. It was the document carefully folded in the envelope that he'd placed in his breast pocket.

Was this the right time to show it to Keinböck? He hesitated; his instinct was to hold off until the very last moment–when it was actually time to head into the vault and activate the transfer. Showing it ahead of time risked devaluing it, as it might be taken differently depending upon the circumstances.

If only the fog would lift.

Keinböck re-entered the office and took the chair behind the desk.

"They persuaded Schuschnigg to postpone the plebiscite for two weeks and notified Hitler earlier this morning," Keinböck said. "He responded by dispatching a special envoy–an adjutant named Keppler–to Vienna with a new ultimatum; they sent him in a plane that the embassy met at the airfield with a car to deliver him directly to the Chancellery. The message was unequivocal: postponement of the date for the plebiscite was insufficient;

Schuschnigg must announce his resignation no later than 3 PM today or Hitler would begin the invasion immediately, announce it publicly and lay the blame on Schuschnigg."

Keinböck gazed at Muller. "So, they're all holed up in the Chancellery: his cabinet; Keppler; the turncoats Seyss-Inquart and Schmidt and their hangers-on, all of them imploring Schuschnigg to surrender in order to avoid a bloodbath. And I suppose there are Fatherland Front supporters there too, urging him to tell Hitler to fuck off."

"Meanwhile, reservists are reporting to their units responding to the mobilization order."

Keinböck stood. "I don't know what I'm going to do with our plan, Muller," he said, opening the door for them to leave. "But right now I've got to get back to running the National Bank of a country that seems to be teetering on the brink of collapse."

They shook hands, and as Muller turned to leave, Keinböck took him by the shoulder.

"I'd advise you to stick around the Palace; it might turn into a busy afternoon."

He waved and strode into his office.

Muller returned up the grand staircase to his office suite. Removing the document from his suit jacket pocket, he opened the safe and placed it carefully back inside, then spun the dial. He went to his desk, picked up some files and tried to read, but put them down, unable to focus. He paced in front of the window, occasionally glancing outside, as if he might see a sign of some kind. But no, nothing out of the ordinary; just pedestrians strolling in the spring sunlight and a steady stream of men in uniforms with packs striding toward their mobilization assembly points. Actually, he thought, the absence of Nazi demonstrators was itself surprising; they must be under orders and waiting for some signal before returning to the streets.

Finally, he descended to the canteen in the basement. He was hungry and ordered a bratwurst with sauerkraut and a stein of beer. Finding a seat was not difficult with so many men having left for the mobilization. He picked up the morning papers from the little kiosk and scanned them, finding little that was new or informative. When he was finished, he returned to the office, making sure the radio was turned on in the event of any announcements. He was nodding in his comfortable overstuffed desk chair when the music over the radio abruptly ended and a burst of static echoed in the office suite.

Muller sat up, fully alert.

After a pause and more static, the voice of an announcer came on the air.

"Citizens of Austria, attention. Stand by for an announcement by the Chancellor, Kurt von Schuschnigg."

There was another pause, more static, then the Chancellor began to speak.

*"Austrian men and Austrian women: This day has placed us in a tragic and decisive situation. I have to give my fellow Austrians a report on today's events.*

*"The German government today handed to our President, Wilhelm Miklas, an ultimatum, with a time limit of 3 PM today, ordering him to nominate as Chancellor a person to be designated by the German government and to appoint members of the Cabinet on the orders of the German government; otherwise German troops would invade Austria.*

*I declare before the world that reports circulated by Germany, alleging disorder by Austrian workers, the shedding of streams of blood and accusations that the situation is out of the control of the Austrian government are lies from A to Z.*

*President Miklas asks me to tell the people of Austria that we have yielded to force since we are not prepared, even in this terrible moment, to shed blood. We decided to order our troops to offer no resistance and the mobilization order is canceled. I have submitted my resignation.*

*So, I take my leave of the Austrian people with a word of farewell uttered from the depths of my heart–may God protect Austria."*

Indistinct voices could be heard in the background, then, softly, the strains of the Austrian national anthem came across the ether, so like, yet so subtly different, from *Deutschland Uber Alles*. In his office, Muller found himself standing, eyes moist, his heart pounding.

Slowly he gathered himself, absorbing what he had just heard.

This was the end; Schuschnigg had resigned. There was no announcement of the appointment of a successor-Chancellor, but

Schuschnigg had said that he and Miklas had yielded to Hitler's demand, so it almost didn't matter. Germany had seized power over Austria; an independent Austria no longer existed.

As the reality struck him, Muller sprang into action. He went to the safe and retrieved the document in its envelope and once again placed it in the breast pocket of his suit jacket. He went to the desk and took out the Luger pistol, slapping one of the ammunition clips into place, putting the other two in his side pocket and shoved the pistol into his belt under the back of his suit jacket. Reaching further into the drawer he removed a hard piece of what appeared to be plaster with a cord attached and, carefully folding the cord, placed in his pants pocket. Then he reached under his desk for the canvas bag. Opening another desk drawer, he took out a pair of small horn-rimmed glasses which he put into the bag, annoyed that he'd nearly forgotten to take them.

He walked out of his office suite and began to lock the door. As he did so, he saw that someone had tucked an envelope under the door. He pulled it out and saw with a start that the envelope bore the imprint of the German Embassy.

Opening the envelope, Muller extracted a single sheet bearing the Ambassador's seal. There was a message written in lipstick.

"Flee. They know."

Marte, he thought. He pocketed the message and locked the door to the office.

There were things to do before fleeing.

Striding down the broad staircase, Muller saw the ground floor of the great hall was in a state of chaos, people streaming in from adjoining corridors, all seemingly speaking at once, hurrying in different directions. As Muller approached the National Bank offices, he saw Viktor Keinböck stand on a chair then step up onto the top of a big desk.

Somewhere, he'd found a bell which he was swinging over his head trying to get people's attention and quiet the crowd. Finally, the din subsided enough for him to make himself heard.

"Ladies and Gentlemen," he said loudly. "You have all heard the news. The government has fallen and Germany is taking charge. None of us knows what that means. Accordingly, as President of the National Bank of Austria, I declare the bank closed for business until further notice. You are all instructed to lock up your files and exit the building as quickly as possible. I wish us all luck. Godspeed."

Keinböck climbed down off the desk. He was surrounded by bank employees and Muller could hear him urging them to depart as quickly as they could. Muller strode rapidly to the first corridor on his right and entered the men's WC. He waited for a man to finish rinsing his hands at the sink and towel off, then, checking to ensure he was alone, he pushed his canvas bag into the large trash container and covered it with used hand towels so it could not be seen. Then he retraced his steps back to the National Bank section of the main hallway.

Keinböck was freeing himself from the last of his employees. As he turned to go into his office, Muller grabbed him by the elbow and motioned toward the vacant office they'd used that morning. Once they were inside, he turned to Keinböck.

"It's time," he said. "Austria is finished; it's now German. Are you ready to act?"

Keinböck looked levelly at Muller.

"Where's the declaration of default and the order to repay the principal amount of the loan?" he said.

Muller pulled the envelope out of his breast pocket and handed it to Keinböck, who took it and extracted the document, flattening it with his hands on the desk. He began to read.

LEAGUE OF NATIONS

150 Route Suisse

Geneva, Switzerland

Mr. Viktor Keinböck

Governor, National Bank of Austria

By hand delivery from the Commissioner General of the League of Nations for Austria

Dated *March 11, 1938*

Dear Governor. Keinböck,

Your attention is directed to the Decision taken by vote of the Council of the League of Nations, Geneva Protocol of July 15, 1936, document C4.41.43, Loan Terms and Conditions

(Final signed instrument), authorizing the governments of France, Great Britain, Italy and Czechoslovakia to guarantee the said Loan to the Government of the Republic of Austria.

The Protocol approved by the League Council expressly provides in Section 5 thereof as follows: "A condition of this decision is that Austria shall take such steps as may be necessary and proper to ensure that the Austrian economy remains independent of the German Reich and that no customs union or similar arrangement shall be permitted to take effect whether *de facto* or *de jure.*"

The League of Nations Commissioner General for Austria has reported to me that as a result of recent actions taken by both the German Reich and the Republic of Austria, the condition stated in said Section 5 of the July 15, 1936 Geneva Protocol, cited above, is no longer being observed and that the Austrian government and its economy have become subject to control by the government of the German Reich.

Accordingly, acting under authority delegated to me as Chief of the Financial Section of the League of Nations in said Protocol, I hereby declare the Republic of Austria to be in default of the terms and conditions of both the Protocol and the loan and I hereby demand immediate repayment of the principal of said loan to the syndicate of lenders in the sum of 570,000,000 Austrian Schillings.

With assurances of my highest respect,

Yours truly,

*Jose Maria Oquendo*

**Jose Maria Oquendo**

**Chief, Financial Section, League of Nations**

Keinböck looked up from the document and fixed Muller with an intense stare.

"How did you get this?" he asked. "It's dated today, but signed by Director Oquendo, who's in Geneva.

"Hitler's actions have taken place a lot more quickly than any of us expected," Muller said, seating himself across the desk from Keinböck. "I've been corresponding with Oquendo in Geneva in my official capacity as Commissioner General." Muller was not going to say anything about Franz's role as confidential emissary in his highly secretive exchange of correspondence.

"Oquendo is the brains behind this plan. He wrote and sent this document to me, together with a document delegating me the authority to date it and deliver it to you when, in my judgment, acting in my capacity as Commissioner General of the League of Nations in Austria, I determined that the pre-conditions had been established."

Keinböck eyed him closely, and Muller continued.

"You remember our plan was that I would formally notify both you and Geneva that, as Commissioner, I was refusing to authorize payment of the quarterly debt service required by the loan on the grounds that I had concluded that Austria would no longer exist as a sovereign nation and beneficiary of the loan."

"Right," said Keinböck, "and refusal to make the quarterly payment would constitute an act of default that would trigger demand for repayment of the loan. That was to be the legal justification for me to use the gold reserves to make the payment."

Muller nodded. "But today is March 11; the debt service is not due to be paid until April 1. So, a notification of refusal to make payment dated today–or any time before April 1–would not constitute an immediate act of default; it would be a notice of *intent* to default and would trigger a demand for consultations by the lenders. If that were to happen, Germany would have ample opportunity to pressure the governments guaranteeing the loan to delay the default notice by pledging to honor the loan terms. Then Hitler could seize the gold, use it for his own purposes and repudiate the loan terms later, whenever it suited him."

Keinböck looked at Muller with a bemused expression and held up the document. "So, what this does is order me to repay the principle because Germany's action in seizing control of Austria violates the premise upon which the loan was agreed to by the League of Nations–that Germany and Austria would remain separate."

Keinböck stubbed out his cigarette.

"And by handing me this document, you've created both a legal obligation on the part of the National Bank to repay the funds and an order to do so immediately.

"Very clever Muller," Keinböck said, and stood with a grim expression. "Then I guess it's time we went to the vault," he said, leading the way.

# CHAPTER 42

They walked back to Keinböck's office. He placed the letter from Oquendo face up on his desk and anchored it with a paperweight.

"I want whomever they appoint to take over the bank to see this letter right away," Keinböck said with a thin smile. "It's not likely to make him very happy."

He reached into his desk and extracted a ring of keys that he placed in a pocket. Then he strode to the wall, slid some books to the left to reveal a safe, which he quickly opened, slipping his new false passport in his pocket and, reaching further in, pulled out a black FN Herstal pistol that he stuck in his belt. He closed the safe and spun the dial.

Reaching for his telephone he dialed four numbers.

"This is President Keinböck," he said into the receiver. "I assume you've been notified that I have ordered the bank closed." He paused. "Good. Before you leave, I need access to the telex room in the vault to send a message. I am coming down via the stairway. Kindly meet me there."

Keinböck replaced the receiver and motioned Muller to follow him.

They descended two stories in the internal National Bank staircase, a badly-lit, damp enclosure.

"I don't want to take any chances with the elevator," said Keinböck.

At the bottom of the stairs, a uniformed guard with a leather strap across his chest opened the vault doorway and stood to attention.

"Governor Keinböck, sir."

Keinböck and Muller entered a low-ceilinged room. Several rectangular tables and chairs were scattered about.

Keinböck turned to the guard.

"Please tell me your name," he said.

"Kurt Bremer, sir," the guard replied.

"Is there anyone else here in the vault area, Mr. Bremer?" asked Keinböck.

"No sir; everyone was ordered to leave," Bremer replied. "The staff closed the vault entry door and locked the system; it's now fully alarmed. I was preparing to lock up here and take the elevator upstairs when I received your call."

Keinböck nodded in satisfaction.

"Very well, Mr. Bremer, you may proceed to take the elevator to the main floor, then lock it up. We will take the stairway when we're done."

Bremer gave a curt nod and strode to the elevator.

When the door had closed, Keinböck walked to the small, glass-enclosed telex office and, using a key from his key ring, opened it, then switched on a light hanging above the teletype keyboard.

Keinböck sat quickly at the operator's stool and pushed the button to activate the large machine, rubbing his hands as it lit up. Pulling a piece of notepaper from his breast pocket, he struck the keys.

"There goes the WRU to the Bank of England," he said.

In a moment, the machine's keys typed a message.

"Perfect," Keinböck said, "There's the answerback."

He fed a perforated strip into the machine and it sprang into action, typing the text of the disbursement message. Keinböck leaned forward to read the text. Satisfied, he hit the transmit key.

He sat back, and a moment later the answerback message confirmed receipt.

"Christ, Muller, who ever thought it would be so easy?" Keinböck said. "570 million Austrian schillings in gold has just been sent to the lenders."

He stood up and shook Muller's hand.

"Now let's get out of here. Fast!"

"Wait," said Muller, "We don't want to risk some attempt to reverse your transaction." He took the piece of plaster out of his pocket and placed it inside the telex machine, carefully unspooling the string attached to it.

"Cordite," he explained. "This fuse should give us three or four minutes, then the small explosion will cripple the machine. Even if they find out what we've done and try to overturn it, this will knock out the dedicated WRU; it'll take days or weeks to fix it."

He lit the fuse with his lighter and they ran to the staircase, bounding up the stairs two at a time. As they reached the top, they heard a muffled sound, but didn't pause and stepped through the doorway into the National Bank offices.

Suddenly, sirens and claxons began sounding.

"It's the fire alarm," hissed Keinböck. "Perfect; that'll keep 'em busy. Good luck," he said and began walking calmly in the direction of the exit.

Muller turned and walked to the WC, which he found deserted. Digging into the trash barrel, he removed his canvas bag. He then went into one of the stalls and quickly changed clothes, stuffing what he had been wearing into the bag. He carefully transferred the brass knuckles into a pocket of the new suit jacket along with the false Rolf Munger passport. He ripped his Paul Muller League of Nations diplomatic passport into shreds, flushing it down the toilet and did the same with the warning message from Marte. He removed identification from his wallet and pocketed the cash before discarding the empty wallet in the canvas bag. He stuck the Lugar pistol in his belt in back and found a suit pocket for the ammunition clips. Finally, he put on the small rimmed glasses.

Leaving the stall, he replaced the canvas bag in the trash barrel, once again taking care to cover it with hand towels. Pausing a moment, he glanced at himself in the mirror above the sinks. He saw a shabbily-dressed youngish man wearing glasses and wearing a nearly shapeless fedora. It would have to do, he decided, as he turned on his heel and exited the WC.

The alarm was still clanging and men in police and fire uniforms were scurrying about the great hallway and the National Bank office space. It was a confused scene and Muller took advantage of it to stroll down the corridor toward the side entrance. The guard who was supposed to examine the identity cards of persons leaving by that doorway was nowhere to be seen, evidently having been distracted by the fire alarm, so Muller simply opened the door and walked out.

Sirens could be heard approaching the Palace and Muller walked, deliberately, in the opposite direction, toward the Danube, making certain his battered fedora was pulled low on his forehead and doing his best to avoid attracting attention.

After walking along the embankment for ten minutes or so, he took a seat on one of the benches and allowed himself to exhale. The telex transfer exercise could not have gone better, he thought to himself. But now comes the hard part; trying to get out of Austria.

He checked his watch. Not yet 5 PM. His meeting with Franz was not until 7, but he decided to begin the process of approaching

Heinrichshof carefully, minding the clandestine steps and checking to be sure he was not being followed.

As he approached the Ringstrasse, beginning the elaborate approach process, his senses were on high alert, and he immediately became aware of an entirely different atmosphere on the street. There were harmless clusters of men apparently returning home from their mobilization points. Most of them seemed light-hearted, happy to be freed from active duty, and not a few were brandishing bottles, drinking toasts to one another and their good luck. But there were also bands of hard-eyed men, many wearing red Nazi armbands, who conveyed a palpable sense of menace. These were not the demonstrators from a few days earlier, marching and singing; these were men with a mission; they carried clubs and other weapons, walking briskly and with determination, as if working from a plan.

As Muller went through his routine, he saw more of these menacing gangs, now often escorted by police, Muller noted, who had either changed sides or abandoned false allegiance to the government. As Muller stood quietly at one of the street corners in the gathering twilight awaiting the next tram, he saw one of the gangs enter an apartment house down the block from where he was standing. He heard the crash of breaking glass and the thump of a door being knocked down, then screams and what appeared to be a family was dragged out on the street where they were punched and beaten until an unmarked Black Maria van pulled up alongside them. The back doors were opened and the family–Muller noted four of five children–were unceremoniously thrown into the van. Several members of the gang took off with the van, perched on the running boards. Others went back inside and soon Muller saw belongings being tossed out of a side window while other things were being deposited on the sidewalk, evidently awaiting pickup by other accomplices. Muller noted several policemen participating in the raid.

Muller watched all this from a doorway, keeping out of sight. Clearly this was no random act of violence; the family had been targeted for attack. It was chilling to watch. He was glad to see the tram approaching from the other direction so he could leave the vicinity.

So far as he could tell, no one was on his tail. He had gone through the entire approach process, taken his time, and to all appearances he was clean. He glanced at his watch; just after 6 PM. So, it was still early. He was about to turn the corner into the street where Café Heinrichshof was situated, a block and a half away on the right, when he stiffened. There were two cars parked on the narrow street, one just before the restaurant, the other just beyond it and he caught sight of a match being flared in the first car, evidently to light a cigarette.

A stakeout. Was he the target? Had Franz been taken and forced to confess? Muller's mind raced.

He re-traced his route back for two blocks, then circled around from the other side, walking slowly and seemingly aimlessly. This time he found a small dimly-lit café where he could sit at an outdoor table in the far corner and see the Café Heinrichshof entrance.

He went to the bar to order a coffee and picked up a newspaper, carrying it back to the table. He lit a Gitane and pretended to read. There were not many passersby. He got up to use the WC and when he returned he saw two burly men in trench coats walking away from the little café. The owner came up to his table.

"You'll have to leave," he said, "Two Gestapo guys–at least I guess that's who they were–ordered me to shut the place because they have an operation being staged down the street." He gestured with his head in the direction of the Heinrichshof café.

Muller stood and handed the owner a couple of coins. "I certainly don't want any part of that," he said, and walked away.

Deciding it was too dangerous to linger in the neighborhood any longer, Muller trudged back toward the Ringstrasse. Then, acting on instinct, he walked across the wide boulevard to the neighborhood on the other side of the broad avenue where the Café Franz was situated–the place where he and Franz had actually held their first meeting after having left Heinrichshof. Was there the chance that Franz–or someone–might use that venue since Heinrichshof had apparently gone wrong? It seemed worth a try, so Muller bought a newspaper that he rolled up under his arm and walked slowly past the entrance to Franz, so he could be easily seen. He stole a glance inside, but saw nothing amiss, and turned at the next corner, flattening his back against the side of the building.

There was a storefront situated across the way with a plate glass window and Muller saw the reflection of a figure walking out of Franz and turning toward the corner where Muller stood. He was carrying a rolled-up newspaper under his right arm.

Muller pulled the pistol from his belt and held it at his side, ready to bring it up to shoot if he had to.

The man never hesitated, however, and simply walked past him but inclined his head enough to say quietly, "He's taken; follow me at a distance."

The man continued to walk along the darkened street away from Muller.

Muller weighed whether he should follow the man's instructions and decided he didn't have many other options.

He had just taken a step in the man's direction when a Black Maria van sped past him, its headlights illuminating the street; a spotlight was turned on by someone inside the van, and its beam aimed directly at the man.

Muller saw the man drop the newspaper and begin to run, but the van was on him in an instant and several occupants jumped out and swarmed over him, beating him with clubs.

Muller stepped back into the shadows of his corner and edged along the wall, moving away as unobtrusively as possible. Then, when he was sure they were out of sight, he began walking quickly along the deserted street. After two blocks, he turned left, back toward the Ringstrasse, where there was more pedestrian traffic and he could try to blend in.

Muller tried to think. It certainly appeared as if Franz and his compatriots had been compromised and at least some members were in custody. That probably meant that he was now in immediate danger. It was now pretty obvious that the stakeout at the Heinrichshof had been meant for him. And there was another problem. Franz had done the planning for his escape, but hadn't revealed any of the details. All Muller knew was he was to be smuggled into Czechoslovakia somehow. But he had no idea whom he was to contact or where.

So here he was, on the run from the Gestapo–only now completely on his own, and without a plan. Muller felt a stab of fear in the pit of his stomach.

He continued striding along the Ringstrasse, trying to figure out what his next step should be.

An ambulance sped by, its lights flashing and siren howling. St. Cecelia hospital was nearby and a plan began to form in his mind. What about approaching Steffi Farber to see if she would let him hide out in her apartment for a few days until things settled down and he could figure out some escape route. He didn't have any better ideas, so he picked up his pace and headed in the direction of the hospital, thinking that Steffi would certainly be on duty there as casualties from the continuing unrest would require treatment.

As he neared the hospital, Muller began to hear band music and singing, and when he turned the last corner onto the plaza in front of the hospital entrance, he saw before him, lit up by a spotlight, a small makeshift stage which faced a crowd of several dozen people–most dressed in Nazi regalia–and a tiny band, made up of eight to ten musicians, playing the familiar *Horst Wessel* song.

Hanging back in the shadows out of sight, with his hat firmly pulled low, Muller made out figures on the small stage, dominated by a large man in a full, black Nazi SS uniform who was clearly in charge–and standing behind the man was Steffi Farber, her white surgical gown bright in the light, and a red Nazi armband on her right arm.

What was this? Muller wondered. It certainly appeared that she was a willing participant in whatever ceremony was being staged.

It was a strangely haphazard scene. Ambulances were parked at odd angles on the plaza near the emergency entrance. One was disgorging a patient on a stretcher in obvious distress, and off to the far side stood a cluster of men and women, some in patient garb, all of them huddled together looking fearful, while the small crowd in front of the stage sang and clapped enthusiastically.

The uniformed SS official held up his hand for quiet and began to speak, his voice loud enough to fill the plaza.

"We have waited years for this great day," he said, "for the day when Austria would become part of the greater German *Reich*, under the leadership of our *Führer. Heil Hitler*!

"*Heil Hitler, Seig Heil*," came the response from the crowd.

"You have seen our flying squads attending to business in our streets this afternoon and evening," the leader continued. "For a long time we have been laying plans to destroy our enemies–the Jews, the Bolsheviks, the trade unionists and those Austrians who dare to oppose us–and today we have sprung into action.

"We will crush them," he shouted, and the crowd bellowed in response.

"This hospital harbored Jews–on its staff, in its offices–even treated Jewish patients, as if that scum deserved medical treatment. Look at them!" He pointed to the cluster of men and women huddled across the plaza.

"Out," he shouted. "Go! You are Jews and have no place here; you are scum that deserve to be sent to Dachau."

Muller saw members of the small audience spit in the direction of the Jews as the official ordered them to leave.

Then the leader gathered himself to continue.

"On this grand night we stand here to celebrate the full Nazification of St. Cecelia hospital. The Catholic nuns, brainwashed by the Pope and his minions, have now understood they must submit to the higher order of the Nazi Party. And submit they will," he went on, "or they will find themselves in Dachau too."

The audience clapped enthusiastically.

"They will be supervised–and this hospital will be run–by new Nazi leadership personified by Surgeon–now Supervisor–Farber, a striking example of the new Aryan, Nazi woman who has dedicated her mind and body to the German *Reich* and its *Führer.*

The crowd applauded and stamped their feet.

Well, Muller said to himself, mind–and body too? He detested this sort of venomous crowd-baiting and his gorge rose in disgust. But there stood Steffi, smiling and clapping, clearly reveling in the moment.

The leader then proceeded to drape his arm around Steffi's shoulder, hugging her and leading her forward to speak.

Steffi moved to center stage, smiling and waving at the crowd as they cheered. "Now is the time for all good Austrians to rejoice in our newfound Fatherland and allegiance to our great leader," she said, raising her arm in the party salute, "*Heil Hitler!*"

The crowd responded and Steffi and the Black-clad leader exchanged a long hug.

Muller watched the spectacle unfold, then slowly, deliberately, slipped further into the shadows and began walking back toward the Ringstrasse.

Fat chance of the new Nazi Supervisor of St. Cecelia hospital agreeing to harbor a fugitive running from the Gestapo, Muller thought to himself. She'd probably turn him in if he approached her now. He shook his head as he reflected, feeling disappointed and bitter at what could only be characterized as a complete sellout to the Nazis.

At one level, he wasn't totally surprised; Steffi harbored deep resentment at having been mistreated and disdained over many years as a mere nurse by the hospital's leaders–the nuns and others, including the Jewish doctors. Revenge is a powerful motive and she had obviously seized the chance to wrest control from her tormentors. As he thought more about it, walking along aimlessly, he concluded that this was how people react to sudden change; they accommodate to new circumstances and look for an advantage: Steffi taking control of the hospital, policemen assigned to shadow Nazi gangs, then defecting and joining them. Muller remembered what Raditz had told him yesterday, that he would have no trouble attracting a crowd of enthusiastic Austrians to cheer Hitler's speech from the balcony at the Palace when he made his triumphal entry into Vienna. Raditz was correct, Muller decided; there would be a rush to embrace the new regime as people flocked to the winning side. It was a depressing prospect.

It also didn't bode well for him, Muller realized. The risks of betrayal would multiply as new converts joined the Nazi ranks; that placed a premium on getting away quickly.

It also highlighted the danger of falling afoul of the Nazi flying squads he had seen operating on the streets. They were ready for this, Muller thought, and they were tightening the noose much quicker and more efficiently than the government–or anyone else–had expected; the possibility of help from potential allies was going to disappear fast.

He'd better look for a quick escape hatch, so he hailed a passing taxi.

# CHAPTER 43

The express train to Prague departed nightly from the East Banhof at 11:15 PM, arriving at the Czech border, at Breclav, at 12:40 AM, an hour and a half later.

That Friday night, March 11, 1938, when Muller's taxi pulled up two blocks away–as close as it could get to the station because of the crowd–the train was already packed, and it was not yet even 9 PM. Railroad officials had added extra cars that extended off beyond the platform and those too were full. Muller elbowed his way into the crowded station waiting room. Needing to relieve himself, he went to the WC and managed to engage a railway employee in conversation as they were rinsing their hands at the basin.

"Any other trains tonight?" Muller inquired.

"None," the man replied. "All the routes South toward Switzerland and Italy are closed because the German invasion is coming from that direction. Trains from Hungary have all been stopped at the border so none of them even got to the Station.

"This is the only game in town," he said. "And everybody knows it," he added ominously, before walking away.

Muller began to squeeze his way out onto the platform, then, reflecting on what the employee had said, reversed course and maneuvered back toward the station exit, fighting crowds determined to get in and board the train.

Moments later, as Muller finally elbowed his way outside the doorway, he heard a sudden outburst of screams and shouting. Looking to his right, toward the locomotive end of the train, he saw a squad of uniformed Brown Shirt storm troopers attacking passengers on the platform with clubs and dog whips, while another gang began boarding the train, hauling people off, and seizing bags and luggage.

This was clearly an organized assault aimed at terrorizing passengers and looting their valuables. Muller saw Railroad Police emerge from their barracks across the plaza and try to deter the attackers, but they were outnumbered. Muller recognized Superintendent Schönen, who had interviewed him after the train assault back in January, trying to muster his men and protect the passengers from the assault. He winced as he saw the Superintendent struck on the side of the head by a club-wielding Brown Shirt and collapse to the ground where his assailant began kicking him.

Then, suddenly, he saw the police begin to back away, and heard shouts and shrill whistles recalling them to the barracks.

Two policemen rescued Schönen and Muller saw them dragging him, his body limp.

The Railway Police had obviously decided to cede the fight to the storm troopers. Defection? Muller wondered. Probably; but with that distraction now out of their way, the Brown Shirts renewed their assaults on passengers and Muller saw they were reinforced by local police who began hauling away people targeted by the gang, shoving them into vans. Maybe they were Jews, Muller speculated; but they could be anybody. Storm Troopers seemed to find enemies easily.

Muller decided that he needed to get away, so he strode rapidly in the other direction and finally found a taxi that had just discharged passengers who were racing toward the station, unaware of what they were heading into.

"Please take me to the Aerodrome," Muller said.

"It'll be crowded there, too, sir," said the driver.

"I'll take my chances," Muller said, shoving a few schilling notes into the driver's lap as an incentive. "Just go."

He concluded that he had no choice at this point but to roll the dice. The Nazis were obviously organized and ruthlessly carrying out raids on people whom they considered enemies. If Marte's warning was correct, the Gestapo was already on his tail; they would only get stronger as they got more organized and German influence in Austria grew. So, finding some place to hole up for a few days didn't make sense; the situation was only going to get worse. He needed to make a run for it immediately.

He had a perfectly good Swiss passport, after all. Yes, it was a forgery, but it had been prepared by Swiss passport authorities, so it ought to pass muster with the authorities here. He was not an escaping Jew or some other Austrian enemy of the incoming regime whom they would want to stop from departing.

No, he reminded himself, he was an even more high-profile target, but one that they currently seemed busy looking for in Vienna itself. Would they patrol the airport looking for him? Certainly, it was a possibility.

But would they expect him to book a flight to Germany? Maybe not; he decided to brazen it out.

As Muller's taxi approached the terminal, he could see aircraft on the ground illuminated by bright spotlights from the aerodrome roof. He whistled softly as he caught a glance of the sleek Focke-Wulf Condor, a new twin-engine aircraft just introduced into service earlier that year by Lufthansa and capable of carrying an amazing 26 passengers. In the distance beyond, he could see profiles of more familiar aircraft–Air France's Bloch 120, the Swissair favorite, Savoia-Marchetti S.M. 83, and a KLM Lockheed L10 Electra.

Could he find a way to get aboard one of those planes?

The terminal was crowded, though nothing even approaching the train station madhouse. A police presence was very evident, as armed men stood guard outside the entry and officers with pistols patrolled the interior. Once he got inside, the cramped terminal was quiet and the atmosphere seemed tense to Muller. Passengers sat hunched over, grasping their tickets tightly, checking their watches, and glancing around suspiciously–and fearfully. Muller realized these were people fleeing for their lives, just like those at the train station; and they were terrified that someone would seize them before they could get away.

Moving to a corner, Muller took off his glasses and held them at arm's length, wiping them with a handkerchief, using the maneuver to scan the room. He saw several men wearing the black leather overcoats favored by the Gestapo. That was not reassuring.

Muller was told by the Swiss Air agent that flights to all destinations except Germany were completely booked. Summoning his courage, he approached the Lufthansa desk and inquired about connecting flights to Zurich through Munich or Berlin.

Munich was completely shut down, he was told. There were seats available on a flight to Berlin, but no assurances of any connecting flights. Explanations by the ticket agent for this strange situation were vague. Upon reflection, Muller concluded that the evasive remarks probably meant that the German aviation system was in disarray because of logistics problems associated with the invasion of Austria–that presumably was already underway.

He was weighing whether he should take the chance of flying to Berlin without any connection, and risk being stuck there for longer than seemed wise, when he spied a blackboard behind the small KLM stall showing a flight departing in 45 minutes through Berlin to Amsterdam. The ticket agent actually smiled at him, saying that yes there was a seat. He accepted Muller's payment and stamped tickets for both legs of the flight, then directed him to the transit visa office, a small enclosure with glass panels and stern-looking policemen inside.

As Muller approached the office he realized with a start that this was the same kind of transit office where he'd been detained in Berlin a few days ago. Well, this was still Austria, he thought to himself–at least sort of. Somehow he doubted that even German efficiency would enable them to take full control over the Aerodrome in only a matter of hours since Schuschnigg's resignation.

So, he straightened his shoulders and, as he was about to enter, froze at the doorway.

There, sitting not fifteen feet from him, just inside the office, was Bill Shirer, tickets in hand, absently filling the bowl of his pipe before lighting it.

Shit! Shirer would certainly recognize him and address him as Muller. That would tip off the Visa clerk, raise an alarm and blow his cover.

He would have to try to create a diversion and get a warning to Shirer.

Opening the door, Muller dropped his two tickets at Shirer's feet and, bending to retrieve them, proceeded to stumble into Shirer's lap, almost knocking him to the floor. They were tangled up together, Muller one knee on the floor, an arm in Shirer's lap. Shirer's pipe had fallen to the floor and they both reached for it.

Muller grabbed it, holding on and pulled Shirer as close as he could.

"Don't say a word," he hissed to Shirer in English. "You don't know me. Please!"

Then he stood up and handed the pipe to Shirer, apologizing profusely in German.

"I'm so sorry, sir; that was very clumsy. I hope you're all right."

Their eyes met for a moment, Muller's gaze intense, trying to reinforce his whispered message.

Shirer stood and brushed himself off, then faced Muller.

"I'm fine, but watch where you're going next time," he said loudly in his accented German, looking Muller over, then resumed his seat and once again began tapping tobacco into the bowl of his pipe.

Muller slouched over to the transit visa window, ignoring the policeman who stood next to it.

"Transit through Berlin on the KLM flight," he said gruffly, handing his tickets and passport though the small opening.

"Reason for traveling through Berlin?" asked the immigration officer in an officious tone.

"To get out of this craziness," said Muller loudly. "I haven't been able to sell any paper for a week now because everything's been shut down and my customers have all been out marching around. Now there's going to be a German invasion.

"Christ," he continued, "how's a salesman supposed to do any business with all this going on? I'd rather be at home in bed with my wife than sitting in a hotel room watching riots out the window."

"Ha!" Muller heard a bellow of laughter from behind him in the room, and saw Shirer rocking in his chair guffawing, and a moment later the whole room seemed to chime in, laughing in sympathy with Muller's outburst.

The clerk reddened, but decided against responding and stamped Rolf Munger's passport.

Muller took a seat, stiffening as he saw the transit office door opened by two men in black leather Gestapo overcoats. The men stood at the entrance and seemed to survey the passengers crammed into the small room.

Muller's heart sank. One of the two men was the Gestapo officer who'd detained him in Berlin. He immediately recognized the pink scar on the man's neck and his broken nose. Shit! This was trouble.

What to do? He couldn't just get up and leave; that would call immediate attention to himself. Could he create some new diversion?

Muller reached into a pocket to extract his pack of Gitane cigarettes, then quickly thought better of it. Gitanes could be a clue they were looking for–and it would likely trigger the memory of the guy from Berlin. So, instead, he began patting his coat pockets, as if searching for cigarettes and finding none. So, he turned to the heavyset man seated next to him and, speaking loudly, asked if he had an extra cigarette.

The man grunted and pulled out a pack of Trommlers, which he shook, offering one to Muller.

Muller took it. "Thanks," he said, accepting the man's light.

Muller's heart was pounding."Trommlers are really good, and I like that design on the pack showing the drummer," he said, wanting to keep the conversation going as a way to divert the attention of the Gestapo agents, still surveying the room.

"Yeah, nice color scheme too," replied the man, turning the pack over in his hand so they could both study the stern Nazi-clad drummer depicted on a bright yellow background. They're sold to generate funds for the Party," he added. "It seemed like a good brand to have in light of what's happening."

"Does it say where the tobacco is from?" asked Muller, aware that the two agents were now beginning to circle the room. "Can I look?" he said, taking the pack from the man's hand and holding it in his lap, looking down to read the small print so his hat covered most of his face.

Muller sensed the Gestapo agents nearing his seat. He found himself suddenly breaking into a sweat. That guy would certainly recognize him.

Keep your head down; act normally.

Continuing to turn the pack in his hand, Muller said, "Look, it says 'Finest Turkish Tobacco', right here." The man bent over to study the pack with him, so they both had their heads down as the Gestapo agents walked past them.

Muller could see their highly polished boots. Keep walking, he implored them.

"I'd have bet it was Egyptian," said Muller, continuing the conversation. Still turning the pack in his hand, he added, "But it certainly says Turkish."

The boots stopped directly in front of him.

Muller's heart was in his mouth; he could scarcely breathe.

The swagger stick held by one of the Gestapo agents suddenly and without warning swatted the cigarette pack Muller and his neighbor were holding, sending it skittering across the linoleum floor.

"Our Führer detests smoking," the agent said loudly. Muller recognized the menacing voice.

He sat up in his seat, reacting to the blow, but as he did, he instinctively threw his forearm up in front of his face to shield his eyes from the bright lights in the ceiling. He kept it there for a long moment, before lowering it, bowing his head submissively.

"Sorry, sir," he mumbled, head down.

"Austrian swine," the agent said. "You will be taught manners."

Then the boots moved on.

From the corner of his eye, Muller saw the agents walk ostentatiously to the doorway, then striding out of the office, they slammed the door behind them.

Muller exhaled. Then he stood, took a few steps and bent over to retrieve the cigarette pack, which he handed to his neighbor. "Thanks again," he said to the man, who smiled in return.

"I'm glad he was more interested in our cigarettes than he was in us," the man said quietly.

Muller didn't trust himself to respond. He just nodded and crossed his arms, hugging himself so as not to betray his urge to tremble. He drew several deep breaths. That had been close.

Moments, later they were led out the gate by a KLM agent, who directed them to the plane–it was the Lockheed L10 Muller had seen from the taxi. Other planes were loading at the same time so there was a lot of activity on the ground as passengers walked toward their parked aircraft. Across the way where the other flights were loading, Muller saw Brown Shirt storm troopers dart into one of the queues, pulling two passengers out of the line, snatching their watches and yanking off a necklace worn by one of the women.

Christ, this was like the train station, Muller thought, and he angrily began feeling for his brass knuckles. An obviously drunk trooper walked unsteadily toward Muller's queue and began shouting at them to stop. The KLM pilot, who was on the ground inspecting the landing gear and checking the wing flaps, strode rapidly to the trooper and planted himself directly in his path.

"You'll have to go through me first," he said loudly enough for Muller to hear. The pilot stood his ground. "These passengers are my guests on a KLM flight to the capital of the German *Reich*," he said. "They are not to be interfered with."

He pushed the trooper in the chest, and the man proceeded to fall backward and sat there, shaking his head, apparently unable to get up on his own.

The pilot turned to the passengers and said, "Board the aircraft quickly please."

They needed no further prompting and quickly filed aboard. The pilot followed them, secured the aircraft door and proceeded up the aisle to the cockpit where he fired up the engines and began to taxi toward the runway.

Glancing out his window, Muller watched with alarm as a van, with Storm Troopers hanging aboard, began speeding toward them. The pilot evidently saw them too and accelerated to the runway, pivoted the aircraft and gunned the engines into a smooth, rapid takeoff leaving the van behind.

In the cabin, the passengers applauded.

# CHAPTER 44

When they reached Amsterdam the next morning, upon deplaning, Muller thanked Shirer for his help. Shirer asked no questions, but simply smiled and observed that it had been only a small down payment on the debt he and Tess owed Muller for getting Steffi Farber to the hospital that night. He then dashed off to catch a plane to London, where, he told Muller, he hoped to make a little history.

After wiring Büro Ha that he would be arriving later that day in Zurich on a Swiss Air flight from Amsterdam, Muller allowed himself the indulgence of telephoning his father at Muller & Company in Zurich.

His father was pleased that he was returning.

"It must have been a successful assignment, Paul," he said, "because yesterday we received a wire transfer through Banque Pictet in the sum of 20,000 Swiss francs. It was from an anonymous donor, asking that it be deposited in an account to be set up in your name. The message accompanying it simply said, 'Thank you'."

# EPILOG

Kurt von Schuschnigg had read his speech resigning as Chancellor from a scrap of paper on which he had hurriedly penciled the wording. He stood before a radio microphone that had been set up the Cabinet Room of the Chancellery and, as he delivered his remarks, he was surrounded by his entire cabinet of ministers, including both Arthur Seyss-Inquart and Guido Schmidt. When he had finished, and the red light went off signaling that Radio Vienna had switched back to the studio, Schuschnigg's stoic calm demeanor finally cracked. He dropped the hastily scrawled speech he was holding and collapsed in sobs, helped to a nearby chair by loyal ministers as Seyss-Inquart and Schmidt averted their eyes.

Then, pulling himself together, he stood, collecting his hat and coat. Overruling pleas that he exit via the back stairs, he informed his former colleagues that he would depart by the main staircase, as he had entered, and directed his car to be sent around to the front entrance on the Ballhausplatz.

Once he was seated in the car, his security officers instructed the driver to go directly to Aspern, the nearby military aerodrome, where a plane was waiting, with engines running, ready to fly him to safety. But Schuschnigg would have none of it. "My place is here in Austria," he said, and turned to the driver. "Home, Franzl, please."

Upon his arrival at the Belvedere, the Chancellor's residence, the building was surrounded by uniformed Brown Shirts armed with rifles and he was informed that "for his own protection" he was being placed under arrest.

***

Confusion reigned at the Chancellery after Schuschnigg's resignation. The Austrian President, Wilhelm Miklas, refused to appoint Seyss-Inquart as Chancellor to replace Schuschnigg, and the Ministers bickered with one another into the evening.

Meanwhile, Hitler's adjutant, Wilhelm Keppler, who had been flown to Vienna that morning to deliver Hitler's ultimatum, had been installed in a separate office in the Chancellery by Seyss-Inquart. From there, he was in near constant contact by telephone with Hermann Göring, one of Hitler's closest confidants, who had assumed personal charge of Germany's effort to complete the Austrian takeover. Göring wanted Seyss-Inquart to form a provisional government and to dispatch a telegram to Hitler asking him to send the German army into Austria 'to restore order'. Seyss-Inquart refused to do either; he maintained that he lacked authority to form a government as he had not been appointed Chancellor and he firmly maintained that the presence of the German Army was unnecessary and was in fact undesirable.

Predictably, this infuriated Göring who proceeded to draft the text of the telegram he wanted, inviting the Army in, and sent it to Keppler, demanding that he get Seyss-Inquart to send it back to him, as a formal Austrian government message. Seyss-Inquart continued to resist, but he did not disavow a message back to Göring from Keppler, telling Göring that Seyss-Inquart had accepted Göring's draft. That was good enough for Göring. Using this fabricated "invitation" as a pretext, marching orders were issued and the German army invasion of Austria commenced just before 9 PM on Friday March 11, 1938.

The next day, the Nazi hierarchy moved into high gear to choreograph Hitler's triumphal entry into Vienna. He would first visit Linz, his Austrian birthplace, and then would be escorted by his victorious troops to Vienna, only a two-hour drive away. Viennese citizens would be invited to celebrate this historic event the same evening with a huge, torch-lit parade around the entire Ringstrasse.

But the start of the procession kept getting delayed and, shortly before midnight it was called off all together, as not even the advance guard of the supposedly victorious German army had yet arrived.

What no one in Vienna knew (and the now tightly-controlled press would not report) was that the German invasion had ground to a halt as it neared Linz. Despite perfect weather and road conditions, and the absence of even a semblance of Austrian resistance, the army's tanks, trucks and motorized heavy artillery began to break down and run out of fuel. Highways became blocked and the massive congestion that ensued prevented repair and refueling vehicles from getting through. The resulting confusion produced a near total breakdown in command and communication arrangements. The army was just plain stuck.

Commentators have since speculated about what might have happened if the Czechoslovakian air force–which was well within striking distance–had attacked the immobile and hopelessly vulnerable German army, strung out along the highways, vehicle after vehicle lined up, one after another, all of them sitting ducks for any adversary.

Of course, nothing of the kind happened.

Hitler was enraged by the army's collapse (and German military commanders were enraged at Hitler for ordering the invasion despite their advice that the army was unprepared).

But despite the delays and the changes in schedule that had to be made at short notice, Hitler's entry into Austria became a triumphal procession. He was greeted by jubilant crowds that cheered him every step of the way. At a luncheon in Linz on Sunday March 13, he announced that he was issuing a decree, that very day, to convert the nation of Austria into a province of the German *Reich.* The announcement was greeted with rapturous enthusiasm. And as Ernst Raditz had predicted to Paul Muller some days earlier, upon finally arriving in Vienna, Hitler delivered triumphal remarks from the ornate balcony of the Prince Eugene City Place to an ecstatic crowd of seemingly joyous citizens of Vienna.

It has often been observed that after the German takeover and in the long years that followed until Germany's final collapse and surrender in May 1945, Austrians became–and remained–among Hitler's most enthusiastic supporters.

***

After bidding farewell to Muller at the airport in Amsterdam early Saturday morning March 12, William Shirer delivered on his promise to make history.

The stunning impact of Hitler's takeover of Austria caused unexpected upheavals in the corporate offices of CBS in New York. William Paley, owner of CBS, had imposed severe constraints upon his European reporters, Shirer and Edward R. Murrow. He limited the number of newscasts they were permitted to broadcast and they were not allowed to speak themselves on the air, but instead had to recruit journalists to read scripts they had prepared. And Paley insisted on broadcasting children's choir music to his American audience, sending Shirer off to remote destinations to set up the live feeds–much to Shirer's disgust.

But the collapse of Austria into German hands had a galvanizing effect and Paley swung into action. After receiving word of Schuschnigg's resignation as Chancellor, Paley telephoned

Erich von Kunsti, the director of the Austrian state broadcasting system, requesting him to provide studio time for Shirer to broadcast a report on the situation. Incredibly, the trans-Atlantic call got through and the two spoke. To Paley's amazement, von Kunsti told him German authorities had seized the system and that he was under arrest, so he couldn't help get Shirer on the air. The line then went dead and Paley, stunned, but fully grasping the seriousness of the situation, sent orders to Shirer to get to London so he could make his broadcast–and do it himself, in his own voice.

That was why Shirer was flying to Berlin and Amsterdam late Friday night March 11 when, in our story, Muller encountered him. From Amsterdam, he flew to London and broadcast his first-hand report of the German takeover that night, only to discover that he'd been scooped by an NBC reporter, named Max Jordan, who had not only delivered the first broadcast on the Nazi takeover, but also managed to broadcast Hitler's victory speech from Vienna, translating it live for his American audience. Public and press reaction to NBC's coverage was overwhelmingly positive.

Paley was determined to mount a competitive counter-attack by CBS, so on Sunday, March 13, he instructed his News Director Paul White to set up a 30-minute live report from European capitals–that very night!

Much has been written about the event that transpired, as CBS commentator Robert Trout introduced Bill Shirer from London and Ed Murrow from Vienna (where he had gotten a line into Berlin patched through to New York, with a Nazi censor standing by his shoulder). They broadcast live and reporters recruited by Shirer and Murrow made broadcasts from Paris, Rome and Berlin. It has been said broadcast journalism was born that night–2 A.M. in Europe and 8 PM on the US east coast. Paley ordered coverage to continue for five more consecutive nights–and ultimately it evolved into CBS Evening News, the longest-running broadcast news program in history.

Shirer finally returned to Vienna a week later and went to his apartment, where Tess and Ed Murrow (and his new daughter Inga) were awaiting him. But he found his way barred by Nazi storm troopers. He discovered that the next building was the home of the wealthy Jewish banker Felix Rothschild. Rothschild and his family had fled, but the Nazis were busy looting it. When finally admitted to his own apartment, Shirer found himself standing by the window with Murrow, glasses of wine in hand, watching the Nazis help themselves to Rothschild's wealth.

***

The March 11, 1938, Friday night express from Vienna to Prague that Muller had tried to get aboard and that was attacked by Nazi gangs, finally departed from the East Banhof, but 20 minutes out, it was stopped and another Nazi gang attacked it, looting what was left and administering brutal beatings to the passengers. Then, upon arrival at the border, where they could see the lights of Breclav on the Czech side, the passengers were forced to de-train.

After a long wait, an announcement was made that the Czech border was closed by order of the Security ministry and all passengers were obliged to return to Vienna.

***

Kurt von Schuschnigg remained in captivity, first in Gestapo facilities, often in solitary confinement, and later, during the war, in concentration camps, first Sachsenhausen, then Dachau, segregated with other prominent captives. He was liberated by American troops in early May 1945. He later emigrated to the United States where he taught at St Louis University between 1948 and 1967.

Arthur Seyss-Inquart became governor of the German province of Ostmark, as Austria was named in the German *Reich.* Following Germany's invasion of Poland, he was assigned to a senior role in the brutal occupation program that followed conquest. Later, he became head of the Nazi administration in the occupied Netherlands, where he oversaw operation of concentration camps and instigated Jewish extermination programs. He was captured by the British in May 1945, tried and convicted of crimes against humanity at Nuremberg and was executed by hanging on October 16, 1946.

***

Bruno Walter conducted his last performance in Vienna until after World War II in February 1938, at the *Konserthaus*, which

Chancellor Schuschnigg attended and where he was greeted by a thunderous ovation, as described in the book. Walter then departed for Amsterdam to conduct the Concertgebouw Orchestra and he was there when Austria fell to the Germans. His daughter, Lotte, was living in Vienna and was arrested by the Nazis. Ultimately Walter was able to arrange for her release. In late 1939, he emigrated to the United States and went on to become one of the most famous symphony orchestra conductors in the world until his death in 1962.

## AUTHOR'S AFTERWORD

This is a work of fiction, but it incorporates a faithful account of the chaotic events leading to the German takeover of Austria in March 1938. Kurt von Schuschnigg was in fact Chancellor of Austria during this period and the tumultuous wave of crises depicted in the book–one after the other during the first two and a half months of 1938 which finally led to his resignation–are rendered with attention to authentic detail.

While it is not customary for novelists to cite sources, I want to acknowledge my debt to *Betrayal in Central Europe. Austria and Czechoslovakia: The Fallen Bastions*, by G.E.R. Gedye, Harper & Brothers 1939. Gedye was a British journalist who was stationed in Vienna from 1926 until he was deported by the Gestapo right after the German takeover in March 1938. As a contemporary account of the Austrian crises, the book was an invaluable resource. The author cites speeches and statements attributed to Hitler and Schuschnigg as quotations. I take this designation with a grain of salt, and while I have included several of his "quotes" in the book (for example, Hitler's tirade at

Schuschnigg), I have used them mainly as guides for a fictional text conveying the intended message.

***

I decided to introduce a fictionalized William Shirer character into the novel for several reasons. Among other things, Shirer was in fact stationed in Vienna at the time the events in the novel occurred. Surely, he would have been a keen observer and might have made the statements fictionally attributed to him in the text. Most important, however, Shirer's wife Tess was in Vienna and actually underwent the horrible experiences of childbirth described in the book–the nuns' insistence on labor for nearly 48 hours without painkillers; the ultimate intervention of a Jewish doctor to perform a cesarean operation, only to have it interrupted in a pogrom-like attack on the hospital where he had to flee for his life, leaving the operation unfinished; and the need for a follow-up procedure to remove an instrument accidentally left in the womb. Shirer describes the ordeal in his biography *The Nightmare Years*.

***

Immediately after Schuschnigg resigned, flying squads of Nazi hit men were dispatched across Vienna to arrest enemies and attack Jews. There are countless contemporary accounts of savage treatment of Viennese Jews during this period. The hospital episode is only one of many. The fearful attack on the last Express train out of Vienna to Prague on March 11 was reported by Gedye in his book and is another example. There had in fact been extensive Nazi planning and preparation for these attacks and, within hours, Austria's borders were closed and routes of escape were shut off, effectively trapping the new regime's enemies.

This led to a problem for your author. If the borders were sealed so quickly–and they were in fact–then how was Muller to escape?

This plot problem became another reason to introduce the fictional William Shirer character.

When William Paley, the President of CBS, ordered Shirer to travel to London to broadcast his report, as related in the Epilog, Shirer faced precisely the same dilemma as Muller. He was not on the run from the Gestapo, of course, but he was trying to escape Vienna at the same time Muller–and everyone else who could–was trying to get out too, and there was no available transportation. But Shirer had the very smart idea of getting out via Berlin. So, he went to the airport where he was able to book a flight that took him through Berlin to Amsterdam and on to London–and his history-making broadcasts.

I decided that should be Muller's solution too. He would have to survive a surprise encounter with Shirer and suspicions of the Gestapo in the airport transit visa office, but using the solution smartly adopted by Shirer in real life, I was able to ensure that Muller escaped Austria intact, along with the prospect of being featured in a future novel.

***

The account in the book of the circumstances surrounding Anthony Eden's resignation as Foreign Secretary in February 1938, are largely factual. Neville Chamberlain did in fact succeed Stanley Baldwin as British Prime Minister in 1937 and pursue a policy of appeasement with renewed vigor, and messianic conviction, ruthlessly enforced by his Chief Whip, David Margesson. This brought him into conflict with Eden, who had by then developed a deep skepticism about Hitler. While admittedly Eden was the original architect of the policy that became known as appeasement beginning in 1935, he had begun to doubt it by early 1938. Eden also resented Chamberlain's cavalier willingness to insert himself personally into foreign policy issues that Eden firmly believed were his prerogative as Foreign Secretary. The two men clashed over Chamberlain's direct negotiations with Italy and his cavalier dismissal of a negotiating initiative from President Roosevelt, among other things. One of the disagreements was over colonial policy, as related in the book, where Chamberlain insisted on offering Hitler colonies in Africa (belonging to other nations, which Chamberlain never consulted about the matter) without any demand for reciprocal concessions from Hitler–which Eden felt should be an essential part of any deal.

There was high drama as the conflict between the two men came to a head in mid-February 1938 and, as portrayed in the book, there was very strong support in the House for Eden to resign and mount a campaign to unseat Chamberlain, which many thought could succeed.

But as was so often the case in Eden's career, he resigned, but then he flinched and couldn't muster the courage to mount a challenge to Chamberlain. Instead, he made a speech explaining his resignation that was so bland as to leave even his supporters wondering why he'd quit in the first place. Bobbety Cranborne took to the floor immediately following Eden and delivered a full-throated critique of Chamberlain's policy. But it was Eden the House and the country wanted to hear from, and the moment passed. Eden then took himself to Cap Ferrat in Southern France for a two-month vacation, playing as much as six sets of tennis every day. Years later he wrote in his diary that he "lacked the spunk" for politics.

The tragedy of Chamberlain's pursuit of appeasement, and the aggressive actions by David Marchesson to enforce Chamberlain's will on the House, are captured in a highly readable volume authored by Lynne Olson, entitled *Troublesome Young Men: The Rebels Who Brought Churchill to Power and Helped Save England.*

***

The Kellogg-Briand Pact outlawing war as an instrument of national policy–the agreement that Muller and Ernst Raditz mocked in the story–was signed in Paris on August 28, 1928. Frank B. Kellogg, the American Secretary of State, was later awarded the Nobel Peace Prize for his leadership in securing adoption of what surely must qualify as among the least effective international agreements in diplomatic history.

***

The movie *Algiers,* which Muller went to see in the novel, was among the most popular films of 1938. Charles Boyer was nominated for an Oscar as Best Actor and James Lee Wong was nominated for best Cinematography. The film is widely credited for being the inspiration for *Casablanca.* As Muller noted in the story, Hedy Lamarr made her American debut in the film and she was a sensation. But in an interesting footnote, not only was Hedy a stunningly gorgeous woman, and of course a glamorous film star, she also went on to be an inventor and, together with the composer George Antheil, developed a radio guidance system for Allied torpedoes, which used frequency-hopping spread spectrum technology to defeat the threat of jamming by the Axis powers. Recent commentators have asserted that the principles of their work contributed to modern Bluetooth, CDMA and Wi-Fi. They were both inducted into the National Inventors Hall of Fame in 2014.

***

Muller's trip to the movies led to the tryst with Marte von Papen, wife of the German Ambassador to Austria, which is of course entirely fictional. But the episode served as a vehicle for recounting von Papen's role in the appointment of Hitler as German Chancellor in January 1933. Historians generally agree that von Papen was in fact the individual principally responsible for persuading Paul von Hindenburg, President of the Weimar Republic, to appoint Hitler, believing that, as Vice-Chancellor, von Papen could manipulate Hitler and keep him from exercising real power. According to one report, upon being warned that Hitler posed a danger not to be underestimated, von Papen is said to have replied, "You are mistaken; we've hired him."

As Marte von Papen observed in the novel, this was Franz' most serious miscalculation, in a career studded with them.

The account, also attributed to Marte in the novel, of how, in a period of only sixty days following that January 1933 appointment, Hitler proceeded to overturn the system and seize control of the entire German government, making himself into Germany's dictator, is an accurate summary of the dramatic events that in fact occurred–and had such far-reaching consequences.

History has not been kind to Franz von Papen. He was viewed by his contemporaries to be 'a vain, irresponsible intriguer' and 'a lightweight'; it was said that 'matters of principle never interested him' and one contemporary characterized him as 'one of the most consummate liars who ever lived'.

The novel endeavored to capture von Papen's role in scheming to undermine Austria's Chancellor, Kurt von Schuschnigg, and becoming a willing pawn in Hitler's elaborate plan to take over Austria.

***

Marte's character in the story also refers to the murderous Night of the Long Knives. This was an orgy of bloodshed ordered by Hitler between June 30 and July 2, 1934 in which at least 85 and maybe hundreds–even today, no one knows the exact number–of perceived enemies of Hitler were killed. Hundreds more–maybe thousands–were arrested, many of them sent off to Dachau and other concentration camps. This event was, and remains, a staggering symbol of Hitler's ruthless exercise of raw power.

On July 13, 1934, Hitler delivered a nationally-broadcast speech to the Reichstag justifying his actions. It is worth quoting an excerpt from his remarks.

*"If anyone reproaches me and asks why I did not resort to the regular courts of justice, then all I can say is this. In this hour I was responsible for the fate of the German people, and thereby I became the supreme judge of the German people. I gave the order to shoot the ringleaders in this treason, and I further gave the order to cauterize down to the raw flesh the ulcers of this poisoning of the wells in our domestic life. Let the nation know that its existence–which depends on its internal order and security–cannot be threatened with impunity by anyone! And let it be known for all time to come that if anyone raises his hand to strike the State, then certain death is his lot."*

The speech was a proclamation to the German nation and the world that Hitler would brook no interference and would not hesitate to resort to violence if he decided it was necessary to achieve his ends.

Germans generally bent to Hitler's will. Many world statesmen averted their eyes.

***

But now, after having trumpeted my fidelity to historic accuracy, I am now obligated to confess that the subplot of the novel–the plan to use Austria's gold reserves to pay off the outstanding Austrian loan in order to keep the gold out of Hitler's grasp–is entirely fictional.

Sorry.

It's fictional, but it's still fact-based. The plot idea had its genesis in a little-known set of actual events that affected the gold reserves of the Republic of Czechoslovakia about a year later.

Readers will recall that in September 1938, British Prime Minister Neville Chamberlain, bowing to Hitler's insistent demands, signed the infamous Munich Agreement, permitting Germany to annex large parts of Western Czechoslovakia (a region known as 'the Sudetenland') to satisfy Hitler's demand to rule over the ethnic Germans residing there. In retrospect, Munich is regarded as a craven sell-out; the ultimate symbol of Britain's failed policy of appeasement. But at the time, Chamberlain was lionized as a statesman, returning to London to proclaim, 'Peace in our time'. As part of the agreement, Hitler had promised that acquiring the Sudetenland fulfilled his territorial ambitions and that he had no further territorial designs. But less than six months later, in March 1939, he occupied the rest of Czechoslovakia, plunging Europe into yet another crisis.

German troops entered Prague on March 15, 1939 and immediately seized the offices of the Czech Central Bank. At the time, Czechoslovakia's gold reserves were stored in the basement vault at the Bank of England, along with the gold of most other nations (as Viktor Keinböck explained to Muller in our story). The Czechs actually held their gold in two separate accounts there. The first was a sovereign account in its own name, containing close to 27 metric tons of gold reserves worth nearly £8 million. The second was an account, also in its name, but held as a sub-account of the reserves of the Bank of International Settlements, which were also stored there. (The Bank of International Settlements was at the time, and remains today, an international bank for Central Banks, and is situated in Basel, Switzerland.) The Czech BIS sub-account held 23.1 metric tons of gold valued at roughly £6 million.

Upon taking control of the Czech Central Bank, Nazi officials directed Bank officials–allegedly at gun-point–to issue two bank transfer orders directing the gold in both Czech accounts to be immediately transferred to the gold account of the Reichsbank (The German Central Bank).

Alarmed by Germany's brazen violation of the Munich Agreement, the British government reacted strongly and the Chancellor of the Exchequer, Sir John Simon, issued a directive to British banks, including the Bank of England, to block all transfers of Czech assets. Accordingly, the instruction to transfer the Czech sovereign gold account to the Reichsbank was blocked.

But for reasons that remain unclear even today, the instruction to transfer the Czech gold from its BIS sub-account to the Reichsbank was executed, and roughly £6 million in Czech gold was transferred to Germany, with no recourse and without a shot being fired.

Reading about the Czech gold incident caused me to wonder whether there wasn't some plausible manner in which Austrian National Bank officials might have been able to re-direct Austria's sovereign gold in order to keep it out of German hands. When Germany had annexed Austria a year earlier, the British government had been in full pursuit of its policy to appease Hitler, so no thought had been given–and certainly no action was taken–to block Germany's seizure of the Austrian gold. I decided that Muller should visit London to make the case for action by the British government to freeze Austria's gold, but of course he failed. Consequently, trying to imagine some other form of government action to forestall Hitler from stealing the gold did not seem to be a viable plot option.

Instead, I hatched the idea of forcing repayment of the Austrian debt to the private sector lenders as the device for keeping the money away from Hitler. So, I went about creating the scenario in which Muller, acting in his League of Nations capacity as Commissioner General, would conspire with Viktor Keinböck, Governor of the Austrian National Bank, to create a scenario constituting a default on the debt and triggering an obligation to repay the principal amount, which would transfer Austria's gold to the lenders and keep it safely out of Germany's reach.

Readers will evaluate the credibility of this sub-plot for themselves. My description of the basic terms of the Austrian loans is drawn from League of Nations archives and is factual–with one vital exception. While the nations guaranteeing the loan insisted, as a matter of policy, that Germany and Austria must not establish a customs union or otherwise integrate their economies, they failed to write those conditions into the terms of the loan. So, the German takeover of Austria did not constitute a formal act of default, and did not trigger an obligation to repay the loan.

In the event, the apprehensions expressed by the characters in the story were entirely warranted and their worst fears were realized. Upon annexation, Germany seized Austria's gold reserves at the Bank of England and used them to pay for its military buildup; then, a few months later, it repudiated the loan terms and stiffed the private lenders.

In the interests of completeness, I should share some additional comments on this plotline.

Jose-Maria Oquendo, the League of Nations financial expert, is an entirely fictional character. But the background briefing he gave Muller in the story is a realistic account of the fall of the Austro-Hungarian Empire and the severe post-war hardships experienced by Austria and the citizens of Vienna.

The tale of the Czech Legion that Oquendo made reference to is also factual. Austrian POWs who were being held in Russia and who were sympathetic to the new nation of Czechoslovakia were organized into a potent army numbering almost 50,000 that did in fact control Soviet Siberia in 1918. It is among the most fascinating stories of that confused and chaotic period when the Bolshevik-led Soviet Union was convulsed by civil war and besieged by foreign armies.

The Viktor Keinböck character in the novel is a fictional characterization of an Austrian official by that name who was in fact Governor of the National Bank when Austria was taken over by Germany. He re-assumed the National Bank Presidency after the war. There is no reason to believe that he ever harbored thoughts of diverting Austria's financial assets away from Germany.

The last League of Nations Commissioner General for Austria was in fact a man named Rost van Tonningen, as referenced in the story, and, in that office, he did in fact have charge of the revenues generated by Austrian customs and the tobacco monopoly, which were to be used to pay the debt service on the Austrian loan. He resigned from his League position in 1936 to become head of the Nazi party in the Netherlands and held positions of authority in the German occupation of the Netherlands during the war. He was captured by Canadian troops, but died in a fall from a balcony of the Scheveningen Prison near The Hague in June 1945, before he could be put on trial. There is some dispute about whether he jumped from the balcony or was pushed.

***

The Swiss intelligence official to whom Muller reported, Hans Hausamann, is patterned after an individual of that name who in fact ran a sophisticated Swiss intelligence network called Büro Ha. The network became an integral part of the Swiss security apparatus after the outbreak of war, especially following Hitler's conquest of France in June 1940, which left Switzerland completely surrounded by potentially hostile powers–Nazi Germany and Fascist Italy–while striving to maintain its policy of neutrality and avoid invasion.

# AUTHOR'S OBSERVATION

As I write these words early in 2018, I am acutely aware of the fact that the eightieth anniversary of the date on which Hitler announced the Austrian Anschluss, March 12, 1938, is only weeks away.

I lack any qualifications to suggest to twenty-first century Austrians how they should acknowledge this event, if at all. But I would feel remiss if I failed to recognize the juxtaposition of time and place and the passage of nearly eight full decades since the events described here took place.

I believe I am entitled to observe that, on that long ago date, freedom was extinguished for many Austrians and a train of tragic events was set in motion with consequences that continue to reverberate today.

And so, I think it is not impertinent to express the hope that Austrians and citizens of other nations around the world might use the occasion to reflect upon what happened not so long ago and to consider what lessons might be gleaned from the events that transpired.

# OTHER BOOKS BY THIS AUTHOR

## THE FIRST VOLUME IN THE PAUL MULLER NOVELS OF POLITICAL INTRIGUE

*Danzig* is a gripping historical novel in the grand tradition. It has generated rave reviews (90% 4 and 5 stars) for its authenticity and its realistic portrayal of high pressure diplomatic clashes between Hitler and Western nations in the 1930s. The story encompasses fast-paced events in Geneva, Berlin, Warsaw and London, as well as Danzig itself, capturing the drama of unfolding crisis that engulfed Europe on what we now know was the path to war.

Paul Muller makes his debut as secretary to Sean Lester, who was High Commissioner of the League of Nations in the Free City of Danzig. The novel portrays the roles played by Lester and Muller in resisting Nazi-inspired crises that threatened to overwhelm Danzig's constitutional freedoms, leading to fierce diplomatic conflict and, ultimately, political betrayal. It's a compelling story of a fateful time.

Excerpts from the reviews:

* "Channeling the best of Alan Furst, *Danzig* is a must read for the any lover of well written historical fiction."

* "Mr. Walker's descriptions made this reader feel as if she were in the middle of the historic drama. The novel builds in intensity until the dramatic ending. It's a terrific read."

* "*Danzig* is a must read for any lover of riveting historical fiction dealing with Hitler's rise. Walker makes the saga of the city and the Polish Corridor come alive. The tensions of the time are vividly described in human terms, making for gripping reading."

* "*Danzig* is an amazing book, putting the reader in the middle of pre WW II in Europe. The time and scene were painted in detail and to perfection. The characters were presented in such a way I felt I knew them and worried for them throughout."

* "Superb historical fiction; good story, good atmospherics. *Danzig* is a sophisticated journey into European power politics during a time of high drama. I think it bears comparison to the best authors in the popular interwar historical fiction genre and I rate it a very successful effort."

* "The author does a great job of making the reader feel what it was like to be in the center of pre-WWII Europe, with Germany flouting the Treaty of Versailles, England following an ill-fated policy of appeasement and the League of Nations powerless and ineffective in dealing with Hitler and his aggression. For anyone interested in WWII history, especially the lead-up to the war and the dysfunction among the European Allies, this is a great read!"

The website **www.authorwilliamwalker.com** offers a link to Amazon Kindle as well as a synopsis, photos and more information.

# ABOUT THE AUTHOR

photo by Albert W. Dungan

William N. Walker brings to his new Paul Muller novel a lifetime of experience as a diplomat, government official and international businessman.

*Danzig*, Mr. Walker's first novel in the Paul Muller series, was published in 2016 to critical acclaim. It was compared to the best of Alan Furst and continues to win praise for its authenticity and historical accuracy. "A Great read for anyone interested in this time period and the events leading up to World War II. It captures the very essence of British appeasement and diplomatic foot-dragging. I can't wait for more from this author."

Mr. Walker was Ambassador and Chief Trade Negotiator for the United States in the Tokyo Round of Multilateral Trade negotiations conducted under the auspices of the General Agreement on Tariffs and Trade in Geneva. He lived in Geneva for more than two years and brings first-hand diplomatic knowledge to the story. While the GATT was hardly the League of Nations, international organizations now, as then, are unwieldy and susceptible to the kinds of infighting and manipulation that we witness in the book.

As a member of the Nixon Administration, Mr. Walker was also a close observer of the political intrigue that destroyed Nixon's presidency. Later, he served as Director of the Presidential Personnel Office for President Ford. After leaving government, he became a partner in a large Wall Street law firm, running a successful international law practice. Later, he established a company, which he continues to operate, devoted to international business that has included transactions in Europe, the former Soviet Union, Turkey, Central Asia and the Middle East. He describes himself as a recovering attorney.

Mr. Walker is a winner of the Distinguished Alumnus Award from Wesleyan University. He is the father of three grown children and lives with his wife in New York City and neighboring Westchester County.

Made in the USA
Columbia, SC
05 April 2018